PRAISE FOR CHRIS FABRY

Not in the Heart

"A story of hope, redemption, and sacrifice. . . . It's hard to imagine inspirational fiction done better than this."

WORLD MAGAZINE

"Christy Award–winning Fabry has written a nail-biter with plenty of twists and turns to keep readers riveted. Fans of Jerry B. Jenkins and Jodi Picoult might want to try this title."

LIBRARY JOURNAL

"A fine piece of storytelling. . . . Down to its final pages, *Not in the Heart* is a gripping read. While the mystery at its core is compelling, it's Wiley's inner conflict that's truly engrossing."

CROSSWALK.COM

"This absorbing novel should further boost Fabry's reputation as one of the most talented authors in Christian fiction."

CBA RETAILERS + RESOURCES

"*Not in the Heart* is the best book I have read in a long time. The plot is unique and creative . . . [and] manages to keep the reader hanging until the last page."

READERVIEWS.COM

Almost Heaven

"[A] mesmerizing tale . . . [*Almost Heaven*] will surprise readers in the best possible way; plot twists unfold and unexpected character transformations occur throughout this tender story."

PUBLISHERS WEEKLY

"Fabry has a true gift for prose, and [*Almost Heaven*] is amazing. . . . You'll most definitely want to move this to the top of your 'to buy' list."

ROMANTIC TIMES, 4½-STAR TOP PICK REVIEW

"Fabry is a talented writer with a lilting flow to his words."

June Bug

"[*June Bug*] is a stunning success, and readers will find themselves responding with enthusiastic inner applause."

"An involving novel with enough plot twists and dramatic tension to keep readers turning the pages."

"I haven't read anything so riveting and unforgettable since *Redeeming Love* by Francine Rivers. Fabry has penned a remarkable love story, one that's filled with sacrifice, hope, and forgiveness!"

"Precise details of places and experiences immediately set you in the story, and the complex, likable characters give *June Bug* the enduring quality of a classic."

Dogwood

"Once the story starts cooking, [*Dogwood*] is difficult to put down, what with Fabry's surprising plot resolution and themes of forgiveness, sacrificial love, and suffering."

"Ultimately a story of love and forgiveness, [*Dogwood*] should appeal to a wide audience."

"Solidly literary fiction with deep, flawed characters and beautiful prose, *Dogwood* also contains a mystery within the story that adds tension and a deepening plot."

BORDERS

of the

HEART

TYNDALE HOUSE PUBLISHERS, INC.
CAROL STREAM, ILLINOIS

CHRIS FABRY

Visit Tyndale online at www.tyndale.com.

Visit Chris Fabry's website at www.chrisfabry.com.

TYNDALE and Tyndale's quill logo are registered trademarks of Tyndale House Publishers, Inc.

Borders of the Heart

Designed by Daniel Farrell

Edited by Sarah Mason

Published in association with Creative Trust Literary Group, 5141 Virginia Way, Suite 320, Brentwood, Tennessee 37027, www.creativetrust.com.

Scripture quotations are taken from the *Holy Bible*, New Living Translation, copyright © 1996, 2004, 2007 by Tyndale House Foundation. Used by permission of Tyndale House Publishers, Inc., Carol Stream, Illinois 60188. All rights reserved.

1 Corinthians 6:11 in chapter 18 is taken from the *Holy Bible*, King James Version.

Borders of the Heart is a work of fiction. Where real people, events, establishments, organizations, or locales appear, they are used fictitiously. All other elements of the novel are drawn from the author's imagination.

Library of Congress Cataloging-in-Publication Data

Fabry, Chris, date.
  Borders of the heart / Chris Fabry.
    p. cm.
  ISBN 978-1-4143-4862-9 (sc)
  1. Organic farming—Fiction. 2. Illegal aliens—Fiction. 3. Drug traffic—Mexican-American Border Region—Fiction. I. Title.
  PS3556.A26B67 2012
  813'.54—dc22   2012020884

FOR AK AND ALL WHO ARE DRIVEN TO THE DESERT.

AND I HAD A LOVER

IT'S SO HARD TO RISK ANOTHER THESE DAYS

Jackson Browne

NOTE: WWOOF stands for Worldwide Opportunities on Organic Farms or Willing Workers on Organic Farms. Volunteers, called WWOOFers, usually are not compensated but learn organic farming and are fed and housed in exchange for their work.

The setting of this novel is Tucson, Arizona, and surrounding towns. But liberties have been taken with certain locations. There is no La Pena, Arizona. The heat, however, is real.

THURSDAY

1

JOHN DAVID JESSUP rode out in the morning half-light, when the sun was just a salmon-colored promise on the horizon. It had been eighty-four days since the last rain, and each hoof-fall of the horse kicked up the dust of a thousand summers. He had no designs on the day or his life.

The local weather reports confirmed the constant negative drumbeat of the farm's owner, Larry Slocum. The man could find something wrong even with a June rain.

"It's just going to run off," he would say to the underside of any dark cloud.

The heat of the morning had awakened J. D. as it always did. Sweating in the stillness, lying on top of the old quilt given to him by Slocum's wife, and straining to feel any air movement from the clacking metal fan he had found in the barn, he felt beads of perspiration run past his mouth and onto the dusty pillow. He had tried sleeping with the door open, but night critters tended to take that as an invitation.

His room was an old schoolhouse Slocum said had been built before statehood, and J. D. believed it. Cattle feed covered half the room. The other half had his bed and a nightstand and a basin he tried to keep full of water. There was no bathroom—that was a Porta-John behind the building, facing the mountains in the distance. His only roommates were the extended family of mice that skittered through the room while he tried to sleep.

There was nothing different about that morning. Nothing out of the ordinary. The springs on the bunk had creaked as he rose and pulled on jeans so stiff he could now lean them against the wall. He'd shaken out his boots, making sure nothing had crawled inside, and staggered into a world he had not known until April, two months before, give or take.

The farm sat at the edge of La Pena, a town south of Tucson and bordering the Coronado National Forest. The Slocum ranch comprised five hundred acres of the best desert money could buy. It had been in the Slocum family for generations before it passed to Larry and his wife, Nora. There was a crude history written up in a weather-worn paperback under the coffee table in the Slocum living room. Stories of ancestors who had emigrated from the old country to the East Coast, then traveled west to fight off the natives and wild animals and stake a claim. Misspelled words and run-on sentences and commas where they shouldn't be.

The story of the farm would probably make a good song if J. D. could ever write again, but he'd traded that creative work for the day-to-day plodding farming gave. A one-foot-in-front-of-the-other existence that beat the hurt down to a numbness in his soul.

Before mounting, he'd taken a sip of water from the canteen hooked to the back of his saddle. It tasted old and hot, and he spit it at a wood rat darting past the barn. Quail were out with their young, clucking and traveling single file in the muted light, like a well-oiled military expedition. Mother led the tiny babies while Father brought up the rear, and J. D. had to look away.

The family dog, Red, climbed out from under the porch of the farmhouse and ambled to a plastic water dish upside down in the dirt. J. D. emptied his canteen into the bowl and the dog lapped. He ran his hand along Red's back before filling the canteen from the spigot by the barn.

He was surprised cattle could survive in such a hostile place, though there was good grazing higher, on the back side of the farm. That a garden would grow seemed impossible, but the ground was like children, forgiving once it found water.

His aversion to the land wasn't just the heat and scorpions but the very lay of it. Born among rolling green hills that exploded with color and then balanced themselves white each year, he felt foreign in the faded brown and gray of Arizona. Instead of preparing to blossom, everything seemed prepared to die, blowing from one flat place to another, shifting in the wind where God wanted—if God even cared about this desert.

The cactus and catclaw and cholla were strange to him. As were the Gila monsters and rattlers. But what he missed most were real trees and streams that bubbled up on their own. The mountains here, all around him, made the land feel like the bottom of some dry bowl. The saguaros seemed to gesture obscenely at him as he rode past each day, a cactus flip-off.

He was a stranger here, and the thought comforted him.

Every other day he rode the fence perimeter, checking for problems and making sure the water line hadn't been punctured by illegals. It was a popular route for both those in the drug trade and those looking for work and a better life. He'd heard stories from Slocum and his wife, the same ones again and again, just like their stories of WWOOFers like himself—a damaged lot who weren't to be trusted.

Red joined him at the first knoll and trotted before the horse as if he were leading them to cross the Jordan. He was a mongrel, long-snouted and curly-tailed, and reminded J. D. of a dog he had loved as a boy. Each sight brought another stab of memory—one of a hundred reminders of the past in this barren land.

The blue sky was cloudless and empty of everything but the contrails of passing jets. He loosened the reins and let the horse go at its own pace through the prickly pear and beavertail and ocotillo and higher to the johnsongrass. Every morning he fought exhaustion. Every night he fought sleep.

If not for the coyote, he probably would have missed her. He just as easily could have glanced away at the moment when fate or providence looked upon a man and winked.

The coyote loped across the trail, unconcerned by the yapping dog, looking back like Red was simply another meal on four legs. Confident, arrogant, the coyote sniffed the wind, then trained its eyes on the horse and rider. The animal finally acquiesced and continued to a rock outcropping, then effortlessly glided across the desert floor, seemingly borne by instinct and an unseen trail.

Just on the edge of J. D.'s vision, when the coyote was a blurry dot among the waves of heat, it stopped, then stepped backward, turning and testing the wind. It was then that J. D. noticed the lone buzzard circling, drifting on an unsteady current.

He pulled the reins, and the horse gave him a side glance before obeying and moving down the slope into the craterous terrain. The sun peeked over the Rincons behind him. The heat made him shiver, and he tugged the brim of his hat lower as if that could cool him. He had turned three shades of red on every exposed part of his skin. That was why he wore long-sleeved shirts and stiff-legged jeans.

The coyote sauntered beside a lump on the ground. Perhaps it was a cow. A patch of cactus blocked J. D.'s view from this angle, but as he rose above the wash and drew closer, he saw that the dot appeared black and too small for cattle. Perhaps a dead coyote blackened by the sun. Or a chupacabra. He had heard that discussed at the farmers' market.

And then he heard Slocum's voice, stories told of an evening by the fire pit. *"It's just another dead Mexican."*

Slocum had discovered a body the previous winter. As he described it, his wife had gone into the house to wash dishes.

"I found one last December, just before Christmas. Sitting propped up against a tree, head down between its knees like it was sleeping. Frozen like a Popsicle."

Not a he or a she—an *it*. Less than a dead cow or dog. This seemed the prevailing attitude in La Pena. In some ways J. D. could understand how it was easier making them less than human. It kept a distance they felt comfortable with when a family staggered through looking for water. J. D. hadn't given it much thought until now. There were too many other things on his mind.

Slocum had called Border Patrol to retrieve the body and told J. D. to do the same if he came across a Mexican.

Instead of tearing into whatever flesh was before it, the

coyote eyed J. D. as he moved closer. But when Red rushed the animal, it snarled and reluctantly trotted away.

J. D. rode around the cactus patch for a better look. What he saw clenched his stomach. Long, flowing black hair spread out from a woman facedown in the dirt. Black clothing. A skirt. Scratched legs and feet caked with blood. An open-toed sandal on one foot, the other bare. Stickers deep in her calves. Who in her right mind would wear sandals and a dress in a desert crossing? Through the hair stretched an arm with a handcuff around the right wrist. No sign of the other cuff.

Who were you? J. D. thought. *And how did you end up here?*

The dog sniffed at the unmoving body and licked the hand. At least the animals hadn't gotten to her. J. D. detected no odor of death. Not yet, anyway. The horse shifted, rearing its head and moving back a step. And then J. D. saw movement. From the dead woman's midsection. Something brown and gray gliding along the torso.

Red barked and J. D. yelled at him to get away, his heart rate climbing. Then came the rattle as the diamondback reversed course and headed toward her feet. Red would not relent, so J. D. stepped off the horse and kicked at the cur, sending him yelping into the scrub.

The snake rose up and eyed him. J. D. hesitated. Should he care for the dog and horse or just take care of himself? They were the intruders here, and the last thing he wanted was to get snakebit.

He dug his battered cell phone from the saddlebag and flipped it open, standing between the snake and the dog. Service was spotty here, but he found two bars. He scrolled through the contacts till he came to the number Slocum had given.

As the call rang, he saw more movement. This time the hand

with the cuff flexed and dug into the dirt. Was it involuntary? A body's last flexing of muscle in the heat?

"Border Patrol," a female voice answered and gave her name.

The snake slithered along the woman's thigh, and she moved her exposed leg. Then the snake rose and J. D. dropped the phone and turned to the horse, reaching for the rifle. In a flash of memory, he and his father were near a clearing with a fifteen-point buck straight ahead. J. D. froze, just as he had then, unable to squeeze the trigger or to breathe.

He shook the indecision off, then grabbed the barrel of the rifle and rushed the snake, swinging the stock wildly as it struck, its rattle fully engaged. He finally connected, and the snake's head snapped back. He dug the toe of his boot into the underbelly and sent it a few feet into the cactus. He felt like a placekicker who had just scored from eighty yards out, but he didn't have time to celebrate.

The woman lifted her head, hair covering her face. She was too weak to pull it back. J. D. moved to block the sun.

"Agua," she whispered. She sounded like a girl, her voice no louder than a bird's.

He grabbed his canteen, the dog now barking with equal fervor at the woman and the snake. He started to hand her the water, then remembered the phone and flipped it closed and shoved it into his pocket. She looked too weak to lift the canteen to her lips, so he knelt to roll her over and support her head as he poured some into her mouth. Her lips were parched and swollen, and with her turned over he could see blood on her shirt or blouse or whatever it was. A lot of blood. He pulled at it to see the wound, but she recoiled.

"Are you hurt?" he said.

She had to spit out some dust and mud to get the water past

her swollen tongue. Finally she drank, all the time looking at him with huge brown eyes.

He fumbled for the Spanish word, trying to bring it back from his high school days. *"¿Duele?"* he said.

She tipped the canteen again and drank. Then she lay back and closed her eyes. He checked her pulse. It was strong. He picked her up, cradling her like an infant to his chest. She was light, but even a hundred pounds of deadweight was difficult to carry. His phone buzzed as he stumbled to the horse. How could he get her back to the ranch?

He let her feet go and held her with one arm while he fished for the phone.

"This is Border Patrol. Did you just call?" a woman said.

"Yes, ma'am, I . . . ran into some trouble. . . ."

"Who is this?"

"Sorry, ma'am, I made a mistake. Called the wrong number. My apologies."

The woman muttered something and hung up.

The sun moved higher, spiking the temperature. It had reached 117 the day before, and with not a cloud in sight, he figured today would be no different. He thought about calling Slocum but decided against it. The man would just haul her to the nearest Border Patrol and wash his hands.

He hoisted the woman, limp as a dishrag, toward the saddle, but the horse backed away. J. D. cursed and grabbed the reins, which only made things worse, the horse circling. He let go of the reins.

"Easy," he said calmly, a hand on the horse's head.

His father's voice came back to him. *"The animal senses your fear. Relax. You don't have to control it. You only have to guide it."*

He tried again, but he misjudged the woman's weight and

had to pull her back. Finally he placed her in the shade of a cactus, removed the saddle, and straightened the blanket on the horse's back. Then he pushed her up with one hand on her chest and another on her backside to place her on the horse. She was a girl, a tiny thing.

He led the horse to a rock and climbed up to sit behind her, steadying her weight with one hand. He tried to go as quickly as he could without jostling her, a hand in the middle of her back. Feet dangling, her body bouncing as they climbed higher, J. D. wondered where the girl had been and where she was going and what all of this meant to him.

"Who are you?" he said.

2

J. D. CARRIED THE WOMAN into the schoolhouse and placed her on his bed, the rising dust troubling him where it hadn't before. It was inhuman keeping her here in the heat of the tin roof, but he had no choice. Her legs were streaked with blood, and he slipped off her remaining sandal and put it on the floor. She hadn't stirred as he rode nor when he carried her into the room. But she was breathing and she had a pulse.

He glanced out the dirty window by the bed and was reasonably sure no one had seen them. The door faced away from the farmhouse, and he had brought the horse up by the mesquite trees to keep hidden. With school out, the kids would soon stir and Mrs. Slocum would be busy in the kitchen or with the goats. Who knew where Slocum was—probably asleep or at the well cussing at the busted motor. It was a full-time job, that dry well. J. D. couldn't understand why he didn't spend the money to dig a new one.

He pulled the fan closer and pointed it toward the woman's face so that her hair moved in dark tendrils. Fighting the old feelings that stirred, he dipped a clean rag in the basin, wrung it out, and began to clean her legs. It was clear she would need medical attention. Her dark cotton skirt was spattered with blood. He worked on her ankles and shins, avoiding the cactus stickers that he wanted to pull out but knew he shouldn't. He'd tried that before on himself with painful consequences.

Her skin was soft, and he could tell by her hands that she was not a woman who did manual labor. He washed her palms of blood and dirt, noticing a black ring on her little finger. It looked expensive. Her left hand was white with chalky dust, and her nails were chipped and painted a light pink.

The handcuff was a problem. It had chafed a dark-red ring and rubbed through the skin by the bone that jutted up on the wrist. Blood and something white oozed, and there was no way to clean it properly. He had a bottle of hydrogen peroxide, but there was no telling how old it was. Brown stains on the cap. When he tested it on his own hand, spilling it on a scratch he had picked up during the ride, it bubbled and fizzed. He poured the peroxide on her wrist and she moved. He poured more, letting it drip on the wooden floor, then set to work on her arms.

The blouse had a streak of white along the top, spotted with more blood. He lifted it slightly and looked for a bullet wound but dropped it when he saw her bra. Yes, she was thin and light as a young girl, but she was a woman.

She wore little makeup—just some eye shadow—and her cheekbones were high. Long lashes and trimmed brows. Full lips. Hair that flowed like water—though it was matted and stringy at the moment.

A pounding on the door. "Mr. Jessup! You in there?"

The voice of Cooper, the youngest Slocum. A waif with a round head and hair that looked painted on. He was a desert child—no shirt, frayed jeans, and feet worn rough on the rocky path that led from the house to the old schoolhouse.

"How many times has your mama told you to wear shoes outside?" J. D. said as he emerged from the shack. He closed the door behind him quickly.

"You're back early. Did something go wrong?"

J. D. moved to the horse to get the canteen, but it wasn't there.

"Where's your saddle?" the child said.

J. D. stopped and turned. "Why don't you stop jawin' at me and go inside and bring me a jar of cool water."

Though his voice had been gruff, the child responded quick as lightning, feet churning, shoulder blades rising and falling like pistons under the thin veneer of skin on his back. He was a loping cheetah.

Cooper scrambled into the house and let the screen door bang with a vengeance.

J. D. waited with a thousand questions and no good answers. Where had the woman come from? What had been hooked to the other end of that handcuff? Where was she headed? Nobody in their right mind would cross the desert in June, though he had heard stories of those who tried.

The door slammed again and Slocum walked out with a steaming cup of coffee. He wore a T-shirt that said *Crime doesn't pay. Neither does farming.* J. D. had never seen him without his Stetson, the biggest in the state probably, and he had a well-trimmed horseshoe mustache that took on a mind of its own when it reached his jaw, flaring out into rogue hair. A wiry, thin man, he walked with a limp from a hip that needed replacement. Too many rodeos and farm accidents. Cooper had told J. D. a rambling story about his dad falling off the roof fixing the tiles a year earlier. He'd climbed right back on to finish the job, even though he'd broken his leg.

Slocum raised the mug a fraction to say hello. Everything was understated, except when you messed up.

J. D. walked toward him into the sunlight. There was a slight wind from the west that made the world feel like a blast furnace on low.

"How's the fence?" Slocum said.

"Looked good."

"You're back early."

"Got up early," J. D. said.

The farmer took a sip of coffee. Didn't make sense drinking something so hot when the earth glowed, but that was the power of the bean. J. D. felt it too.

"Where are they?" Slocum said.

J. D. hadn't seen the cattle, but he told him where he thought they'd be, at the back fence line where there was still a semblance of grazing.

"I need to get a new protein lick over by the canyon bottom. They've gone through that grass like a fire." Slocum said it like he expected him to run back right away.

J. D. put his foot on a wooden step. "I was thinking of heading into town."

"What you need in town? You remember we're slaughtering chickens later this morning. It's all hands on deck."

He couldn't think of anything to say that would convince the man. "Just need to go."

"Still got that pump to work on too. We don't get water moving in the line, we're gonna lose every one of them Tohono O'odham melons. Most of that cabbage is done burnt."

Nora Slocum came out, wiping her hand on her apron, carrying a Ball jar of water from the refrigerator. He could tell because it was misty on the side, water beading.

"Cooper said you wanted a drink," Nora said. "You want to come in and get cool for a change? Eat your breakfast with us?"

J. D. took the water and drank a little. "That's kind of you, ma'am, but I think I'll take it over to my place if that's all right."

"Suit yourself," she said, shaking her head and turning.

A roadrunner bounced between the barn and the house and paused before darting into the desert. The two men watched it silently until Slocum spoke again.

"You up to doing the market by yourself tomorrow?"

"I expect so. Just give me the list of prices."

"Last WWOOFer we let do this ran off with the money box. Never did see him again."

J. D. had heard that story a dozen times, plus the one about the guy from France who had tallied up a six-hundred-dollar phone bill before heading west. They had another kid from California they let drive their truck. He raised their insurance by smashing the side of a Porsche at the Harkins Theatre off I-19.

"We'll load the meat after supper tonight," Slocum said. "Vegetables and salsa in the morning."

J. D. nodded and smiled. "You two going on vacation?"

"What's a vacation? I don't even know the meaning of the word."

Nora brought J. D.'s plate in one hand, wrapped in cellophane. Eggs with salsa and diced potatoes. She threw spices onto whatever she cooked like they would go bad if she didn't. In the other hand was half a melon with a grapefruit spoon in it, also wrapped in cellophane.

"Thank you, ma'am."

"What time will you be back?" Slocum said.

"Won't take long. Before chicken-slaughter time."

"See to it," Slocum said. "And if you're headed for the liquor store, get me a twelve-pack."

When he returned to the shack, the woman was sitting up, moving the handcuff back and forth on her wrist. He handed her the Ball jar, and she drank the whole thing in one gulp. He held out the plate and pulled the cellophane away from the melon. She shook her head.

"Go on and eat it. You gotta be hungry."

She studied her wrist.

"Comer. Para ti."

She looked up at him with those eyes, big and brown and a world of hope behind them. Or maybe it was fear he saw. She took the plate and stabbed her fork into the potatoes, cut the eggs and ate around the salsa, then went ahead and scarfed it down too.

He offered her the melon but she waved him off. He put it in the small, empty refrigerator and turned. "I want to get you to a doctor."

Her brow furrowed. *"¿Médico? No. No quiero médico."*

"You're dehydrated, all scratched up, and I . . ."

She stared at him like he was an alien from another world.

"No miedo. I can find a *médico.* Somebody safe. *Seguro. ¿Comprende?"*

She shook her head and rattled off something in Spanish so

fast that his head spun, but her voice . . . it was like an angel talking. Crisp and fluent and full of fire and passion. Someone had told him once that the voice is the breath of the soul, and hearing her speak made him believe it.

He pointed to her legs. Some of the blood was gone, but there were open gashes and stickers in deep. Her legs were swelling. "Infected. These could get infected. Make you sick. *Enfermo. ¿Comprende?*"

She grimaced, reaching to pull out the stickers. He took her hand and held it, and she looked up again, this time in pain.

"You need a *médico*." He looked into her eyes and could feel he was making contact. Maybe his voice could get through to her. His soul pouring into hers. "Trust me."

Something came across her face, like the sun breaking through a dark cloud. Then she nodded and handed him the plate. He told her to wait, that he would pull the truck around. He said it three times, hoping he had the right word for *wait*.

3

HIS NAME WAS GABRIEL MATOS MUERTE. He walked into the bedroom of his employer without hesitation. The man was propped against the headboard with breakfast on a tray across his lap, a computer beside him. He wore bifocals and kept his eyes on the screen as Muerte walked in, as if he was expecting the visit. Water ran in the bathroom, and the bed was rumpled beside the man. Muerte knelt by the side of the bed.

Sanchez spoke first, still staring at the laptop. "Is there a problem?"

"Yes. It's about last night. The exchange was not made."

The man looked up and removed his glasses, shifting enough to spill a generous amount of orange juice on the tray. "What do you mean? You said everything was in place."

"We're not sure what happened after they reached—"

"You're not sure? Where is she? Is she safe?"

"A Border Patrol agent was killed."

"I see nothing about that here." He pointed to the computer. "How do you know?"

"It wouldn't be in the American press yet. It was late last night. His body probably has not been discovered."

"What happened?"

Muerte shrugged. "Our driver took her through the border checkpoint. They went to the arranged meeting place. Something happened there. That's all we know."

"You should have gone with her."

"In hindsight, yes, that would have been better."

"This was a simple exchange. That's what you said. How long have you known this?"

"Only this morning."

He reached for the phone. "Have you called her?"

"She doesn't answer. She may have turned it off."

"Turned it off?" He spoke absently, without emotion.

"I believe she is still alive. As soon as I heard, I looked for the signal and I have seen movement."

"Where?"

"Across the border. Moving farther north."

A deep breath. "Get her and bring her back."

Muerte nodded.

"And what about the money?"

"We will find the money."

The man placed the tray on the floor angrily and stood, wrapping himself in a satin robe that hung on the headboard. He strode to the window overlooking the valley of the town of Herida. Sunlight was just peeking over the mountains.

A woman opened the bathroom door and stopped when she

saw Muerte. She wore a long, white robe and quickly glanced at Sanchez. "What's wrong? Someone was killed?"

"Get your clothes and leave," Sanchez said, still looking out the window.

"What?" She said it with equal annoyance and shock.

Before she could utter another word, Muerte turned and pulled a 9mm pistol from his belt. She gasped and put her hands in front of her.

"Stop," Sanchez said.

Muerte kept the gun aimed at her forehead. One shot there, one in the heart, and it would be over. A quick death. "She heard too much. We have to protect you and the girl."

"She heard nothing." Sanchez walked across the room and placed a hand on the woman's arm. "Now get your things together. Please."

When she had gone, Sanchez sat on the edge of the bed, elbows on knees. After a moment he said, "You think I am weak."

"It does not matter what I think."

"But that *is* what you think. About Maria."

"You made a decision. I respect what you're trying to do. I know the pressure you're under. You're thinking of her future, your own future. But I will protect you at all costs. And I will deal with this situation personally."

Below them, inside the compound walls, hired men went about their tasks in white uniforms. Worker bees doing what they were told, heads down, sensing they were being watched. Muerte would have ordered the men to carry the woman's body away. He had done it before.

"Was this the Border Patrol agent we had an agreement with?" Sanchez said. "Was he the one killed?"

"I don't know. All I was told is that the exchange never

took place. Someone must have intercepted them before the rendezvous."

"Then the package is gone."

"Perhaps."

"And she may be dead."

"There is movement on the signal. I am following her."

"The killer may have stolen the tracking device."

"True. I won't know until I get there."

"Where?"

"A small town north of the border, between Nogales and Tucson."

"And you have someone there?"

"I have someone heading there, yes."

"I want you to handle this. I want you to bring her back. And the money as well. And handle whoever did this. Take care of it."

"I'm leaving now."

The man ran a hand through his graying hair. "This is not what we needed. The Americans are already concerned about the violence."

"There were risks involved. But I am not concerned about the spineless Americans. We can handle them. I am more concerned with who may be behind this. We have to consider the possibility . . ."

"What possibility?"

"That she has been kidnapped. That she is being held. What they will require of you to allow her release."

This thought made the man sway, and he reached a hand to the glass table to support himself. "You told me there were risks with these people, but you never said they could be capable of such a thing."

"You know that is a possibility anytime she sets foot off the compound. Even inside the compound it is possible."

"I felt it worthwhile to take this risk. Sending Maria was a show of good faith on our part."

"Perhaps it will still work out for the best. Perhaps it is not as bad as we fear."

The man clenched his teeth and pointed a finger at Muerte's chest. "You bring her back. Do you understand?"

Muerte nodded.

"And find who did this. Take care of them."

Muerte left the man pacing the bedroom and yelling for his housekeeper. He walked toward the stables, dialing a contact on his cell, and heard the whirring noise of an open car window on the other end.

"Where are you?" Muerte said.

"Just getting here. There are police and Border Patrol vehicles everywhere. . . ."

"Get out of there. Find the girl."

"You said you wanted me to locate the satchel."

"Find the girl. Do you have her location?"

"She's been in one place all night."

"Check the coordinates—she is moving again. Just outside a little town called La Pena."

"All right. I will find her and bring her back—"

"No. Listen carefully. Are you listening to me?"

"Yes, Mr. Muerte. Always."

"Find her, retrieve the satchel if she has it, and dispose of her."

The noise on the other end lessened. A window closing. "Say that again, please?"

"You heard me correctly. Make it bloody, make it messy. Make it look like revenge. But do not let her get away."

"So your plan has not changed?"

"This is what I've been waiting for. You will be rewarded for this."

"I'm at your service. But one question."

Muerte was silent, so the man asked anyway. "Who was she dealing with? Wasn't she carrying money to pay for a future shipment?"

"That you do not need to know. Find her and make this happen. Communicate with no one but me. Do you understand?"

"Yes."

"I will join you this afternoon."

4

EVERY TIME THEY RAN OVER A CATTLE GUARD, the woman jumped at the noise. And they ran over quite a few to get to the main road and then quite a few more as they turned off it. It took J. D.'s truck a few minutes to get cool, but he could tell the air calmed her. Because of the stickers in her legs, she had to sit low in the seat and her skirt rose. He tried not to look.

They pulled up to a farmhouse, the shocks squeaking from the ruts made by rain the year before. He pointed at the handcuff and said, "I'm going to take that off. Stay here."

She stared at him with those big eyes, and he realized this was a girl whose whole life was in his hands.

He left the truck running with the air on and walked behind the house to the shop. He had seen the door was open from the road.

Harlan "Win" Winslow was a retired jack-of-all-trades,

which meant he had plenty of time to help anybody with anything. Planting, harvesting, castrating cattle, fixing a tractor, and landscaping were all in his repertoire. That's how J. D. had met him—the man had helped Slocum fix his air conditioner back in April as J. D. arrived.

Win was a member of a local cowboy church, a loose gathering of people who liked their religion simple and didn't mind horse apples near their place of worship. Dressing up meant a clean T-shirt and a freshly dusted pair of jeans. J. D. knew the group met at the barn on Win's farm, and he'd considered going just to frost Slocum, who hated religion. But even the warmth of Win and his friends couldn't push him toward church people. Win had asked J. D. a few questions when they'd met, but when J. D. gave him silence, it set the tone. It didn't seem to bother Win or keep him from engaging.

Win smiled and removed plastic goggles as he shut down his sander. Dust settled from the wood on the workbench. He shook J. D.'s hand and patted his back. "Good to see you, J. D. How's everything? Slocum's water pump working?"

"It's still down, but he's actually taking it seriously now that he's losing money on his produce."

"I should head on over there after my siesta; what do you think?"

"Couldn't hurt anything as far as the crops are concerned."

The man studied him with the moist eyes of the aged, looking deeper than the surface. His hair, what was left, was slicked back. Broad smile. As eager as hungry cattle to a hay wagon. "Well, you must have come here for something other than small talk."

J. D. was already scanning the tools. He hemmed and hawed, then gave up trying to hide. "I'm trying to get a handcuff off."

"Handcuff?" Win looked at J. D.'s wrists.

"Not for me. It's a long story. I figured a guy who worked Border Patrol as long as you did might have squirreled a key away. You wouldn't have anything like that, would you?"

"You think I'd retire without a good handcuff key?" He gave a laugh that rattled in his chest and filled the workroom. Over the workbench was a pegboard, where every size tool known to man hung neatly. Wooden tools and rusty metal ones, some ancient. Win opened three drawers in a dust-covered plastic chest before he pulled out the key.

"What, pray tell, do you need a handcuff key for?"

"To get a handcuff open."

"Makes sense." He handed the key to J. D. "Slocum's wife didn't hook him to his tractor, did she?"

J. D. laughed. "I'll be right back." He stopped at the door to make sure Win didn't follow him, but the man just tipped his hat, pulled the goggles down, and went back to sanding.

At first glance the truck was empty, and J. D. scanned the flat terrain. Then he took a breath as he spotted her, slunk down in the seat. He opened the passenger door and slid the key inside the handcuff. When he pulled the teeth through and it released, he felt like he had just climbed the first rung of a ladder he wasn't sure would reach the roof.

The woman smiled and rubbed her wrist.

"Alto aquí," he said.

She nodded.

J. D. returned the key to Win. The man took a look at the lone handcuff and the mangled chain that hung from it. "Somebody beat the stuffing out of that thing."

"I imagine they did. Thank you for your help."

"J. D., enlighten me. Who's in your truck?"

"I got a situation. I'm not sure anybody can help. I don't want to drag you into it."

"You've already dragged me." He handed the cuff back. "If you're wondering if I can keep a secret, I can."

"I better not."

Win took a step forward. "It won't do any good to carry a load alone. Especially if it's heavy lifting."

J. D. pawed at the ground with a boot. "I found somebody on my rounds. Near dead. Cactus sticking out of her legs."

"Her?"

He nodded. "I need to get her looked at before she gets an infection."

"An illegal?"

"I don't know. She's not from this side of the border, that's for sure."

"Let me take a look," Win said.

J. D. stopped him. "She's flighty. I think you might scare her."

"At least I'll be able to talk with her."

"True. But I don't want to get anybody in trouble. Slocum would kick me off the ranch if he knew. Might even be illegal to give her a ride to urgent care."

"Not illegal to give people water. Perhaps removing a handcuff is a gray area."

J. D. hooked his thumbs into his belt and stood his ground.

Win leaned against the bench. "You know, my great-uncle was killed out there near the Slocum ranch. Back then it wasn't drugs; it was liquor. During Prohibition there was a steady stream flowing back and forth over those mountains. He got the drop on one, shot him off his horse. Then the one behind him shot him in the back. He turned and put a bullet through the man's head. Right here." He pointed above one eye. "But my uncle bled out before he could find help. Me and my little brother found him still sitting in the saddle. He was a tough old bird."

"That's supposed to convince me to let you meet my friend? You must hate Mexicans like everybody else around here."

"I don't hate nobody. Those people coming across the border are just looking for something better than what they've known. I don't begrudge them. The ones I'd like to get ahold of are the drug runners. You've heard about what's going on down in Hermosillo and some other little towns? How our church and others are getting involved? People need to know the love of God no matter what side of the border they're on. Now let me take a look."

They walked out to the truck and J. D. opened the door. Win nodded toward the girl and spoke, checking her leg wounds and wincing. She was skittish at first, then seemed put at ease by the man's fluent Spanish. She smiled and J. D. thought there couldn't be a better sight in the world than a pretty woman smiling.

"I know a doctor down in Benson where you can take Maria," Win said with a nod. "I'll call him."

"Benson's a long way," J. D. said.

"Yeah, but you take her to the urgent care in La Pena and everybody in town will ask Slocum about his new maid. And why he's hiring illegals."

"What should I do? I mean, after he fixes her up?"

"What do you want to do?"

J. D. looked away. "Help her, I guess."

"Why you, J. D.? Why don't you let somebody else take care of her?"

He took off his hat and wiped his brow. "I don't know. I kind of feel responsible."

"Have you asked her what she wants to do?"

J. D. shook his head. "My Spanish isn't that good."

Win spoke to the girl, but J. D. could only pick up a few words, they were flying by so fast from both of them.

Win turned. "She says she doesn't know many in Tucson. Just needs to heal up a couple of days and she'll be on her way."

J. D. nodded.

"Can you keep her out of Slocum's sight that long?"

"I think so."

"She can stay here. Might be a better deal for her. It's cool in that back bedroom. My son moved out."

"Where'd he go?"

"Basic training. I say good luck to the Marines—they're going to need it the way that boy eats."

J. D. smiled. "I'll let you know what we decide. You'll call that doctor?"

"I'll dial him now." Win gave directions to the office, made sure of J. D.'s cell number, and said some final words to the girl before he closed the door. To J. D. he said, "You be careful. There's a storm coming up from the south and it ain't bringing rain."

J. D. nodded and got in the truck. He made his way to I-19, then headed southeast on I-10.

"Win's a good guy," he said finally. "But he's *religioso*."

She looked straight ahead.

"Win said your name's Maria." He reached out a hand. "Nice to meet you. I like that name. I'm J. D."

She handed him a dead fish and turned back to the landscape, which was lonesome desert. Every now and then came a farm or a subdivision, but mostly it was cactus and dust.

A murky haze hung over the mountains in the distance, and heat rose from the roadway.

He scanned through some FM channels, then hit the local AM talk station that rattled in one speaker. Another record scorcher for Tucson with no end in sight. Preparations being made for a speech by a politician—a governor running for president would make an appearance in Tucson on Sunday to talk tough about the border. And a breaking story reporters were investigating about a shooting overnight near Nogales.

News was change, but a shooting near Nogales seemed to him as normal as the sunrise.

There wasn't a car in the parking lot when they pulled up to the gray building. The sign said *Everyman Healthcare of Benson*. A doctor, a dentist, and a chiropractor were listed at the front. J. D. checked the hours and Thursday wasn't listed. Probably a golf day for the doctor.

He cursed and tried to explain to Maria, but she didn't seem to understand. While he was searching for any Spanish word from high school, his cell phone rang. It was the doctor saying he was almost there. A few minutes later a guy with a ponytail pulled up in an MG. It looked early sixties and out of place for Benson, except for the noise from the tailpipe. The man waved them inside as he fumbled with his keys.

Dr. Hodding Mercer introduced himself. Under his name on the door it said *Internist*. "Win called and said you needed help," the man said, glancing at Maria's legs as he worked the keys. "Those look nasty." He looked up at her. *"¿Fueron al desierto sin llevar linterna?"*

She smiled. *"Sí."*

The door opened and he ushered them inside a small waiting

room. The carpet was worn down to the pad, particularly at the front desk.

"This is my day off, so we shouldn't be bothered." He looked at J. D. "Does she have a change of clothes?"

"This is how I found her."

"You saw the Walmart coming in. Let me check her and then you can get her some shoes and clothes. There will probably be a prescription."

J. D. settled into an uncomfortable plastic chair and put his head against the wall. The office had been haphazardly decorated with Southwest fare—handmade pottery and paintings of cowboys on horses chasing cattle. Manila folders grew on a wall behind the front desk, piled and overflowing on invisible shelves. The wall clock was small and white with a cactus for the hour and minute hands, and the tick-tick of the second hand lulled him.

The hum of the air conditioner and the cool air on his skin caused him to close his eyes and drift. And in the drifting she came to him, her skin milky white, gliding like some apparition. Perhaps it was the doctor's office that conjured her, the smell of antiseptic and waiting rooms. Perhaps it was simply the longing of his heart. He could never prepare for these visits and was always left wanting more when he awakened.

She watched him drifting as his eyelids fluttered. He wanted to reach out to her, but he couldn't move. And then he felt a hand on his shoulder.

"Excuse me," the doctor said.

J. D. sat up quickly and wiped at his mouth. "You done already?"

He shook his head and the ponytail wiggled. "She had a nasty graze wound on her shoulder. A little lower and she'd have a broken clavicle or a punctured lung."

"She going to be okay?"

"She's very lucky; that's all I can say." The man handed him a prescription. "Fill this at the pharmacy. Pick up some clothes, too. Shoes, sweats . . . she can't wear what she has on."

J. D. got a Coke and stood in line at the Walmart pharmacy until a lady who spoke with a German accent took the prescription. She said it would be twenty minutes, so he grabbed some sweatpants, a T-shirt, and sandals that looked like they would fit Maria. He sat on a little metal bench near the pharmacy and watched people walk the aisles looking for Depends and Ensure and diabetic supplies. He noticed a blood pressure device around the corner and put his arm in. His pulse rate was 66. Blood pressure 106 over 70. Not too bad considering his family history and all the Big Carl cheeseburgers he had eaten in Tucson.

His cell rang. It was Dr. Mercer.

"A car just pulled up. The girl is scared. You'd better get over here."

Maria was talking in the background.

"Is it Border Patrol?"

"Don't ask questions. Come to the back of the building. Hurry."

J. D. put his Coke and the clothes on the metal bench and ran to his truck. The store was only a couple of minutes from the doctor's office, and as soon as he came in sight of the building, he saw a maroon Escalade parked sideways in two handicapped spots near the front. Definitely not Border Patrol.

The driver's door was open, and as he drove past, he spotted a computer between the front seats. He continued to the back exit and parked. He tried the door—locked—then peeked in a window, but the shades were drawn.

The pop-pop of automatic gunfire clenched his stomach. He couldn't move. Then someone screamed. He pounded on the door and Maria ran out and leaped into his truck.

J. D. called for the doctor.

"Get in!" Maria yelled.

Stunned, he jumped in and gunned the engine, spinning loose gravel and sand. The Escalade was still in front, door open.

"You speak English?"

She couldn't stop shaking.

"Okay, talk to me. Who was that guy?"

"He's a bad man. Sent by another bad man."

"Why? What have you done?"

He turned at the Walmart parking lot, but she waved him toward the road. "No, don't go here. He'll find us. Keep driving."

Instead of heading to the interstate, he went south on Route 80 and floored it. He guessed his blood pressure had risen. She kept looking back. When J. D. pulled out his phone, she grabbed it.

"Don't call the police!"

"That doctor risked his life to help you. The least you could do is send the police."

"No police."

He shook his head. What in the world had he gotten himself into?

They passed houses and pecan trees and several farms, then slowed when they hit St. David. They were almost to Tombstone when he took a right along a little country road he knew intersected with Route 90. Slocum had sold cattle to a man near here and showed J. D. a loop back to the interstate. Then J. D. remembered a checkpoint they'd have to pass through and decided against it.

"What are you doing?" she said when he turned in the middle of the road.

He told her about the checkpoint. "You have your papers? A passport?"

She didn't answer.

"No way he's going to find us out here," J. D. said. "Now tell me about this guy. Who is he?"

"He is very bad."

"Where's he from?"

"He lives in Herida. Where I'm from."

"And why would a guy from your town want to kill you?"

Silence.

He pulled off the road and parked. The sun was high now, blistering the landscape. The air-conditioning barely put a dent in the heat, and the stopped truck just blew hot air.

"Is the man from your town the one who put a bullet in your shoulder?"

"I don't know who did that."

He took a deep breath and wiped his forehead. "Look, Maria, I don't know who you are and I don't know your town in Mexico, but up here it's not normal for people to shoot you for no reason. Though that may be changing. I need to know more."

"Take me back to that man's house," she said. Jaw set. Eyes wild. "The one who speaks Spanish. I didn't ask you to help me."

"I know you didn't ask me, but that's what people do. You need a hand; we try to help."

"Take me back."

He threw it in gear. "Suit yourself."

They were nearing the turn when he saw the Escalade. The driver was glancing down at something when he passed, and

J. D. ran through the Stop sign and gunned the engine. A car honked from behind and flicked its lights. Seconds later the Escalade returned to the T in the road and raced toward them.

The car following hugged his tailgate. Behind it but gaining was the Escalade. A semitrailer ahead of them was going fifty. Double yellow. He swerved left to see three oncoming cars and a dip in the road. When the three cars passed, J. D. mashed the accelerator to the floor. He shot around the truck as the semi lost steam uphill, then passed just before another semi met them head-on.

"This bad man—what does he want from you? Money? Drugs?"

"I don't know," she said.

"Maybe we should pull over and have a talk with him." He said it as a joke, but she didn't smile.

"You don't talk with madmen. He will kill you just like the doctor."

"How do you know he killed him?"

"I know it because I know this man."

When they got to St. David, J. D. kept the accelerator mashed, hoping they might get stopped by the local police, but for once there was no cruiser waiting behind a rock wall or some shady tree. Just his luck. The semi they'd passed was behind them, but he saw no Escalade, and when they reached the interstate, J. D. headed east, trying to lose the car in the desert.

They pulled off at the next exit, halfway to nowhere, and sat on the shoulder where they could see the interstate. "I think we lost him," J. D. said.

"He will find us."

"How's he going to do that?"

She shrugged. "He just will."

"Where did you learn English?"

She looked out the window.

"You sound like you could have gone to school on this side of the border. I wish my Spanish was as good as your English."

"Do you have a gun?" she said.

"Slow down, Annie Oakley. I know we're in the Wild West, but you can't go shootin' up the place."

"If he catches us, he will kill us."

She turned to him with those brown eyes that made him wonder again about this mess. It had to be more than just an illegal looking for a better life. She looked as innocent as a schoolgirl. But her head worked differently than a schoolgirl's.

"We need a gun or we have no chance."

"Let's head to Walmart for the prescription, and you can pick me out a nice Remington with some pink shells." He smiled, hoping for some crack in her stony face, but there was none.

He parked behind the blue-and-gray building near a line of cars jockeying for an oil change or tires. The truck wouldn't be seen from the street. They walked through the automotive door and he told her to find what she wanted while he got the prescription, but she stayed as close as a baby calf to its mother.

They walked to the front, where his Coke and the clothes he'd picked were still sitting on the pharmacy bench. He paid for them as well as the antibiotic and bottle of Percocet.

"What is J. D. short for?" she said. "What are the names?"

"John David," he said.

A woman rang him up, and he slid his credit card and signed. He took Maria by the produce section near the front, opened the white bag with the antibiotic, and popped out a couple pills. "Go in the bathroom and change. And take these while you're in there."

"Will it make me go to sleep?"

"The Percocet will, but not the antibiotic."

She grabbed his arm. "Don't leave me alone."

"I'm not going anywhere, but I'm not coming in the ladies' room with you. Now go on. I'll be right here."

A lady at the customer service desk eyed them and he tipped his hat. "We paid for the sweats already." She glared as he leaned against a display of red, white, and blue cupcakes. They were getting a jump on the July 4 holiday.

The front door opened and closed with each new customer, but out of the corner of his eye he noticed the maroon Escalade roll past the door and stop in the fire lane.

How in the world did this guy find us?

J. D. walked to the women's room and opened the door an inch or two. "Maria, time to go. We've got a visitor."

She was already dressed. "I told you."

To the right was an emergency door that would sound an alarm. He took her hand and led her back through the produce and around frozen foods.

"You should buy a gun," she said.

"Yeah, if we had an extra hour to shop, maybe I would. You have to fill out forms and get cleared. I've seen it before—they escort you up front to check out. I guess we could load it at the cash register, but it doesn't seem like a good plan. Your friend will be waiting."

"He's not my friend."

"Yeah, I know."

They made it to automotive, looking back down the long aisle to the entrance. He couldn't see the Escalade.

J. D. scanned the parking lot, then waved her out. He drove over the curb, across a trash-strewn field, and through the ditch, onto the same road as the doctor's office. Maria kept watch behind them and didn't react when they passed the office. Yellow tape was up at the front and back doors, and an ambulance sat with its lights off.

"That doesn't look good," J. D. said, expecting her to say, *I told you so.*

He continued on the road, figuring it would lead farther away from the Escalade and toward a cross-street that intersected the main road, but it only took them back in the scrub brush to a housing development. He wound around for twenty minutes, keeping an eye on the gas gauge. The last thing he wanted was to be pumping gas when that old boy found them.

He made it to the interstate. There was a Kentucky Fried Chicken to their left and she stared at it, so he went to the drive-through and ordered her a three-piece meal, the wind kicking up and blowing heat like a hair dryer each time he rolled down the window.

She wolfed the chicken and potato wedges and biscuit without so much as a thank-you, but he was glad to see her eat. That was a good sign. Her fingers were greasy and she wiped them with an alcohol-soaked napkin she found in the packet with the plastic fork.

Maybe it was the chicken, maybe the alcohol, or it could have just been the sight of her. His mind returned to another drive-through and another beautiful girl. As far away as it seemed from here, from the front seat of his truck, it was as close as his own beating heart. He turned away from her so she wouldn't see the water in his eyes.

5

MUERTE WAS ON THE PHONE as he reached the border and waited in line at the crossing, keeping up on the progress, or lack of it, with the girl. Some things you had to do yourself. He had no control over the broken plan from the night before, but the mess at the doctor's office could have been avoided. It only drew attention, and this attention was not what he needed.

After showing his papers and enduring the trained dogs and the inept search of his vehicle, he immediately drove into Nogales to a nondescript three-bedroom stucco with a garden full of sunflower plants. A nice touch, he thought. Suburban. Familial. Just one of a cluster of homes that looked like the rest. There was a covered patio in front where a man and his family could sit in the evening and no one would know what happened inside.

The garage opened as he arrived, and a man named Ruiz

waved in welcome as Muerte pulled into the cavernous, empty space. There were wheeled dollies and boxes in one corner. Otherwise it was a clean slab.

The man shook his hand and led him inside the house. The floors were travertine and wood and his footsteps echoed. Two bedrooms had air mattresses shoved in corners with sleeping bags thrown on top. There were children's toys scattered about and a few books tossed in milk carton crates. Ruiz and his wife and children made this their home. The only computer in the house sat on a table in the dining room.

The third bedroom had a television on the wall and a pool table perfectly placed in the middle. But Ruiz asked Muerte to help him move the table to the side and removed the sixteen-by-sixteen tile underneath to reveal the mouth of a tunnel connecting to another home 120 feet away on the other side of the border. Muerte had okayed the digging of the tunnel but had never seen the elaborate construction. It was impressive in design. He'd pictured some dirt-strewn entrance, but the wood and concrete were remarkable.

"You've told no one I'm coming, correct?" Muerte said.

"Absolutely no one. Even my wife does not know."

"She is where?"

"She took the children to school and then went to work. At the hotel."

Ruiz seemed nervous and excited to have such a distinguished guest and offered something to eat, which Muerte politely declined. Then Ruiz demonstrated how they unloaded packages that came from the tunnel into trucks that fit into the extended garage. It was all done under the cover of the home, in the dead of night. It had been their most successful distribution point, but everyone knew it was only a matter of time before the tunnel would be discovered. That put Ruiz and his family at high risk, but the man trusted Muerte's connections. He and his family could be out in minutes, and they were willing to sacrifice the potential discovery for their short-term financial gain.

"I need an extra weapon," Muerte said.

"I have a TEC-9," Ruiz said.

"That will do nicely. And the grenades? The C-4?"

"In a box in the garage. Are you sure you are not preparing for a war?" Ruiz laughed.

Muerte stared at him. He needed an alternative if he didn't recover the weapon. "The rifle. It has not been found, correct?"

The man looked at the floor. "I did not have anything to do with the transfer."

High-powered rifles and AK-47s had been sold by undercover agents in the US with the purpose of tracking their route into the hands of the Mexican cartel. It was a sting operation gone horribly wrong for the Americans, but deliciously right for the cartel and even better for Muerte. Heads had rolled in Washington after a Border Patrol agent had been killed with one of the rifles in 2010. But Muerte did not want the discomfort to end there. The next target would pay for the ineptitude and pay dearly. In fact, the whole country would pay.

First things first. He had to take care of the girl and retrieve the satchel before putting his plan into action.

Muerte put a hand on Ruiz's shoulder. "I'm not accusing you. You have nothing to fear. I've put out the word about it. We'll recover it or one like it."

Ruiz relaxed and led him to the box in the garage. He unzipped several bags to show him the cache and Muerte examined the TEC-9.

"Please put the rest in the trunk for me."

"Yes, sir."

Muerte loaded the weapon and took a garage door opener from a shelf. Ruiz stored the boxes and bags. When he turned, Muerte shot him once in the forehead, and the man fell backward at an angle. Muerte dragged him a few feet to the side so he wouldn't back over the body. Then he stacked boxes at the garage entrance to block the view from the street. He backed out, hit the button to close the door, and drove toward Tucson.

6

J. D. HEADED TO the Winslow farm. He knew Slocum would be full of questions about the Mexican girl with all those bandages. Plus, Win had offered Maria a place to stay.

Something gnawed at the back of his mind about this woman. Like a song without a chorus. An unresolved melody. Something he couldn't chart on the chord progression of the day.

The radio news had already picked up on sketchy reports about a doctor shot and killed in Benson. He knew the speculation was that it was drug related. Waves of doubt crashed onto the shoreline of his life along with a sickness that wound around his soul. Would the police find surveillance video of him and Maria at the office? He hadn't seen cameras in the building, but he hadn't been looking. Did the doctor have a family? A wife?

Children? Grandkids? What about his patients, the "everymen" of Benson?

He slowed as he neared the Winslow farm. A plane passed overhead and he watched it slip through the sky. How many were inside that metal tube? How many people were hurtling hundreds of miles an hour above the earth with not a care in the world as to how they would get back down? They had put their lives in others' hands they didn't even know. There were parallels to his own life there, but he shook off the thoughts and focused.

"I think we need to call the police," he said as they pulled into the Winslow driveway.

"No police."

"Why not?"

She didn't answer.

"You can't just say something like that and then shut up. It doesn't work that way."

The truck got hotter as they slowed and the gas gauge neared empty. He had watched it dip like water running out of a bucket. And with the price of gas, it was an expensive bucket.

"Why didn't you tell me you spoke English?"

"I didn't know if I could trust you. I was afraid."

"Fair enough."

"And it was fun to hear you try to speak Spanish." She glanced at him with a hint of a smile. "I like watching you figure out the words."

"I'm glad you got a kick out of it."

A hawk flew past them and circled over prey. There was silence again, nothing but the hum of the motor and the whir of the hot air through the vents.

"We need to call the police."

"*No police.*"

"It strikes me that you're the kind of person who doesn't get told what to do. Am I right? Your mama give you whatever you wanted? Your daddy not able to tell you *no* once in a while?"

She looked toward the barn and the chickens surrounded by wire mesh that ran all the way up to the coop. Because of coyotes, you couldn't just put up a fence. You had to protect the birds because all they did was peck at the dirt. Just waiting to be grabbed by something hungry with sharp teeth.

"I don't know how they treat people where you're from, but that doctor helped you and it cost him his life. And it's probably going to cost mine before this is done."

She bit a fingernail and studied the chickens. "I didn't ask you to help me."

"True, but I'm here. I'm mixed up with you. I think I deserve to know what's going on. I want to help you, but I have to know who I'm helping. And why you're in this mess."

He stared at her silky black hair and slender arms. She was an uncommonly beautiful woman, but it seemed every time he looked at her, there was some discovery, like each angle brought out something new he hadn't seen. Hauling her back from death had been like picking up a wounded rattlesnake. Sooner or later the fangs and venom had to appear. But that wasn't right either. With a rattler you only had to deal with one head. This girl was a hydra, and there was no telling how many heads were on their way.

"Suit yourself," he said. He grabbed the door handle and put a foot on the hot gravel.

"Wait." She clutched his arm—a strong grip, unlike her handshake, and with it came a shock and a tingle echoing like his first electric guitar. An uncle had given him the Fender knockoff and an old amp with a frayed power cord. If he was holding the guitar when he plugged it in, electricity radiated up his arm.

"I will tell you what I know," she said. "But there are things I don't know."

"You mean you lost your memory?"

"No, I remember too much." She took her hand away and leaned forward to follow the hawk.

He sat and closed the door, staring at her profile.

She turned, her eyes misty and full of hurt. "I did not want that man to die. He was very kind. He comforted me. He did nothing but help me, and I was the reason he was killed."

"Well, you didn't pull the trigger, so you can't blame yourself." It was the best he could do at consolation. "How do you know the guy who shot the doctor?"

"I don't know him. I know *of* him."

"Why would he want you dead?"

"Because of who I am."

"Who are you, the queen of Mexico?"

She smiled, and the flash of white took his breath. "I am not a queen. I am a woman who wants to live."

"There's a lot of women who want to live that don't have a guy with an Uzi following them. Why does he want to kill you?"

"Because the man who hired him ordered it."

"And who's that?"

"His name is Muerte."

Now he was getting somewhere. Names. Reasons. "What does Muerte have against you?"

She stared at her hands and so did he. Soft and delicate and unaccustomed to hard work. When she didn't answer, he said,

"How did the guy with the gun find you? How did he know you were at the doctor's office?"

"I don't know."

"Well, the more you talk, the less I feel like *I* know. But we know that doctor is stone-cold dead. And if you really care and you're sorry about what happened, we should call the police. They're the only ones who can help us."

She rotated the black ring on her pinkie. "You don't understand."

That's for sure. "Most people who come across the border are looking for a better life. But it strikes me that you're not here to get a job and send money back to the family."

"I live near a small town, and there are many who want to come here to work. But I had a passport. No longer—I lost it last night in the desert."

"Really? How do you lose a passport?"

She didn't answer.

He tried again. "What brought you to the Slocum place?"

She furrowed her brow.

"The farm where I found you is owned by a man named Slocum. It's where I work. Why'd you choose that farm?"

"There are some things you choose. Others that choose you. Do you understand?"

"You stumbled onto us."

"Yes, I stumbled onto the farm. But I think there was a reason. If it had been another farm, I might have died. But you found me. I think there was a purpose in that."

He laughed. "When you figure it out, tell me."

"Why do you laugh?"

"Because I've been looking for the answer to that one for a while." He said it leaning back and stretching his arms; then he noticed the stains of his underarms and the mildewed-basement smell of his shirt and quickly lowered them. "I've been looking for the purpose of things my whole life and I've yet to come up with any."

"Maybe it was God's will that brought you to me. I prayed and asked him to help me, and you came."

"Is that so?"

"When I first saw you, I thought you were an angel."

"Well, there's a first time for everything, I guess. I didn't know you were *religioso* like Win. You two ought to get along well, but I'm betting he's going to be on my side of this."

"What side?"

"The side that says we need to call the police. Explain what happened last night, how you got into the desert, the guy in the Escalade, the whole shooting match. No pun intended. They'll protect you from this Muerte and get you back home in one piece. Maybe even help you find your passport that's—"

"No. If I go to the police, worse things will happen. You have to believe me. These men will not stop. And I'm not the only one they want to kill."

J. D.'s cell phone buzzed.

"There are others," she said. "Muerte is pure evil. And I believe—"

She stopped midsentence and J. D. looked at where she had set her eyes. Win had stepped off his porch and was walking toward them, one hand holding a phone to his ear, the other waving like there was a fire.

J. D. rolled down the window and Win leaned in.

"You heard about the doc?" J. D. said.

Win nodded. "The Benson police just called. They wanted to know why I had called his cell phone."

"What did you tell them?"

"That I had a friend who needed help." Win looked at the bandages on Maria. "What happened down there?"

"To tell you the truth, I'm not sure," J. D. said. "But there was a well-armed lunatic after her. The doc got in the middle."

Win winced and shook his head. "The police are headed here. I need to tell them what I know. About you. About the girl." He stole a glance at Maria.

"What are you going to say?" she said.

J. D. saw the surprise on Win's face. "Yeah, she knows more English than the two of us put together."

Win's voice softened. "Maria, we want to help you. *I* want to help you. But we have to—"

"You are not helping if you go to the police. You are not helping if you have me arrested. I will be killed."

Win shook his head. "Things aren't that way here. The police will help locate—"

"No," she interrupted. "This will only make it worse."

"I'm going to answer their questions," Win said. "I'm obligated to tell the truth and before God I will."

"How does talking to the police make it worse?" J. D. said.

"You don't understand."

There was an awkward silence until Win said, "Iliana is making carne asada. Why don't you join us? We'll clear all of this up when the officer gets here."

J. D. pulled up to the house, and Maria slowly got out and followed Win inside. Iliana Winslow was a small woman with short black hair. Every time J. D. saw her, he wanted to rename her "Our Lady of Perpetual Smiles." Chubby cheeks and a broad grin. She hugged Maria and welcomed her.

"Thank you," Maria said. "Could I use your restroom?"

Iliana showed her the bathroom, down a hall toward the back, and the two men sat at the table. The aroma of spices and sizzling meat filled the kitchen. Her cooking was the reason Win had to punch another hole at the tip of his belt.

J. D. told them about Benson, the chase by the man in the Escalade, how he appeared again at Walmart. "I swear, it's like he knew exactly where she was."

"Do you think it's drugs?" Iliana whispered, clutching a spatula like it was a rosary.

J. D. nodded. "I don't know what else it could be. But she's not carrying anything. Why would they want to track her down and kill her? Doesn't make sense."

"Perhaps she has drugs inside?" Iliana said, still in a whisper. "The newspapers say people swallow packages and come across the border."

J. D. shrugged. "The X-ray machine over at Slocum's isn't working, so I couldn't check that." Neither of them smiled.

"She was wearing a handcuff," Win said.

"Half of one, you're right."

Win ran a hand through his graying hair. "The world makes no sense. Violence, drugs, bloodshed. Dr. Mercer was a good man trying to help people." He stared out the window. "Like Bible times. Look at the news. It's either Sodom and Gomorrah or a flood or hurricane."

J. D. leaned back to look down the hall. The bathroom door was still shut. The toilet flushed and he put his elbows back on the table. "What will the cops from Benson do with her?"

"Question her," Win said. "If she's done nothing wrong— and it sounds like she hasn't—they'll eventually send her home."

"She says she lost her passport in the desert."

Win lowered his voice and scratched at his stubbly beard.

"I'm not sure you can believe everything you hear. Something's off with her, J. D. And you can see, the deeper you go into this, the worse it'll get. For both of you."

J. D. glanced down the hall again. "Well, it's over now. We'll take what comes."

"You'll be all right with the Benson law."

"I helped her, though. Drove her down there. You don't think they'll have a problem with that?"

"She was nearly dead. Dehydrated as far as I could tell. What were you supposed to do, leave her?"

"From what she says, sending her back across the border is a death sentence too. Not sure why, but she seems confident that's what'll happen."

"Well, I don't think I want to know the particulars. Maybe she brought this on herself by carrying something across the border. Maybe she's a victim. Only thing you can do is make sure she doesn't make you a victim."

"Sounds kind of cruel. Just look out for number one? Aren't you supposed to be your brother's keeper, do unto others and all that?"

Win stared at him. "I'm asking God to give us wisdom about her. About what to do. I've been praying since you came here. But if you don't know what to do, you start by obeying the authorities."

J. D. sat with his thoughts and his past swirling like the cumin, cilantro, and jalapeño pepper mixed with the beef juice. Then his ears pricked as the engine of his truck fired. When he made it to the door, there was nothing but dust on the driveway.

7

J. D. HURRIED OUTSIDE and Win followed. Maria turned right out of the driveway and a plume of dust billowed behind her on the road. Which way she would turn when she got to the hard road was anybody's guess.

"I left the keys in there," J. D. said. "But she won't get far. Truck's almost out of gas. I'll give her to Main Street in La Pena before it runs out."

"I'll call the police and report the vehicle stolen," Win said.

"No, don't do that. She's liable to meet them on the way in, anyhow. Can I borrow your car?"

"Use the Suburban. Keys are in it."

The Suburban door creaked open and J. D. stepped in, then looked over his shoulder through the open window. "Tell Iliana to save some meat. I'll be back as soon as I round up my truck."

"Be careful, J. D. Remember, don't become a victim."

Win stood in front of his farmhouse like a sentinel and J. D. felt a twinge in his gut. That was a picture of an easy friendship in the rearview mirror. Despite J. D.'s silence, the man and his wife had taken him into their lives like he was a lost son come back from a forgotten war. And they still had no idea what he'd done or been through. Or maybe they did. Maybe something inside had drawn them to the rough road he was traveling.

The Suburban coughed and sputtered to life and a voice came over the stereo. Some preacher on an AM station talking about trials and the love of God. The book of Job. J. D. was halfway down the driveway before he found the Power button.

The steering was loose, as were the shocks, so the vehicle bounced and shimmied down the driveway like a ride at the county fair. He gunned the engine when he made the turn onto the road and cut it hard but still nearly ran into the ditch on the other side.

He didn't pass any cars on the dirt road, and when he got to the blacktop, he worried again if she would've headed to town or gone south. The southern route led to a lake and a campground, basically a dead end, but she had no way of knowing that. There would be no dust to track her and once he committed, he was stuck with the decision.

He turned left and raced toward the lake, knowing that just over the ridge was a wide-open area where you could see for a mile. He came up over the ridge, his heart sinking when all he saw were a few longhorns in the distance and the rolling desert with the wires running beside the road.

He did a three-point turn and nearly hit a javelina scurrying from the brush to cross the road. Maria was getting farther away every second, but he also knew there was a finite amount of gas in the truck. She had no money, so he would find her eventually. But he didn't know if he could convince her to talk with the police. If he dragged her back to Win's place, she might head out on foot. A girl like that might cross the Sahara in flip-flops.

He punched the gas but swerved as something flew through the air toward the truck. A bird in flight had hit a power line, and it tumbled to the ground, wings spread, toppling end over end until it collided with the hot pavement. Feathers flew. It was like his life. Flying along unaware of hidden dangers, things growing in the dark he couldn't see. He'd thought of writing a song about God watching sparrows fall but not giving a hoot about humanity. He would probably never put it to paper.

He passed the dirt road he had turned from and continued down a winding hill, past a farm with a sign that said *Fresh Eggs for Sale*. Most people here lived on farms, but several developments had begun and were then abandoned when the housing market collapsed. Clumps of two and three homes and then plastic PVC pipe sticking out of the ground with the phone lines already buried but nobody to talk.

Fences lined the roads and he hit a cattle guard. He passed a winery and a little white church—convenient for the Communion tray, he supposed—then a clearing opened up and the road meandered down and up another hill in a V. At the bottom of the hill, off to the side of the road, was his truck.

"Bingo," he said softly. He felt a lightness, something like the relief of finding a wandering puppy just as coyotes began howling.

He couldn't tell if Maria was still in the truck, but she wasn't in the pasture by the road. He barreled down the hill, his front wheels bald and wobbling, and noticed another vehicle topping the ridge ahead and speeding toward the bottom. It only took a second to recognize the maroon Escalade and that the other side of the V was a lot shorter.

He cursed and mashed the accelerator. The Suburban picked up speed, bobbing and weaving down the undulating roadway, but the Escalade beat him. The driver's door opened and a dark-skinned man with closely cropped hair got out and moved toward the truck. Now he saw movement inside. Maria was trying frantically to move to the passenger side, as if the distance would protect her.

The gun came up and the man braced himself as he sprayed bullets. Glass shattered and exploded. Maria had to have been hit.

In that split second, acting on something from the gut, J. D. made his decision. Whether it was a protective instinct to help the innocent or levels of grief and revenge that rolled like waves, he did not know or care. He simply gritted his teeth, kept his foot on the accelerator, and bore down on the man.

The gunman looked up, then jumped toward the Escalade. J. D. slammed into the open door of the vehicle. A sickening crunch of the door and then a thud as the man caromed off the hood of the Suburban and went airborne. J. D. slammed on the brakes and screeched to a halt in the middle of the double yellow, but he had already gone fifty yards.

He ran back, heart pounding, trying to breathe. The man lay a good twenty yards behind the Escalade at the edge of the road, his head twisted to the side, blood gushing from glass wounds to his face. J. D. picked up the gun on the other side of the road and ran to the truck.

He found Maria hunkered on the passenger-side floor, wedged between the glove compartment and the seat, looking up at him with tears streaming.

He reached out a hand to help her. "You all right?"

She nodded. Somehow the bullets had missed. Maybe an angel had protected her. Maybe the guy was a bad shot.

J. D. put the gun on the passenger seat and ran to the man lying on the road. He hadn't moved and his eyes were open and staring into the sun. J. D. put a hand to the man's neck. No pulse.

Footsteps behind him. Maria holding the gun. She looked down with hatred and lifted the barrel.

"He's dead. He's not going to bother you."

She said something in Spanish he didn't understand, but he didn't really need a translation.

"We need to go," she said.

He stood. "Maria, this is the guy. The police have their man. You don't have to worry. They'll match the bullets from that gun, don't you see? Wait here and we'll explain what happened."

"Stay if you want." She slung the gun over her shoulder like it wasn't the first time she'd done it and headed for the Suburban.

He glanced back at the Escalade. The tinted window had shattered and the computer lay on the floor, still on.

"Maria, they'll protect you."

She stopped. "No, they won't. They can't. I told you he would be back. And Muerte is coming. Stay here if you like. I don't need your help now."

"You don't need my help? You'd be dead if it wasn't for me!"

"Then I say thank you. From the heart."

She tossed the gun in the Suburban and got in. J. D. looked at the dead man, at the glass, the door smashed and barely hanging on the Escalade, the violence that made no earthly sense at all. Two men had died in the space of a couple of hours and he had been part of it. If he went with her, he'd be a desperado.

Stealing a friend's truck to go . . . where? Where did you hide from such things?

But staying with the body felt like giving up. Waiting for the police to question him was waving a flag he didn't even know he had. And he knew what he decided next would likely change the course of his life and maybe hers. Or had he changed course that morning when he brought her in from the desert?

Maybe his course had been set as soon as he came to Arizona.

Or perhaps this decision had been made for him months ago when he tossed dirt on the casket and walked away from life. Maybe all of this was just fate turning the doorknob.

Maria closed the door, and the Suburban coughed and sputtered and coughed again, the starter struggling to fire the points and plugs. And it was then that it hit him full force. He wasn't throwing anything away because there was nothing left. What was Slocum going to do, fire him? He only worked for the food and knowledge of how to farm. He had no real ties here, just acquaintances at the farmers' market. And the Slocum kids. Though he had been distant and gruff, they were attracted to him and the feeling was mutual. Win and Iliana too.

He walked slowly up to the vehicle and saw her watching him in the side mirror.

He opened the door. "Scoot over. I'm driving."

8

AS HE DROVE INTO THE COUNTRYSIDE, Muerte tried to focus on
the computer screen, but the road became unpredictable. Full
of curves and turns. He tried to zoom in on the signal but hit
the wrong button and cursed as it expanded.

He was trying to get from a view of the entire US back to
this area of Arizona when he pulled up behind an older car with
a female driver, slow as frozen molasses. She sat so low that all
he could see above the seat was her hair. She was a turtle with
a Lincoln Town Car. A small dog stood on her backseat, sniff-
ing at the air, its tongue hanging out on the right side. Twin
troubles of heat and genetics were working against the dog.

The road was coursed with solid yellow lines because of
the unnerving blind curves. Muerte let off the accelerator and
switched to his phone app, looking up to make sure the old

woman hadn't slowed more. The girl was close. She was somewhere ahead on this route.

He pulled out to pass, and at that moment an SUV barreled up a hill toward him and he swerved back, just missing the vehicle. The computer clattered to the floor and he cursed again. His heart pounded and he caught the old woman shaking her head in front of him, her silver hair matted like a snowy cap. The speed limit here was fifty, but the curve they were coming up on had yellow signs that said thirty-five and her brake lights flashed. He pulled past her in the curve, glancing at her as he went by. She was talking to herself, or maybe to him, and it was all he could do to resist pulling the gun and taking her life. It would have been so easy. Like shooting a crow sitting by carrion.

He came up over a ridge where it looked like he could see all the way to the Mexican border. The world spread out from here and the view made him wish he had taken care of the girl long ago. She could have had an "accident" on the farm and he wouldn't be going through this trouble. In the distance he spotted two vehicles—one on the right, one on the left. He recognized the maroon Escalade and pulled up behind a body. Miguel lay dead beside the road.

He expanded the view of the tracking device on his phone. The girl was traveling behind him now on the same road. She had passed him. Muerte closed his eyes and struggled to remember the make and model of the SUV. It was his gift. An ability to recall fragments of details from flashes. The surprised looks of those who had no idea this was the way they would die. Dead men with gold fillings. He could remember which molar in some instances. There was no license number, just a flash of color—a two-tone tan. The word *Suburban* and the face of a man driving. Facial hair. A mustache and beard. Or perhaps it was just growth and not a full beard. Caucasian. A cowboy hat. She had gained help on her journey.

Something squeaked behind him, metal on metal. The old woman, braking. The car took a painfully long time to stop, the brakes like fingernails on a blackboard. Muerte stood over the body and stared at her, willing her to keep going. When she didn't, he motioned for her to move, and the dog jumped at the back window with its head at an angle, whiteness covering the left eye with a cloudy film. Its tongue slapped the window and a cascade of saliva ran down the glass.

The woman hit the Power button for the passenger window and the glass inched down. She spoke over the barking. "Is that fellow dead?"

Muerte gripped the pistol behind him and leaned down. His stare should have been enough to move her, but she seemed confused. Ancient hands gripped the wheel. Her skin was opaque and wrinkled, and fat hung from the undersides of her arms.

"If you know what's good for you, ma'am, you'll keep driving."

"Is that a threat, mister?" She scanned the scene. "What happened here?"

She studied Muerte and then rose up a little to see the body. Muerte took a breath and counted to three, glancing at the road, giving her time to move. When she didn't budge, he brought out the gun.

"I don't know what's happening to this country," she said. She stepped on the accelerator and crawled between the cars, talking as she drove, the window still down.

Muerte nudged Miguel with his foot but he could tell the stare of death. He took the man's wallet, retrieved the laptop from the damaged car, and moved to the truck. The passenger door was still open. He pulled out the registration under the name John David Jessup and shoved it in his pocket. He thought about dragging Miguel's body into the Escalade and torching the car but decided it would take too much time, and there was no telling when someone else would come upon the scene. Besides, by the time the authorities figured out what had happened here, the girl would be dead and the country in shock. It would take a long time to make the connection between this road mishap and what he had planned. Maybe they never would.

The image on the screen moved toward the city, so he swung the car around and drove away quickly. Another two miles down the road, he passed a police car heading the opposite direction, its lights off. He slowed his breathing and checked his speed. He couldn't let paranoia overcome him. He was simply another car on the highway. A hunter, in control.

He would wait until the girl and her friend stopped, wait until they landed, like flies, and then he would strike. Hard. Catch them unaware, finish the chapter, and move to the next.

9

SMALL DECISIONS LEAD TO BIG ONES. That's what J. D.'s father had always said. Integrity comes in inches, not miles, and is built over time. Brick by brick, day by day, one decision after another. The mortar holding it all together is truth and love for your fellow man. If you care for others more than you care for yourself, you're on the right track.

These were J. D.'s thoughts as he drove, reflections of his life, words from his father that sounded good growing up, things J. D. had seen at work every day. Integrity was cumulative, compounding like interest on a debt, growing in the heart and mind as his father said. He had tried to live by the rule, but at some point another equation took over, almost the converse of the postulate: It only takes one decision to begin unraveling the cord. One misstep can lead from integrity to devastation and encompass everyone in a man's path.

There had been a series of arguments, of fallings-out between J. D. and his father. The two were as different as night and day, and his mother struggled to become both dusk and sunrise to bring them together. His brother, Tyler, had been the uninterested bystander.

In spite of his desire to live as an island, wanting his choices to affect only himself, J. D. knew he was connected. The ripples of his life touched the beachheads and inlets of a thousand hearts. Just like his father's life. The one he had not measured up to. And he was beginning to understand he never would. He would never be the man he wanted to be, the man his father wanted. Life didn't allow that now.

But he had also seen through his father's facade. The parent who said he only wanted the best for his son had shown he simply wanted a problem-free, worry-free retirement without encumbrances. The man's own cord had unraveled, and J. D. saw the spiraling free fall of his father's life with all the feathers and the hard pavement underneath. J. D.'s choices had revealed these hidden cracks and fissures. He hadn't seen it when he was younger, when he was reaching for the top, striving for success, but now that he was at the bottom he could. And that was a gift—one he would never have put on a list, but there it was.

He drove in the noisy silence of the Suburban toward the city. Even with the windows up, there was a whistling of wind through the sunburnt window molding. The air conditioner had desperately needed recharging ten years earlier. He was sweating in places he didn't know he had. But going toward people instead of away from them seemed right. Hide in the middle of the crowd rather than behind a saguaro. There were problems with that plan, but it was the best he could come up with under the circumstances.

Still on I-19, his cell rang and he answered.

It was Win. "Did you find her, J. D.?"

"I did, but there's a long story behind the finding I'm not ready to tell."

"Where you at?"

"Can't tell you that either, compadre. Probably better you don't know. But I'm going to have to borrow your vehicle. You okay with that?"

"Sounds like you're already on your way and it doesn't matter if I'm okay with it."

"You're probably right."

"How far you going?"

"Can't say. Just need to get out of town."

"Are you in trouble, J. D.?"

"It appears so. Feels like I'm coasting toward trouble downhill with the engine in neutral."

"And you have bald tires and wheels out of alignment. I know the feeling."

"Well, it'll work out." He said it with a measure of dread.

"Yes. But . . . I'm concerned."

"I know how to take care of myself, Win."

"All right. Just know that's a farm truck. It's not meant for the open road. I drive it around here but there's no registration. Add some oil when you fill up."

Maria rolled her window down, and J. D. had to plug his left ear and hold the steering wheel with his knee.

"There's something else you ought to know," Win said.

"What's that?"

"There's a loaded .45 in the glove compartment. I keep it there for coyotes."

J. D. looked at Maria, her hair swirling in the hot wind. Like a vision of something that fell from heaven or crawled up from hell—he couldn't tell which.

"I'll get the truck back to you. But I can't say when."

He could picture the man's face, grimacing with regret. "I'm praying for you, J. D. That you'll go to the police. Let them handle this."

"It's not just her now, Win. I'm mixed in too. Do me a favor and call Slocum. I won't be back today or at the farmers' market tomorrow. Explain what happened."

And then it hit him. He had a stash of cash in the schoolhouse. For an emergency. He thought about asking Win to retrieve it, but he couldn't do that. The police would be at Win's any minute. In fact, they might have heard the whole conversation.

"Good-bye, Win. Thanks for everything."

He flipped the phone closed, and like a flash of lightning, Maria grabbed it and tossed it out her window.

"Why'd you do a fool thing like that?" he said. "That's our lifeline."

"It's also a way to locate you. It will get you killed or arrested. The same with your credit card. They will find you. And if they don't, he will."

"You talking about Muerte?"

She nodded.

"Who is he? How do you know him?"

She shook her head, and he interpreted the silence the same as his words to Win. The less he knew, the better, at least from her perspective.

"You keeping quiet isn't helping—"

"Your friend is right. You should go to the police. Drop me at the next exit."

"I'm not dropping you anywhere." He glanced at the mountains all around them and the blue sky so clear it looked like a glass bowl over them. "So what do you suggest we do?"

"I try to stay alive."

"This isn't just about you. I'm throwing in with you, as they say back home. Good or bad, we're together."

"Why?"

"I don't know. Maybe I feel sorry for you."

She didn't respond.

"You said yourself that maybe God brought us together."

"What do you believe about God?"

"I don't think it matters what I believe. It's an exercise to make sense out of stuff we'll never make sense of."

She was quiet, so he went on. "But if you're right and the big guy is up there pulling the strings, there's a reason I'm mixed in with you. And the question becomes, how is he going to help us survive?"

She said something he couldn't hear, then turned to him with those big brown eyes all cloudy and red. "I said I don't know." She choked it out before turning to stare out the window again. He thought she was probably thinking of the place where she grew up or maybe her mother's tender kiss at night or a favorite dog she had as a little girl. Who can know what goes on inside the mind of a beautiful woman with secrets?

They passed a sign for a Quality Inn and another cheap hotel, but it was too close to La Pena. There was a Holiday Inn at the Duval Mine exit, but he kept driving, kept the engine gauge moving upward toward hot.

"We could head up toward Phoenix. Maybe stay at Casa Grande. Someplace this Muerte guy wouldn't think to look."

Maria shook her head. "I need to stay here."

"And why's that?"

She didn't respond. When they passed the Harkins Theatre, she was all eyes, taking in the restaurants and stores.

"When's the last time you went out to see a movie?" he said.

"We have only a small theater in the town where I live. They play old movies."

"Well, when this is all over, what do you say we go?"

"I would like that, but I don't think this will ever be all over."

J. D. shook his head and banged on the steering wheel. "All right, let's talk. You and me. A sit-down, come-to-Jesus meeting."

"I don't understand."

"'Come to Jesus' means we come clean. You tell the truth about what's going on. You and I are dancing around it. You're scared of what's about to happen with Muerte, and I don't know who he is and what you're mixed up in. The only way we're going to get through this is for you to tell me what's really going on."

"All right," she said. "If you tell me the truth, I will tell you the truth."

"Deal."

Her back was straight now as if she was ready for a fight. "Are you married?" she said.

He took a deep breath. "I was."

"What does that mean?"

"It means I was and I don't have a wife now. I don't see what that has to do—"

"You wear a wedding ring."

"Right, I do."

"If you are not married, why do you wear a ring?"

"That's a long story."

"Now it's you who is dancing. Tell me."

"All right, I'll tell you about the ring after you tell me about Muerte and why he wants you dead. Deal?"

She nodded. "Let's go somewhere safe. Where we can have this come-to-Jesus discussion."

He kept going toward I-10, then took one of the first exits heading toward El Paso. It looked like the Route 66 of his childhood with souvenir stands and Wild West memorabilia.

They came to a stretch of fast-food restaurants—chains and local taco stands that were the gateway to hotels and motels you wouldn't find on the Internet. The cheapest was $21.95 a night with no questions asked. The sign outside the one he picked said ESPN and HBO were available and the pool was open year-round, but nobody was staying there for the pool or what might happen to be on TV. In fact, nobody was staying there at all, it looked like.

He could hear the roar of the interstate leaking through the back window of the office as he paid cash for one night. The desk clerk said they needed to keep a credit card on file for any damages. He was a slight man with a rubber tube under his nose, an oxygen pump seeping fresh air into him while he tapped a Camel on the ashtray. Looked like a dangerous combination to J. D., but who was he to judge?

"What if I don't have a credit card?" J. D. said.

The man got a faraway look and stared at the green computer screen. "Everybody's got a credit card. Can't buy anything these days without a credit card."

"Well, I'd just as soon pay a cash deposit if you'll let me."

"Can't do it. Manager would have a fit."

"Then I'll just head on over to your competitor. They said I could pay cash."

The man pushed a key across the counter with the number 12 on the plastic fob. "Give me enough for two nights and I'll refund it if you leave tomorrow. First floor, down the way." He pointed his cigarette.

J. D. gave him the cash and then another twenty. "If anybody comes asking about us, or if you see a Mexican fellow hanging around, call the room, okay?"

The man took the bill and stuffed it in his shirt pocket. He studied the girl in the front seat of the Suburban and J. D. could see the tumblers turning in his brain.

"Don't make me regret this," the man wheezed. "I got a job here and I want to keep it."

"I understand."

J. D. thought about getting two rooms, the voice of his father talking about integrity again. *"Don't let it appear wrong to anyone. Don't take a chance."* But J. D. decided against it. If somehow Muerte found them and Maria died, he'd blame himself. He decided to keep her close no matter how it looked.

Room 12 had two double beds, one with a "Magic Fingers" machine mounted on the headboard. Inside was hotter than his place at the ranch and had a wet-carpet smell, but once he turned the air conditioner on, it cooled. There were orange bedspreads, an ice bucket and plastic bag on a little table with two chairs. He couldn't get the curtains closed all the way, so he pushed the table near the wall and propped up one of the chairs to hold them together.

He placed the automatic on the bed closest to the window and walked outside to check if anyone could see in. Then he drove the Suburban three full blocks away and parked on a residential street that looked rougher than a cob. He retrieved the handgun from the glove compartment and placed it in the back of his jeans, letting his shirttail cover it. It would be just his luck if he shot himself in the rear.

The shower was going behind the closed bathroom door when he returned and he wondered if she was still there. He stood at the door, ready to call out her name or knock. Then the toilet flushed and he relaxed. He tossed the key on the table and hid the pistol in the nightstand under the Gideon Bible and the Book of Mormon. He lay on the bed, his boots on, and listened to the air conditioner hum. It wasn't the Hilton, but the room was a step up from Slocum's place.

Exhaustion reached him like a wave, something he tried hard to keep at bay on the farm. Of late they had been stopping outside work at eleven because of the heat, but he found it hard to stay inside. He gravitated to the shade tree behind the farmhouse where the kids would find him and bring a cool drink, then stay out to push each other on the tire swing. The sounds of their giggling and calls to go higher took him back where he didn't want to go. Just a hand on the tire was all it would take to make them happy, and he couldn't give it.

What had become comfortable and normal was gone. How had his life fallen apart so quickly? The answer stood in the plastic shower stall fifteen feet away, naked as the day she was born. He pushed that thought away when he heard her crying. At least he thought he heard soft sobs through the thin walls.

He clicked the TV remote and was about to flip the channel when the local news teaser appeared.

A woman with blonde hair and thick makeup looked into the camera. "Here are the stories we're working on in the Action 4 newsroom." Video of yellow police tape at Dr. Mercer's office flashed on-screen. "A beloved Benson doctor is dead and police are following leads on the shoot-out that took his life. Details at six." There was nothing about the man in the Escalade.

He switched to ESPN and watched grown men kicking a soccer ball and grown men and women in the stands by the thousands, and he thought there was no hope for the world. Like watching cows graze. Actually, the cows were more interesting. At least with golf, the ball went in the cup at the end of each hole. Plus you could make fun of the clothes.

Maria walked out barefoot, her hair wrapped in a towel. She had pulled up her sweats, revealing scratches and bruises on her legs. She had removed the bandages. She looked through the peephole, moving like a cat, no wasted motion, and it reminded him of high school and his first sweetheart, a gymnast. Just the way she walked down the hall with her books clasped tightly to her chest could have been an Olympic competition.

"See anything?" he said.

She shook her head and sat on the edge of the other bed.

"You getting hungry yet?"

"No." She dried her hair with the thin towel, droplets falling on the bedspread and leaving little dots. "Are we safe?"

"You're asking me? From what you say, I don't think we're safe anywhere, but you won't go with me to the police."

"No police."

"Right. I seem to remember you saying that a time or two." He told her where he had parked. "How do you think that fellow in the Escalade found out where you were?"

She shrugged.

"It could have been dumb luck that he showed up at Walmart and before that found us out in the sticks. But for him to be heading toward Win's place is wrong. I think he was tracking us."

"Maybe your truck had something on it."

He scratched his face, covered with three or four days' worth of beard. The shower felt inviting, but he didn't have a change of clothes.

"He was driving around with a computer, I know that. Wish I'd have thought to take it. But what's to keep somebody else from doing the same thing?"

She stood and threw the wet towel on the bathroom floor and got another one.

"You don't have some computer chip planted somewhere in you, do you?" he said.

"Computer chip?"

"You know, those things they put just under the skin of a dog or a cow so they can track it if it runs off or gets eaten by a coyote?"

She shook her head.

"You ever felt any weird bumps? Maybe on your back?"

"Are you asking me to undress?"

"No, I'm not asking that at all."

She smiled. There was someone she looked like when she smiled, an actress or a singer. Dimples showing in both cheeks. "Are you blushing, J. D.? You are. You're blushing."

"Forget I asked. I'm just trying to figure out how he found us."

She turned her back to him and pulled the hem of her T-shirt up, moving her hair to one side. "Take a look. Do you see bumps that may be computer chips?"

"Put that down; I believe you. I don't need to see."

"Look at my back." She sounded like she meant it. "Stand up."

She had a tone in her voice that came from privilege, like she'd had practice ordering people around. He got up and moved toward her. She was about five-seven, so he didn't exactly tower over her. In the dim light there were traces of water from her hair on her skin. Her hair smelled like the cheap hotel shampoo, and he bet she had to use all of it just to get up some lather. It had been a long time since he had been this close to a woman, and the sight excited and pained him.

"It was a dumb idea. How would the guy get a chip in you, anyway?"

She let the shirt fall and turned, running her hands over her arms. "It's not a dumb idea. The people in our town were frightened that children might go missing. It was a story I heard as a girl."

"So your mom or dad could have implanted something when you were a kid." He looked at her legs as she ran her hands along the backs of her arms and her elbows.

A car door slammed outside and J. D. pushed past her to the door. In the distorted view through the peephole, a man in a St. Louis hat got out of an exhausted Ford Taurus wagon. Luggage strapped to the carrier on top and bike wheels sticking out on the back and rust all around. A woman in the passenger seat yelled at the kids behind her as the man stretched and scratched himself.

"Is it him?" Maria said.

J. D. opened the curtain slightly to get a better look at the Illinois license plate on the front of the car. "Is he a Cardinals fan with three kids?"

"What is a Cardinals fan?"

"It's not him. Or if it is, he's got a good disguise. What's Muerte look like?"

She was checking her legs now, still looking for the chip. "Dark hair, a mustache, and that thing down on the chin . . ."

"A goatee?"

"Yes. Always shaved. He uses lots of cologne. He hates to get dirty. Always washing his hands. Stocky build, like a block of ice. Square shoulders. About your height. Maybe a little shorter. And there's a scar—" She gasped and touched something on the bottom of her calf. "Feel this."

He ran a finger over the smooth skin and noticed a tattoo near her ankle. A stallion's head, its mane flowing. "Feels like a chigger bite. Maybe he's tracking chiggers."

The mention of the word *chigger* made her scratch.

"I don't think you're going to find anything."

Maria went into the bathroom and closed the door. J. D. took a deep breath. Something was stirring, something old, and he knew he had to keep his head or things could go downhill fast.

Maria returned and sat on her bed.

"Didn't find it?"

She shook her head.

"Maybe it was just luck that he found us," he said. "Or that guy in the Escalade followed us and I didn't notice him in the rearview. Do you know his name?"

"No. Just that he works for Muerte across the border."

"Wonder if he had kids?" He said it absently, not expecting an answer. "Wonder if they had something on him to make him do that kind of thing or if he was just plain mean."

"How old are you?" she said. It came out of the blue, like a leaf fluttering toward the ground in the fall.

"You want to know my shoe size, too? I'm an eleven. And I'm thirty."

"Do you want to know how old I am?" she said.

"My mother taught me never to ask a woman's age. But my guess is you have to be at least eighteen."

She rolled her eyes and frowned. "I'm twenty-five. I get that a lot." She told him the year she was born, like that would prove it in a court of law, and he studied the high cheekbones and slender nose, the burnished, impeccable skin. Even in the muted light of the room, she glowed like an angel.

"I believe you," he said. "I didn't mean you looked like a kid, just not twenty-five."

"Now tell me about your wedding ring," she said. "Are you married?"

"I told you I used to be. But I'm not now."

"You're divorced? I want to know. I am curious about you, John David."

"Don't call me that. It's J. D."

"If we are to trust each other, I have a right to know. You said you would answer my questions. Why do you wear a ring if you are not married?"

"It's not a crime to wear a ring when you're not married. You wear a ring and you're not married, right?"

"I wear it on my little finger, and it's not a wedding band." She thought a moment and dipped her head, her dark hair veiling her face. "Maybe you think she will come back to you. You wear the ring in the hope of what might be in the future."

"Maybe I wear it so people won't ask me questions. Ever think of that?" He said it with an edge he didn't expect. "I've just never taken it off, that's all."

She lifted both hands in surrender and walked toward the bathroom. "No more questions then."

But he wasn't through. "Since we're on a roll here with all the trust that's oozing from you, why don't you tell me about that bracelet you were wearing? The one around your wrist when I found you." It seemed like a year since the morning.

"Bracelet?"

"The handcuff. What was the other end hooked to?"

She turned and cocked her head slightly. "It was something I wore that I didn't want to take off."

He heard something outside and rose to check it. The wind had kicked up, blowing dust and mesquite beans and trash around the parking lot. The thin door moved. The lock was flimsy and the weather stripping had worn from the edge so that sunlight shone through and hot air blew inside.

"It was a satchel, a leather case," she said with remorse as if she regretted their argument. As if she wanted to thank him but couldn't. "The other handcuff was hooked to the handle. It was long and heavy."

"What was in it? What were you bringing across the border?"

"I don't know."

"That makes no sense. How could you not know? Who gave it to you? How'd you get through customs? You have to know what was in there."

"I have an idea, but I can't say for sure. It was locked and I didn't have the combination. But I knew it was important. He wouldn't have sent me with it if it wasn't."

"Okay, and who is *he*?"

She looked at him, then at the floor. "Muerte. He was part of it. He suggested it, in a way."

"So you know him personally. What is he, some guy you dated? You worked for?"

She frowned. "He is not my boyfriend."

"Is he the one who handcuffed you?"

"No, I did that myself."

The story wasn't making sense. "So you came through the border handcuffed to a satchel and they let you waltz through?"

"I did not put the handcuffs on until after we made it across the border."

"We?"

"Yes, there was a driver."

"But the Border Patrol didn't check it? The dogs didn't go wild?"

"The driver I was with had a contact at the crossing."

"Maria, this is pretty confusing."

"It is not that difficult to get through the border when you know the right people."

He imagined a handshake and a subtle exchange of cash, but that seemed unlikely. Too many cameras. Was she making this up?

"So where'd you get the handcuffs? Or is that just part of your accessories where you're from?"

She had a far-off look now. "The driver. I took them from him."

He let the information sift through his mind. Everything about her said she was telling the truth.

The phone rang. It was an old ringer, one that clanged and rattled. Maria was startled but J. D. got another feeling.

10

MUERTE DROVE TOWARD TUCSON, pulling off the interstate twice to view the location of the tracking device. He used his phone instead of a laptop. When the signal became stationary, he proceeded toward his hotel, a historic inn located near the university. The news media had made the nearby medical center a focal point a year earlier when a congresswoman had been shot. Most of the victims had been brought here after the gunman opened fire.

He continued past his hotel to see the hospital. He wanted to get a view of what it looked like without the world's attention. He smiled as he passed a grassy area where flowers and teddy bears and scribbled messages had once been displayed. The world would again mourn at this spot in three days.

He checked in to his room, which was immaculately clean. He watched the locator as he called in an order at the four-star restaurant downstairs with the room phone, then left the room after noting that the girl's location hadn't changed.

The tables in the main dining area were crisp and clean, and at this hour the room was nearly empty. He asked to be seated near the fireplace, where he could see the entire dining area. His seared breast of chicken with prosciutto tomato relish came almost immediately, garnished with garlic mashed potatoes and early squash harvested from local farms. Tonight, to celebrate the first stage of his plan, he would have the Mediterranean seafood paella for dinner, along with a bottle of cabernet sauvignon from a Napa Valley winery and perhaps, if his work went particularly well, a crème brûlée to top off the meal. He did not allow himself haphazard sweets. They made him soft and he needed to be in control of every movement. This was his one indulgence, a dessert tied to the memory of his first assignment for Sanchez.

The hacienda sat on a hill overlooking the valley. The father had been a local constable, and Muerte knew when the family ate dinner together at the hacienda. Muerte was to send a message to anyone who would stand against Sanchez. Alone, disguised as a deliveryman, he had taken out the security guards at the front of the residence with two perfectly placed shots. He had to use three more bullets than he wanted on dogs prowling the residence, and things got messy in the kitchen when the cook, a burly man with arms like tree trunks, tried to block his entrance to the dining room. All were silent deaths, the men and animals collapsing in heaps where they stood, except for this man. His massive body fell against the doorway and into the room.

The man at the head of the table had jumped up in horror and protested, though Muerte could see resignation in his eyes. After the head of the household, Muerte took care of his wife and three children, who looked at him with mouths agape, frozen in their seats. Sanchez had not been happy with the killing of the wife and children, and looking back, Muerte conceded that he should have left at least one living witness who could have described the horror, could have warned others not to try to stand up against the cartel. But it had been his first job. He had learned from his mistakes.

With blood on the tablecloth, he waited for any movement in the rest of the house or grounds, then retreated through the kitchen, spotting several individual servings of dessert for the family. He picked up a spoon and tasted the concoction, something he had never had growing up in Mexico City. He ate an entire serving and took the next with him, along with a silver spoon with the family crest. He had saved it as a memento as one might save a baby picture.

I should keep something from the girl when this day is over, he thought now.

When he had completed his meal, he went back to his room. He had set the temperature to sixty-two and now the air was crisp the way he liked it. He hated being hot as he slept. He used the restroom, washed his face, and dried it, studying himself in the mirror. A little stubble had begun to appear on his cheeks and he used his razor to clean the spots.

When he neared the hotel on the east side of town where the locator showed the girl to be, Muerte slowed and looked for the truck he had seen earlier. It was not in the parking lot or on the street near the building. Had they figured out the tracking device and left it in the room? He checked to see if the device had moved in the past hour, but the sensor wasn't precise enough to reveal minor movements. He parked across the street and waited, evened his breathing. *Stay in control. Do not panic.*

A Taurus station wagon pulled in and a man in a red hat got out and stretched. The passenger-side door flew open and a child stuck his head out and vomited. Muerte turned away, then noticed slight movement in the window near the Taurus. He noted the room number and watched the family get their luggage and enter the dilapidated hotel. Then he made a U-turn in front of the office, looking in at the aged desk clerk and deciding he would not engage the man. Better to simply proceed and complete his job.

His job. That sounded good to him. Not taking orders from Sanchez any longer, but making decisions himself.

He pulled to the curb on the street, a few steps from the parking lot and perhaps ten yards from the door of room 12. He would have liked a weapon with a little less firepower, but his main concern wasn't to avoid detection; it was to take care of the problem. If the noise of the gunfire drew spectators, he would simply eliminate them.

He strode confidently toward the door, holding the TEC-9 close to his body. No hesitation, no stopping to listen at the door or any other movement that would give them time to react. He planted his left foot on the concrete walkway and thrust his right boot firmly near the doorknob. The kick splintered the sun-scorched wood like balsa and the door flew open, the sunlight revealing squalor. There was no one on the beds.

Muerte pulled the trigger and sent a spray of bullets into the bathroom wall and tile and plaster fell. He listened closely for any sound.

Nothing.

He stepped to the bathroom and pushed open the door with the gun muzzle. Beside the sink were bloody bandages. Steam on the mirror. Open shampoo and conditioner bottles on the shelf. Missing tiles in the wall and plaster on the floor. An open window at the back of the room—small but big enough for an adult to crawl through. He cursed and looked out on the alley behind the hotel. He hadn't checked for the truck there.

When he exited the room, one of the children from the Taurus stood in the doorway of the next room, staring at Muerte. The child was pulled back inside and the door closed. He heard the distant sound of a siren.

He hurried to his car, looking back for the desk worker, who wasn't in sight. Probably on the floor praying. Muerte checked the tracking device and cursed again, banging the steering wheel. It had changed positions. They were somewhere east of him moving quickly south. But the siren was coming behind him. He gunned the engine and pulled away.

11

J. D. DROVE AS FAST as he dared in the residential area. He had never been in this part of town and was flying blind down narrow streets with sun-faded cars hugging the curbs.

As soon as the phone had rung in the hotel room, he knew. Something in his gut, some inner intuition, had told him they shouldn't stop, but he'd pushed that down and let his desire to rest win. The allure of a shower and someplace cool had been too enticing and now he kicked himself for the indulgence.

The desk worker on the other end of the line had mentioned a car across the street and a man wearing sunglasses watching the hotel.

"What's he look like?" J. D. said.

"Can't see too good," the man wheezed. "Looks Mexican."

J. D. almost dropped the phone. He wanted to run, but the fellow was chatty.

"Hang on, looks like he's pulling out. Yeah, he's leaving—no, he's turning around and coming back." The man cursed. "He's pulling in the turnaround. He's right out front." The man had moved and his breathing was shorter now. "Definitely Mexican."

J. D. had enough of the play-by-play. He hung up and grabbed the Uzi from the bed and rustled the handgun from the nightstand. "Your friend's outside," he said to Maria. Her eyes flashed with deep fear.

He shoved open the bathroom window and Maria climbed up on the sill. He pushed on her backside to help her through. Such a light woman. Nothing to her, really. Her T-shirt caught on the metal windowsill, ripping as she quickly turned and dropped to the asphalt. He was right behind her, and then they ran through the alley toward the Suburban.

Like a fighter would pull his arm toward a wound, they'd stayed close to the buildings. When he heard the muted spit of gunfire, he stopped and turned. She grabbed his arm and pulled him across the street in a dead run. She was thin, but there was strength to her. And not just muscles. Inner strength. He could sense it, and it both encouraged and frightened him. What had it taken for her to get to this place? And what would it take for her to overcome what was following her? What would it take for both of them?

He reached Twelfth Avenue, and instead of heading back toward the interstate, he drove south past liquor stores, bars, taco stands, and locked businesses with bars on windows. Shuttered real estate offices and seedy gentlemen's clubs lined the street. Even the gas stations looked scared.

"What does this guy want?" he said.

"He wants me dead."

"There's got to be more to it than that." He let the statement hang, searching for some reasoning. "That satchel you were handcuffed to—what happened to it?"

"I don't have it."

"I know you don't have it. I can see that. What did you do with it?"

"I threw it away."

"Where?"

"Somewhere in the desert. Near where you found me, I think. I put the chain on a rock and used another to break it and then I threw it away."

"Down a ravine? Behind a cactus? Where?"

"There was a hole. It had a wall around it."

"You mean the well? Did it have brick edging?"

"I think so. It was dark, so I couldn't see well."

"You ever stop to think that might be what he's after? Maybe he doesn't want you dead—maybe he just wants what's his."

She kept turning to scan the street. "He is after *me*. What do I have to say to get you to believe me?"

"Might help if you start with the truth."

She glanced at him, then back to the roadway. "I'm telling the truth."

"This guy evidently knows you pretty well because he can pick out a needle in a haystack just as easily as that guy at the doctor's office. No matter where you are, they show up."

He kept driving and glancing in the rearview mirror that hung at an odd angle. That sent his mind scurrying back to Win. The police were probably at his house, questioning him and Iliana. What did they know about Maria? What was her connection with the doctor in Benson? What did they really know about J. D. Jessup?

As he'd gotten to know them in the past months, he'd told them his hometown and bits of information, but they didn't know much. He hadn't told anyone the real reason he had retreated to the Slocum farm. They weren't the best organic farmers in the area, and if he had known more coming into the situation, he wouldn't have picked them, but once he was there, he figured he could learn all he needed.

He hadn't expected to meet people like Win and Iliana. Sweet people who just accepted him, no questions asked. Look where that had gotten them. When they tried to come up with answers for the authorities, they would have little to go on. J. D. had dragged them into this mess without knowing the ramifications, all the problems that accompanied kindness. But what was he supposed to do? Just keep riding? Let her die in the heat?

He wished he could call Win and talk. Explain a little more. The police would probably get bits and pieces of information from his truck and head to Slocum's farm to try to tie him and the girl together. But there wasn't any tying together. It was random, all happenstance, like the rest of his life. There was no focus or purpose; it just happened. Living and dying without reason.

"What if we take off and head east?" J. D. said. "I got some cash saved up we could use."

Maria shook her head. "He will find us. And if not him, someone else he hires. He will not stop until he kills me."

"Why? What have you done?"

"It is not what I have done; it is what I know."

Now they were getting somewhere. "Okay, what do you know?"

"If I tell you, then you will know. And he will kill you."

"Listen, I don't think his bullets discriminate."

She scrunched her face like she didn't understand the word.

He drove on as the scene turned from blight to plight, descending into a world of both cactus and barrios. They passed a vacant lot that looked like a place where serial killers came to bury their victims. Scrub oak and mesquite and cactus, the landscape of Pima County.

"I'm not religious, but I believe the truth will set you free. I'm giving you permission to tell me, even if it scares you. I want to help you, but I can't do it if you're going to string me along. What do you know about this man that makes him want to shoot you like a dog on the highway?"

The sun was still high in the sky, a red ball of fire in the cloudless blue. This time in June it hung there a little longer before it made its quick descent over the mountains to the west. There were mountains all around this valley, so you couldn't direct people by telling them to drive toward or away from them—they were everywhere.

"He is with the cartel," Maria said, breaking the silence. "I believe he is working with another group to take over the cartel that operates in our town. Perhaps the Zetas. I don't know how he plans to do it, but that is his objective."

"I've heard about the Zetas. Not a nice bunch."

"They are ruthless."

"And how are you mixed up in all of this? You run drugs for them across the border?"

"No. A family member knows Muerte. That's how I was introduced."

"An uncle? A brother? Somebody in your family is mixed up with the drug trade?"

"The town is paralyzed by the drug wars. If you're not with them, if you don't help them, you are against them. If you want to live, you stay hidden or you look the other way."

"So you joined them?"

"No, I am against what they do, which is why I agreed to come across the border." She saw the look on his face and moved closer, with more passion in her voice. "I chose to come here because I thought I could stop them."

"Stop them from what?"

"I'm not sure. They're planning something. I overheard Muerte."

He shook his head at his luck. This girl was a jigsaw puzzle, and the more edge pieces he found, the more he felt like he shouldn't empty the box. Just put it back on the shelf and walk away.

The best thing he could do was drive straight to the nearest police station and turn himself and Maria in and be done with it. Let the chips fall. Explain what had happened and head back to the farm. Win would get his truck back and the Border Patrol would send one more Mexican over the fence.

But if she was right about Muerte, that would just make her a fish in a bowl. And it would probably put the police and Border Patrol agents in danger. The law wouldn't believe her or protect her until they saw she was right, and then it would be too late. And when it was too late, most people would chalk it up like Slocum: another dead Mexican and one less mouth to feed in a holding cell.

"What about your family? Your mother and father? Brothers or sisters? They'll help you."

She hung her head and shook it as if something deep inside had pained her.

"It'd be worth a try to call somebody up and explain what's going on," he said. "You can talk with your mother, right?"

"My mother is dead."

He wanted to ask what happened but decided to keep going. "What about your dad? He's probably worried sick."

She sat, taking in what he was saying like some silent reservoir after the monsoon. A dry wash soaking up water. She seemed troubled but content with the inconsistency, content with the trajectory they were on, away from danger. "My father cannot help me."

He sighed and stared at the Check Engine light that had been on since the hotel. He wasn't made for this. He had no experience. He was an artist turned nomad farmer, not a protector or vigilante.

"What's that smell?" Maria said.

J. D. noticed it too—an acrid, sulfurous tinge to the air. He slowed and shut off the air conditioner but the smell remained. The water gauge was fine. He rolled down his window, thinking the odor might be from some nearby industrial plant, but the hot air outside wasn't to blame.

"I don't know much about engines, but I'll bet something's getting hot under the hood."

He pulled into a Circle K and parked near the air hose to look for the hood release, but it wasn't there. He found a frayed metal cord hanging down underneath the steering column and pulled at it, but he couldn't get a good grip. In the side of the door was a pair of pliers and he used them to give the cord a jerk. The hood moved slightly. He hopped out and got his fingers underneath the hot metal, feeling for the latch. He wished he had a pair of gloves.

As soon as he lifted the hood, a wave of rotten-egg smoke rose. Win or Slocum could sniff at the dipstick or run a finger through some pooled liquid under the chassis and tell what was wrong. He, on the other hand, knew next to nothing. He could get the hood open most of the time, but that was the extent of it. When the smoke dissipated, he saw the battery leaking. That wasn't good. It was filled with acid. Would it explode?

A voice from behind startled him. "Got a problem?" The man wore dirty coveralls and his hands were black with grease and dirt. His El Camino sat nearby, and J. D. marveled at how many older cars and trucks were still running in the dry desert air. VW Beetles. He'd even seen Gremlins and a Pinto in near-perfect condition. On the bumper of the El Camino was a faded Impeach Obama sticker. J. D. guessed the guy had altered the size of the fuel tank because the numbers on the pump were whizzing by like a fat man's on an amusement park's guess-your-weight scale. A black dog wagged its tail inside the car and panted, turning its head at any movement on the street.

"It's not my truck," J. D. said. "Belongs to a friend of mine."

The man stuck his head over the battery, dirty hair hanging down. His skin was sunburnt and leathery like he worked outside all day. "Terminal cap's leaking. Desert does a number on batteries. You don't have to worry about your tailpipe rusting out, but every two or three years you got to replace the battery. Most of the new ones are sealed nowadays. That looks like the old type. How long's it been in there?"

J. D. found a sticker on the side that showed it was three and a half years old.

"Well, you've gotten your money's worth."

"Will it explode?"

"Not unless you arc it. I don't think so. But it'll keep leaking and cause you some problems with the acid dripping. Plus the smell of it. I'd get it changed out fast. They'll do it for you at just about any auto shop."

J. D. thanked the man and closed the hood, seeing that

Maria wasn't in the truck. He checked the street, then the little store. He didn't see her. He walked in and noticed restrooms at the rear, then caught something black to the right, outside the big window by the potato chip display. She was feeding coins into a pay phone.

"Where'd you get the money?" he said when he reached her.

"In the ashtray."

"Who are you calling?"

"You told me to call my family."

He thought that was a good sign. He went back inside the store and let the cool air wash over him again as he grabbed a bag of corn chips and a box of donuts, then two bottles of soda. Just something to tide them over if they drove into the desert. Insurance, really. He didn't have a plan. He didn't have any idea what he was going to do except take one step at a time. Keep moving. Stay as far away from the guy with the vendetta as he could.

"I'm looking for a car parts place," he said to the girl behind the counter as she scanned his purchases. There were wrinkled hot dogs rolling in a glass case by the cash register and an open tub of orange liquid that people put on their nachos. It was supposed to be cheese, but there were so many chemicals in food these days. "Any place around here where I can get a battery?"

She thought a minute as if she had a hard time connecting the words. "There's one of those car places out that way, I think. Auto or Pep something or other."

"How far?"

"I don't know—maybe a mile?"

He thanked her and walked out to hear Maria speaking Spanish in an animated voice. He could pick out a few words but couldn't follow most of it because of the speed. Might just as well have been Swahili. He kept his eye on the street and pulled the truck next to her in case the guy drove by, guns blazing.

She hung up and put the change in a cup holder. He drove south. She didn't speak, and he didn't tell her what he was looking for as the shadows of evening stretched out toward the distant brown hills. He spotted the Pep Boys a few minutes later. There were five bay doors in use and four guys who had stripped down to their T-shirts and hung up their uniform shirts. Fans were running full blast, but it was like waving a hat at the mouth of hell.

But the waiting room was frigid and there were two kids playing with cars and dirty dominoes. Maria sat and stared at the television while J. D. found a cheap battery. He had three twenties and a few ones and a couple of fives left, and the one on sale that would crank the Suburban was $79.95 plus tax. He wished he hadn't bought the chips and donuts. Instead of trying to scrounge up the change, he told them to put in the battery and some oil and he'd pay with credit.

"I need it quick as you can do it," he said.

"We'll get to it," the man said without looking up, a signal he could wait his turn. If J. D. pushed, the guy would drag his feet, so he waved Maria to come out of the waiting room. She reluctantly stood and entered the land of tire rubber and floor mats.

"What did he say?" J. D. asked.

"What did who say?"

"The phone call at the gas station. Did you talk with your father?"

She wandered to an aisle away from the register and picked up a key chain with her name on it. "My family can't protect me."

"That's what they said?"

She didn't make eye contact. "There may be a safe house. A place where I might survive."

"Look at me."

She put the key chain back. There was a hardness to her eyes, like a stone cliff overlooking a pool of water. There was also a sliver of hope amid the stone. A ridge of pumice along the edge that might lead to something more.

"Do you trust him? Can you believe what he's saying, or is this a trap?"

She looked away again. "I don't think I have a choice. I have to trust that this will help me."

He stared at the key chains, names swinging on a rack. "You do have a choice."

"You don't understand."

"Tell me then. What don't I understand?"

"The danger you're in. If you stay with me, you will die. You may die no matter what happens."

"That's comforting. You should speak at one of those positive-thinking seminars." He smiled but she didn't return it. "Maria, I'm not afraid of dying."

The mention of her name brought a response, but just as quickly she shut down.

"That sounds like something an American would say. Until you realize what dying looks like."

"I thought we were the only ones who were racist," J. D. said.

"What do you mean?"

"People here, the ones who don't know any better, judge you because of your skin color. And here you are telling me I'm just another ignorant gringo."

"That is not racist; that is the truth."

"Well, excuse me, but that doesn't sound much different

from every redneck in these parts and what they say about Mexicans. I've heard it on the farm, in bars, and other than jobs, it's all they talk about at political meetings. It's not right to judge people because of the way they look. And I'll be the judge of whether or not I want to get involved with you. I don't need you making that decision because you think I'm stupid."

"I didn't say you were stupid."

"Yeah, you did. I'm an American. I don't understand the danger."

She folded her arms and looked at the floor. "I'm not ungrateful for what you've done. I am thankful for your help."

"You've got a funny way of showing it."

"I will try to do better. But I think it is best if you take me to this place where I can be safe."

He could see it beginning, like the sky opening up at sunup, a little shard of light. He could be done with this, done with the bullets flying and the uncertainty, done with her. But something inside didn't want to be done. She had become a stowaway somewhere inside his heart, and he didn't want to let go. He knew why but couldn't stop the feelings from rising.

Once they pulled out, Maria gave him the location of a gas station on East Speedway where her contact would meet them in two hours. Over toward the Rincons near Tanque Verde. He knew exactly where it was. It wasn't that far from the farmers' market where Slocum would set up the next morning.

"Who are the people you're supposed to meet?"

"I spoke with them."

"Who are they?"

"They know me. Friends I know in Tucson."

"I thought you didn't have friends in Tucson. That's what you told Win."

"These people are with a church that comes to our town. The Tabernacle."

"So they gave you their address and told you to hurry on over? That doesn't add up. It's better if you stay disconnected with all of that and stay with somebody Muerte and your family don't know."

"Muerte already has information about you."

"How do you know that?"

"Because I know him."

Back to third base. Back to the ignorant American.

"Just take me there," she said. "Do you know where it is?"

"Yeah, I know how to get there." He checked his watch. "Let's get something to eat first."

"Someone can pick me up if you won't take me. That might be safer for you."

"I'm taking you. If that's what you decide, I'll drive. But I don't want you going into an ambush."

"These people care for me."

He cut over to the interstate and took Kolb Road north. They passed the boneyard of Davis-Monthan Air Force Base, a menagerie of aircraft scuttled in neat rows of ghost squadrons. He pulled into Chuy's, a chain Mexican restaurant, then thought better of it. No sense risking their lives and a room full of people for a good burrito.

He drove on past a bank sign that showed the temperature as 102. Nine in the evening and still 102. He turned onto Broadway, headed east, and found a Carl's Jr. They ordered at the drive-through, then sat in the parking lot of a Sunflower Market and ate, watching people walk in and out of the grocery.

"I'm not going to be able to talk you out of this, am I?" he said when he had finished his cheeseburger.

Maria shook her head. "This is best. For us both."

He resisted the urge to argue. "Where will you go when it's over? Back home?"

A shrug. "I don't see how. I will figure out something. Can we leave?"

He checked the street as they pulled out. Looking over his shoulder was a full-time job, and it would be a relief not to worry about it anymore.

The better part of him, the part that had willed him to move forward and not wither, didn't want to abandon her. Something deep was calling to him, a familiar song that felt like home in a barren, foreign land. He could drive for days and not see a single person he knew. But walking beside a broken and poured-out woman, he felt some moisture in the air after a long drought. And she was intent on going her own way. It was his life repeating itself. The familiar ache he had tried to bury and walk away from in order to live, in order to breathe.

At Speedway he turned right and hit construction horses, flashing lights, and a lowered speed limit. There was always construction somewhere in the city. He passed the gas station and went through a light to a dip in the road that said not to enter when water was present. What a joke. There hadn't been enough water for a gnat to get a good mouthful in months.

"It was back there," she said.

"I know where it is. I didn't see your friends in the parking lot."

"They won't be in the parking lot—they are too smart for that. I told them about this truck. They will come when everything is all right."

"I don't like it. Where are they taking you?"

"It is better you don't know. You should be glad to get rid of me. I've only caused you and your friends trouble." She asked the time and he told her. Almost exactly two hours since she had been at the pay phone. He pulled into a wide, sandy area at the side of the road where vendors sold honey or homemade burritos and hot dogs. People trying to scrounge a living. When he turned off the engine and lights, they were in darkness with a billion stars peeking through the dirty windshield.

J. D. folded his hands across the steering wheel and looked into the sky. "You asked about my ring."

"You don't have to tell me."

"I was married for six years. To a woman who stole my heart the first time I saw her. Still has it. Taking off the ring is something I haven't been able to do. It's like looking in the rearview mirror when you back up. Just instinct."

"What happened to her?" Maria said.

Deep breath. "She got sick." Three words brought memories and he rubbed his forehead to stave off the onslaught, speaking before the pressure became too great. "The funny thing was, she was always the health nut. Real careful with everything she ate. Exercised every day. She had this little dog when we got married. Said I had to accept them both—they came as a package. She'd take it for a run, and then it got older and it could only walk. At the end the dog had to be pushed around in a baby stroller. She loved that little thing."

He looked out at the stars through the mist in his eyes. It felt good to talk about their life together, to admit that she had walked the planet beside him. At the same time it hurt, like a dull knife through a scar.

"I can tell you loved her a lot," Maria said.

He nodded. "I thought we'd always be together. I didn't want to keep going after she was gone."

"But you did."

"Yeah, so far. Maybe I was too scared to do anything else. But you're right. I did. And I kept the ring on because I couldn't get the strength up to take it off."

She placed a hand on his arm and something surged through him. "You have great strength. I can sense it. If you hadn't found me, I would be dead."

He turned to face her. "Maria, I've got a feeling about this. If you leave, something bad's going to happen. I'll see your picture in the paper. And they'll ship your body back to Mexico in a pine box. I don't want that to happen."

She put her hands together and nodded. "I don't want to be in a box, but I can't put you in any more danger."

"Let me decide that."

"You and I both must deal with the past." She took off her ring and gave it to him. "My mother gave me this when I was little. I have kept it to remember her. To not forget the place she has in my heart. I want you to have it."

"I couldn't take it."

"I have kept it on because she is watching over me. You've given me the strength to remove it. Please."

He held out his palm and she dropped it. It had a weight but was tiny, and he wondered if he could even get it on any of his fingers. But that wasn't the point.

"Thank you," he said.

He reached for the ignition but she opened her door. "I want to walk. You stay here."

"No, if they don't see the truck, they won't know you're there."

"They will know," she said.

J. D. got out of the truck and slipped the ring into his pocket. Maria came around the back and looked into his eyes, the moon shining off her face and making it glow.

"You need a flashlight," he said, the ache rising. "You never know what's crawling around out here this time of year."

"I'm all right," she said. "I'm not afraid of what's on the ground."

"You should be."

She smiled and hugged him, then walked toward the gas station. He waited until he could no longer see her in the darkness, then rummaged through the glove box to find Win's flashlight and followed, driving slowly beside her, pointing the light at her feet. She laughed and shook her head, but he kept pace. Finally he pulled over and shut off his lights at the intersection. There was no one on the street, just the buzz of fluorescents and the crimson glow of a Redbox machine.

Maria crossed the street like a cat prowling for dinner. He watched for movement around the building, holding his breath, hoping Muerte didn't jump out of the shadows and mow her down.

She stood by an ice machine and looked back. He wanted to gun the engine, grab her, and drive away, but he didn't. He put his hand over his pocket and felt the ring. His whole body felt the low rumble of the exhaust and the vibration of the rough-running engine. A bullbat flew past him and up toward the streetlight, where the moths were thickest.

Headlights from the bridge appeared, and a car flew through the intersection as the light turned yellow. Maria peeked inside the store, then moved back to the shadows by the ice machine.

J. D. glanced at the night sky and tried to pick out some

constellation, but he had never studied the alignment of planets and stars. It looked like a black bowl of soup.

When he looked again, she was gone. No car. No machine gun piercing the night. Gone like a phantom. He rolled up to one of the pumps and sat. He went inside and asked the cashier if he'd seen a woman come into the store and the man shook his head. He plunked one of his twenties on the counter and told him the pump number, then went back out and leaned against the Suburban as he filled up.

Where does a man go who has seen something he wants slip away like sand in an hourglass? He was a fool to think that way, but there it was. He could spend the rest of his life searching for the feeling so strong it nearly drove him to his knees. It was like finding a vein of gold in a hill he hadn't mined. He wasn't looking, wasn't asking, but it appeared and disappeared in the same day.

A farmer can get beat by the wind or too much or too little rain. His livestock can be felled by disease or by standing in the wrong place during a storm. Fires rage through like tornadoes. A thousand things can sink a farm, but none so deadly as a broken heart.

He had been so dead inside he could hardly say his own name. The move to the farm had been an effort to make something happen, and for two months he had slogged through life. In the span of a single day he had felt a surge toward living and then the release of it.

"Good-bye, Maria," he whispered.

And with that he got in his truck and drove away.

12

MUERTE PULLED TO THE ROADSIDE and stopped, placing his gun by the door out of the officer's view. Only if he approached from the passenger side would Muerte be in trouble. But the trouble would be the officer's. How many times had he eliminated an official or officer in Mexico? It was not as common north of the border, but he would not be taken into custody.

The flashing patrol car lights caused a dull throbbing in his temples and he thought about pulling away as the officer exited, but he didn't need a high-speed chase. That would only involve more police.

He sat and watched the rearview mirror and willed the man forward. Muerte believed that if he could envision something, if he could conceive it with his mind, he could cause it to happen. Humans used a fraction of their mental abilities. He would harness that power and use it for himself.

Getting pulled over by the police changed many things. It sent his plans about the girl into a tailspin. It jeopardized the bigger plan. This made his next move even more important.

The officer approached cautiously with his hand on the revolver at his side. Muerte switched to view the side mirror, then rolled down the window. Heat invaded the car. He endured the blast and smiled convincingly.

"Good evening, Officer. Is there a problem?"

"I need to see your license and registration, sir." There was nothing genial about the man. He looked to be in his thirties. Caucasian with perhaps a distrust of anything south of Tubac. A slight build. A shadow's growth of beard, which told Muerte the man had been on duty for some time. He was tired and ready to go home to his wife and children, if he had them.

"I wasn't going over the speed limit, was I, Officer?" He said it jovially, his best English, while reaching into his jacket pocket. The officer brought the gun out of the holster and pointed it toward the ground, ready.

Muerte pulled out a fistful of cash and held it in his right hand, high enough to be visible, as he probed his other pocket. It was probably more than the officer made in six months. Muerte continued the search for the registration until he was sure he had the officer's attention. He caught the man staring at the cash.

Lowering his voice to just above a whisper, he said, "I can make it worth your while to let this infraction slide, whatever it is. Broken taillight. Failure to yield."

The officer cocked his head slightly to get a better look at the money.

Don't go moral on me, Muerte thought. *You will take this money. I am willing you to take it.*

This would not have happened in his homeland. The officer never would have stopped him in the first place. And if he had by mistake, he would have sent Muerte happily on his way. But this was not his homeland.

"All right, step out of the car, sir. And keep your hands where I can see them." The officer reached for the door and opened it. The TEC-9 clattered to the pavement but Muerte had already grabbed the Glock inside his jacket. As the officer stared dumbfounded, Muerte lifted the pistol and shot him twice, once each in the chest and head, crumpling the man to the ground.

Careful not to let his face be caught on some dashboard camera, Muerte grabbed the gun, closed the door, and pulled back onto the road, scanning for witnesses. He could see none, but as he reached a stoplight, someone ran across an empty parking lot toward the cruiser. He thought of turning around but decided to put distance between himself and the officer. The police would now have his license number and vehicle make. That would be traced back to Sanchez. He could live with that. In fact, this new wrinkle probably aided his overall objective, but it did not get him any closer to eliminating the girl.

He pulled out his phone, which could also track her location. Somewhere east.

He phoned his contact and explained the situation. "Things have changed for me. I need a different car and two of your best men."

The man told him where to drive and he was there an hour later, waiting for them at an excavation site that looked like an abandoned strip mine. Three cars trailed dust in the moonlight as they drove toward him. They shook hands; then Muerte retrieved his belongings before one of the men poured gasoline throughout the car.

Muerte opened Miguel's laptop and leaned against the Audi A8. "I have something important for your men. It could mean a great deal of money. In addition to what I am already paying for your help. But you must understand: if you fail, I will kill you."

The three men smiled. And just as quickly they turned serious when they saw he was not joking.

He explained the tracking device and how to find it. "This is the location of a young lady." Several clicks of the mouse and her picture appeared. Muerte could tell they were admiring her. One said something vulgar under his breath.

"Do not let her beauty fool you," Muerte said. "She is as cunning as a wolf. And twice as dangerous. Do you have a knife?"

"Yes," the older man said. "You want us to kidnap her and bring her to you? Or we could hold her until you—"

"I want her shot on sight," Muerte said. He handed over the laptop. "Bring her head to me. She is also carrying a satchel with her. The contents are very important to me. Do you understand?"

The men looked at the photograph again and nodded. Muerte took a lighter from the youngest man, flicked it on, and threw it inside his car. The *whomp* sent black, acrid smoke into the air and lit the night. The heat was intense, even seconds after the fire began.

He got into the Audi and held the door open. "Use the computer to track her. I expect this to be done by morning. Call me, no matter what time of night." He threw a burlap sack at them.

The youngest picked it up. "What's this for?"

"Her head, of course."

13

J. D. DROVE WITH THE WINDOWS DOWN, pavement rushing underneath whining tires, running toward something. He stayed on the main road until he got to a perch where he could see Win's place. A police car was still there. At Slocum's farm it was worse because yellow crime tape surrounded the old schoolhouse and lights illuminated the squalor. It was a set trap, and the cheese was the money he had squirreled away. He doubted they would find it.

The longer he thought of Maria, the more it ate at him. He could just give up, toss up his hands and let her go, but he felt like he owed it to himself to investigate. Follow the trail. He drove the back road, a tractor path that took him close to the well, and parked in the moonlight by the wire fence. The engine chugged and rattled even after he turned it off, and he watched the dust dissipate around him and move like a cloud toward the hill. It was about as remote as you could get on the planet. He'd been to Moab, Utah, and that had felt as lonely as he could stand. This was worse because except for some cows and Slocum's family, few had ever walked the area.

He used Win's flashlight to find the fence, avoiding the stickers and thick cholla. A low grunt stopped him in his tracks as a family of javelinas passed. The adults were huge, and when he shone the flashlight in their eyes, they scurried away. He located the water line and followed it toward the rocky over-hang. Slocum had showed him the well when he first arrived. The man seemed skeptical he could actually hold his own on a horse, but it had come back to J. D. quickly—a lesson from his father that actually stuck, the way to feel one with the horse. Slocum's black mare had been gentle and forgiving as his memory returned.

The well had been dug by Slocum's grandfather and pro-vided plenty of water for the livestock until it ran dry. Slocum's father had run the water line a few years before he died, and it was a constant chore to keep the pipes flowing.

J. D. lost his way once, when his eyes stung with sweat and he couldn't place the landscape. It was one thing to have the hot air moving through the truck, but out here the stillness and heat drenched him and he wondered how anybody ever stayed in a place like this. He'd heard September was the best month and that you could walk barefoot outside at Christmas, but anybody walking barefoot here in any season had to have their head examined.

He found the well. The boards on top had been tossed aside, along with the rock that held them down to protect some tipsy cow or coyote from falling in. The well was beat up on top, so he figured this was where she had gotten rid of the handcuff.

Those chains were thick and it would have taken a good deal of strength and a heavy rock to bust loose. Seeing this made his heart swell for her as he imagined what she'd been through. He glanced west at the way she had come with no flashlight and wearing a skirt and after whatever had happened with the driver who brought her across the border. He shook his head.

J. D. shone the light deep into the well's belly and saw a satchel hung up on some tree branches. He couldn't see all the way to the bottom, but he imagined snakes in the mix of glop and rocks. The bottom was probably fifty feet down. There was an old pulley, broken and hanging by a thread at the top of the well. Beside it on the ground was a rope, but until then he hadn't thought a whit about how he would pull the satchel up. He leaned over the edge and stared, sweat dripping through the LED beams like it was raining. Then he sat by the well and turned off the light, just listening to the quietness and staring at the stars and the lights of the city in the distance and the hazy gray of the sky clutter. In town they couldn't see what he saw. The vastness of the universe and twinkling galaxies beyond. All you had to do was look and there it was.

Maybe life was as simple as that. Just look up. Don't ask questions. Don't try to feel. Place yourself in the hands of whoever or whatever fashioned all of that. It was all predetermined. One death simply fertilized the ground for another man's soybeans. One choice meant nothing in the span of eternity.

Or maybe the choice did matter. Maybe the choice was whether or not to love and, in doing so, trusting whatever hands you placed yourself in when there was no money-back guarantee. There was no guarantee of any kind as far as he could tell, except that your heart was going to break and spill out in the end. All the things he could have done, all the things he forgot to do, all the things he didn't do pressed down on his chest until he had to stand to breathe again.

He picked up the rope and snaked it down the well. It was close to reaching but not close enough. Would the ratty thing even hold the weight of the satchel? He walked to the truck and rummaged in the back until he found a toolbox and inside what looked like a pick with a small handle. It was sharp and curved on the end; what Win had used it for he couldn't imagine. He also found a bungee cord that looked long enough to reach, and he returned to the well, tied the tool and the cord to the end of the rope, and let it down.

It took him twenty minutes to determine the bungee cord wasn't working. The satchel had landed on its top amid the branches, and every time he got the hook in the side of the satchel to turn it, it came loose. He pulled the rope up, untied the bungee cord, and thought for a minute. Then he pulled off his boots and slipped off his jeans, tying them to the rope and running the sharp end of the pick through a thick patch near his cuff, and let the whole thing down. The first time he hooked the satchel with the pick, it moved and he let out a yelp. But instead of pulling it up, he nearly dropped it to the bottom. Carefully he swung the rope with one hand and held the flashlight with the other and tried to focus on that pinpoint where the handle and hook would meet. After several tries and sweat drops cascading, he had the satchel near the top of the well. He grabbed the handle and pulled it over the edge as if he had landed a prize bass at a fishing contest. He sat in the dust and cradled what felt more like a suitcase. It had a good weight to it.

He fiddled with the lock but knew the combination would take him years to figure, so he took the sharp end of the hook and began to pry, cursing and banging when it wouldn't budge. He even tried making a hole in the leather, but that was futile.

He left his jeans and stepped into his boots to take the case back to the truck, where he found a hacksaw blade and a handle. Careful not to break the blade, he sawed the lock.

Just as the pin snapped, headlights shone on the path behind him in the valley and his stomach fell. He was okay being caught. It would be a relief in a way. But how was he going to explain how he had found a suitcase full of money, if that's what it was? Or drugs? He pulled back the latch quickly and opened the case. Pieces of a gun and a scope. A really expensive gun. Shiny, like it had never been used. No cash. No drugs. Just the gun and several shells that looked big enough to bring down a rhino at full gallop. What in the world had he gotten himself into?

He threw the case in the truck and started it, keeping the lights off and pulling farther up the hill around the rock outcropping leading to a butte at the end of the property. The tractor trail wound another half mile through the back country toward the Mexican border. He got out and watched the scene from the outcropping. Just him in his boxers and boots, a sorry sight. In the distance he heard the lowing of cattle but he couldn't see them. He wished he'd had the presence of mind to untie his pants and put them on, but he hadn't planned on visitors.

The car below parked near where he had, close to the fence, and in the darkness he saw two figures step out and head toward the well with something glowing. The first one held the light in front of him and the next one followed as they walked toward the well. Straight to it, like drawn by a magnet. Maybe they were police with night vision goggles.

The two made it to the well and shone their light inside. The car didn't look like a cruiser—he could tell that. It also didn't appear to be Border Patrol. They would have dogs with them.

"Who are these guys?" he whispered. "Whoever you are, leave my pants and wallet alone."

One of the men went back to the car and zigzagged through the mesquite and cactus to the well. Perfectly silent, J. D. heard them speaking Spanish, but it was nothing he could make out. Something flashed and flames flickered beside the well, and they dropped the burning thing inside. Fire in the desert was not good this time of year.

In the silhouette of the flames the two men hovered over the scene. Then a click and automatic gunfire echoed through the valley as one of the men fired into the hole. What he was shooting at, J. D. couldn't tell, but he instinctively ducked and kept his face in the dust.

The two walked back to the car, turned around as best they could in the ruts and humps of the path, and rolled away, dust floating toward the night sky.

J. D. watched them drive out of sight and watched some more, thinking he might see the police meet them. He checked his watch. It was a long time to sunup and he had a choice. Several of them. Instead of mapping out his whole life from that point, he decided to take the next step, which was to get his pants.

He drove down the arroyo and searched in the dirt for his jeans. When he looked in the well, he saw the charred mass still smoldering. Great. His wallet was gone and with it his credit cards and the little cash he had. At least he had gas in the Suburban. The ring was gone too, and he felt a pang of remorse.

Something about the ring had made him feel like a little part of Maria was still with him.

He pulled the rope up but the end of it had burned through. As he dropped it on the ground, he stepped on something and shone the light down to see a round object with a hole in it. The ring had either fallen out when he took off his pants or the men had found it and tossed it away. He was going to shove it in his pocket but realized he had none, so he wedged it on his little finger but it would only go to the knuckle. He held the flashlight over the well to see what they had shot at but smoke and branches blocked the view.

He started the Suburban and checked the gas gauge. Something told him to drive straight toward any police car he could find. Men with automatic weapons weren't to be trifled with. He had no ID, no cash, no credit cards, no pants, and more importantly, no hope.

He put a hand on the steering wheel and stared at the ring. No, he couldn't leave her. He couldn't live with the questions. He couldn't live with giving up again.

He had no idea how he would find her, but he had to try. Before others did.

14

THE CLOCK SHOWED just after midnight when Muerte awoke to the ringing phone.

"We located her," the man on the other end said.

He couldn't remember the man's name. *Think.* Pablo. Yes, that was it. "Where, Pablo?"

"We followed the tracking device to an abandoned well in the desert."

"Is she dead?"

"Yes."

"Do you have her head?"

Hesitation. And as soon as he heard it, he knew she was alive.

"We couldn't see to the bottom of the well, but we sprayed it with more bullets than you can imagine. She could not have survived."

"Did you see her body?"

"No, we could not. It was too deep. But we think someone must have disposed of her there. At any rate, she is dead."

"What about the satchel?" Muerte said.

"It was not there. However, we did find a man's wallet."

When he heard the name, he turned on a light and located the truck registration. John David Jessup.

"Excellent," Muerte said. "Bring me the wallet."

"Where would you like us to bring it?"

He told them, then tossed the phone on the bed and opened his computer. He typed in the man's name and came up with an electrical contractor, a Facebook listing, a dental office in Rhode Island, and a musician. He typed in the name and *Arizona* and came up with the musician, a man in Mesa who sold sports memorabilia, and an attorney whose name wasn't even close.

He clicked the musician and followed a link to a Nashville newspaper article about the rise of J. D. Jessup. There was a picture of the man, along with his wife. Muerte could tell he was trying to look like the rugged outdoor type but that it was a sham. He had probably spent his early years inside, practicing piano and obeying his mother. Another photo showed the wife in a hospital gown, sitting in a wheelchair trying to smile, her face wan and thin.

Muerte noted the date of the article, a year and a half old, and looked hard at the man. Could he be helping Maria? And how much could he know about her? Had she conspired with him before she came into the country?

Muerte paced the room, thinking, planning. He picked up the phone and dialed another number, then hung up when the voice mail message sounded. Almost immediately the phone rang.

"I have something urgent I need you to research." He gave the woman Jessup's name and what he knew. "I want to know everything about him. Why is he in Arizona? Where does he live? What kind of soda does he drink? And as soon as the sun rises, contact our friend with the Zetas in town. I need their help in another matter."

The woman had sounded groggy, but when he mentioned the Zetas, she snapped awake. "Is everything going as planned?"

"Not quite. Maria escaped. She had the weapon."

The woman cursed.

"I am offering one million dollars, US currency, for the person who locates her and can bring her to me. Spread that word to the Zetas and beyond."

"One million?"

"Yes. One million if she is found alive. Or one million if her body is brought to me. I also must locate the package she was carrying. It's imperative that I find it quickly."

The woman typed furiously, sounding nervous as they talked, as if she would be the next person with a bounty on her head. She wasn't far off in that estimation, though Muerte tried to calm her.

When he hung up, he felt satisfied, accomplished. It wasn't pleasant to admit the girl had slipped through his fingers, but it was the truth. He would call Sanchez as soon as the sun was up. He would say that Maria had run into the desert and was hiding. It was only a question of who would find her first. He would again promise his absolute allegiance to the family and assure the man his daughter would return. Only Muerte knew her body would be in a different condition than when she left her father's house.

Before he went back to bed, he used the phone app that tracked the girl and saw it was static as the two had said. In the desert. If it changed, he would see it when he awakened.

15

J. D. SEARCHED THE SUBURBAN for loose change, but Maria had taken most of it when she used the pay phone. He found a couple of quarters in the glove box and some change in the ashtray and the rest in the cup holder and under the driver's seat. He counted out $3.60 to his name.

If he'd had a towel or an oily rag, he would have girded himself with it, but finding none, he walked into the Walmart on Speedway and Kolb wearing his boots and boxers and T-shirt. A newspaper headline screamed, "Benson Doctor Murdered." There was no greeter at this time of night, but a woman in a blue shirt and khakis sat next to the exit using a nail file and looking over her glasses at him.

"Welcome to Walmart," she said across the carts, glancing at his thin shorts.

He pulled his T-shirt down a bit and kept going. The

woman probably saw all kinds overnight, people in various stages of dress and undress. From the look of those gathered at the checkout, he blended well with the crowd, but he still felt naked in the fluorescent light.

To the right, past the customer service desk and the McDonald's, was the sports paraphernalia, the Arizona Wildcats shirts and hats. Baseball caps and shot glasses. He found what he was looking for on a rack marked Clearance. Shorts and T-shirts had been marked down several times and were actually in his price range. He found a pair of gray sweatpants for $2.97. He stepped into them, holding tight to the change in his left hand as he tried to get his boots through the elastic at the bottom of the pant legs. He kicked off both boots and tried again. When he had the sweats on, he took Maria's ring off and shoved it into a pocket.

At the checkout he grabbed a Snickers bar and snapped the tag off the sweats and handed both to a woman old enough to be his mother. She scanned the tag and tossed it in a plastic trash can, blipped the candy, and told him the total, then reached out to steady herself with a sun-splotched arm. He placed every cent he had in her hand, having to flick off a few pennies that were held by the sweat and grime, and she looked at them like he had given her a handful of mouse droppings.

"Having a rough night?" she said without looking up.

"You could say that."

She separated out the quarters, followed by the dimes and nickels, then spread the pennies out and took them by fives.

A man came up behind him holding a box of caramel popcorn and a diabetes test kit, which seemed a killer combination. He wore a tattered T-shirt with a skull on it and a dirty cap over stringy hair. A look as vacant as the parking lot. Someone had pulled the plug on the gene pool and it felt like he and this man were swirling down the drain.

The woman handed him four pennies. J. D. set them by the credit card reader and said to the man, "Help yourself."

He ate the candy in three bites and tossed the wrapper in the backseat of the Suburban. Only in America could you clothe and feed yourself with stray money from an ashtray. And make phone calls.

He watched the gas gauge float and the dashboard get brighter as he curved his way toward the mountains away from the city. On Old Spanish Trail he passed saguaros and a restaurant—The Bone-In. A coyote crossed the road and loped into a pasture near a sign with a cow on the front and the words *Open Range*.

His eyes were heavy and stinging and he felt himself drifting, so he finally stuck his head out the window as he roller-coastered along the road's undulations.

He spotted an ominous brown sign: *Fire Danger Extreme*. The word *Extreme* had a red background, which made it seem more apocalyptic. This was a constant through the summer. If weeds didn't choke the crops, grasshoppers would. Or the wind. Or a drought would dry everything to chaff, or they'd get too much rain and the flooding would take the plants, roots and all. And if not that, fire could ravage the land and smoke would linger along the mountains like dry hope. There was very little belief that a man could actually raise a crop and make a living at farming, but for whatever reason the people who lived close to the ground kept doing it as if they had no other choice.

Past the sign a hill took him down toward a wash and cool air swept over him—just for a second, but it was a hint of something to come, a ray of hope in the heat. On that two-lane country road he felt there was something new on the horizon.

She came to him as sweet and real as summer sweat, her hair blocking the sun as beams of light shone through golden strands and sutures. Laughing at the power she had over him, at the life she could call forth or leave sleeping, she kissed his chest, warm and supple lips and freckles, the blinding whiteness of her teeth, dark eyebrows, and the hairline tracking the borders of her face. A continent of love.

She moved closer to his lips, his cheek, and rose, a golden shadow. *You sleep enough for two lifetimes,* she said.

That voice, close to his ear, soft as a cloud and fluttering like a tiny bird feathering into the wind. Her breath on his skin, in his mouth. Breathing in, he took it like a whispered kiss from God.

This was what he missed in sleep. This was why he cursed the hot nights with the metal fan, keeping him from her, wrestling with exhaustion, with himself. This was where he wanted to be and no act of will could take him. It was only in surrender that he found her, but surrender was the most difficult. Surrender was submission to the truth.

He reached to touch her again, but she was up, sitting beside him, turned away. Her spine was a series of mountains rising and falling, her skin tight over the range. Too tight and stretched thin, like a drum's.

It's time to get up, she said. *It's time to sing.*

It's time to sleep, he said. *The songs are gone. None are left.*

She shook her head and the long-flowing hair reminded him of an old folk tune, the color in the morning when we rise.

There are always more songs, she said. She tapped on his chest and then splayed her hand out, and he felt the coolness where warmth should have been. Trapped but waiting.

His heart swelled and his breath came more quickly; then his body relaxed, some portal opened, and there was washing like a tide.

Surrender. Bright surrender.
Down by the shores of time and sorrow.
Quickly fading, love's awaiting, bones and blood called forth.
I sleep with dead reckoning of sunken ships and whaling
    vessels slipping through the undertow.
    I wander at night along the beach of memory.
    And I wait.
She is my school. My penitentiary.
    The prison I'm locked inside. I will never escape.
    I never want to escape.

Words came disjointed and in cascading succession as the night sang to him, crickets and frogs joining the chorus like an orchestra, antiphonal waves of sound and heat rolling across the landscape. Rolling toward him.

Wake up, she said. *It's time.*

And he did.

FRIDAY

16

J. D. OPENED HIS EYES and stared at the crack in the steering column and then at the open windows to his left and right. Where was he? How had he gotten here? He looked through the mud-splattered windshield at the barn and the playground and it came back. The drive south and the men at the well. He looked at his sweats and felt the remnants of chocolate and peanuts.

There's always a song, he thought, and he looked for something to write on or with but could find neither. *Surrender. Time and sorrow.* Words that stuck from the dream. But what was the use? He would never be able to recall them from the subconscious, where the music played in spite of him. There was something there, something coming to life if he was thinking of lyrics. But these were shadows, black-and-white images on a wall of memory moving and playing with some fire that had been left smoldering.

A bark scorpion climbed along the seat and he flicked it out the passenger window. In his head he held up his arms to signal a field goal, but he didn't have the energy. The morning was dead calm and a hazy light shone over the Rincons. Not a cloud in the sky, just the moon behind him and a few lingering stars chased by the sunlight.

He sat up in the driver's seat and surveyed his surroundings. He had parked on a dirt road behind the barn at the farmers' market and there was already movement as a truck backed in to unload. The organic coffee roaster with dreadlocks would be there soon, setting up on the edge of the tent. In this heat, people would tear down and head home by one in the afternoon, so you had to get things set up before the sun got too high.

The spice guy would be nearby, selling tins of venison rub and chili powder, recipes his father had sold after his father before him had developed the mixes out on the trail. The man wore a Stetson and played guitar like he meant it. Others could play and sing the songs, but it took something special to mean it. J. D. figured he had some kind of life story that made the words resonate like the strings on his Martin. The peaceful, easy feeling of verse and chorus and back around again that you couldn't teach.

J. D. had caught most of that as a kid from a three-fingered man who worked at a gas well on his father's property. J. D. heard he could play and dragged his Silvertone through the bramble to sit near the slush pond on a stump and watch the man pick in a way he had only heard on the radio. Maybe it was easier to follow three fingers, but the man had given him something more than technique in those visits.

The man, Hollis, had said music was something that came from deep within, and even if you didn't have all the equipment others had, it would find a way out, just like gas and water under the ground.

A Prius backed up to the edge of the tent and Goat Milk Girl exited. She was younger than most of the vendors and moved with a kick in her step, an inner confidence that comes from knowing you're one of the beautiful people on the planet and no doubt one of the healthiest. J. D. had heard she was an elementary schoolteacher by day and a yoga instructor by night, but those were just rumors. All he knew for sure was that in her spare time she raised grass-fed goats that never touched corn and soy. She sold the fruit of her labors on the weekends in glass jars with hand-printed labels. Happy men went home with a gallon of milk each weekend to the glares of disgruntled wives. She also made soap from the milk, scented with lavender and rose petals. She brought her favorite Nubian, Sadie, with her, a white, scraggly-looking animal that was a hit with the children at the playground who would wander over to pet her or take her for a walk around the barn.

On the other side of the barn were crafters, vendors selling knives, cutting boards, metal signs, Native American jewelry, wind socks, and cactus ornaments. Pulled pork sandwiches and bratwurst and cold drinks for fifty cents a can in an ice chest. There was even a fellow selling ink pens he had made from .50-caliber shell casings.

Inside the barn were more exotic artisans, quilters and leather tanners and sculptors of wood. A few times he had seen an author selling books in a stall like a woman would sell her grandmother's apple butter recipe. Just words on a page, slathered on and cut straight so they came to the edge and no farther.

Selling books looked like a lonely profession from what J. D. could tell, and it reminded him of the product tables he'd had at venues on the road.

There was also Karl, an older man who reminded J. D. of his father, white-haired and wiry, who walked at an angle because of a bad hip. He sold homemade oatmeal-raisin cookies and tortillas, flat corn pressed out and baked, then shrink-wrapped in packages of a dozen. During the chili festival in the fall he would sell three hundred packs, or so J. D. was told, but most weeks it was only fifteen or twenty. The man really wasn't in it for the money. You can tell that when people smile while unloading.

He stepped out of the Suburban and stretched, the wetness heavy on his back. How long had he slept? It felt like days, but when he checked his watch, he saw it had been a few hours. Could he have dreamed all of that and made the connection with her so fast?

A hay bale barricade ringed a small playground area with a slide and a couple of swings. Something for the little kids to do while their parents sold trinkets and produce. He walked toward the Rincon Country Store, a mini market nearby that sold only regular gas, then realized he had no money. His body ached for coffee but he would have to hold out for a sample of the organic, fair-trade stuff.

On his way back to the Suburban he heard the low rumble of Slocum's diesel truck. This wasn't going to be easy to explain, but he was man enough to face Slocum and try. He hadn't set out the previous morning to abandon the farm or his obliga-tions. Far from it. He had done everything Slocum had asked and more in the past couple months. But in the course of a life, things work out differently than you plan.

J. D. washed his hands at a spigot by the barn, then walked up behind the truck and began unloading vegetables. Plastic cartons of organic carrots, cabbage, beets, and squash.

When Slocum saw him, his mouth dropped. "Look what the cat drug in." He shook his head. "What are you doing here?"

"It's a long story."

"I'll bet it is." He stared at J. D.'s sweatpants that didn't seem to go with his boots. "You know the police are looking for you. They was at the house half the night."

"I've had more than the police looking for me." He grabbed a carton full of string beans and carried it to a cart. The bed of the cart was beveled with plywood bases on both sides that rose at forty-five-degree angles so shoppers could see what they were buying. People would paw through the produce to get just the right head of cauliflower or broccoli.

The family could easily live on the meat and produce they raised on the farm. If the apocalypse came the next day or in a year, they would survive because they knew how to work the land. But to pay the water bill and have electricity to run the air conditioner that kept them from being boiled to death in that old farmhouse, they had to have cash. Plus, buying the feed and seed and gas for the farm machinery took money they didn't have, so they sold what they could and raised enough to pay the note and other bills and scrape by.

Slocum followed empty-handed. "If you'd have listened to me, you wouldn't be in this mess."

"You're probably right about that."

"I told you if you find a Mexican, call Border Patrol. Why didn't you?"

"I did. That's when I thought she was dead, but when she moved, it seemed a little cruel."

"Cruel? How do you come up with cruel? Somebody breaks the law, you call the law."

J. D. set up the two tables that would hold the cash box and a scale to weigh produce as he answered. "When I saw her, I remembered that fellow who came through a few weeks ago from Nicaragua. The guy trying to get back to his family. Just crying and wanting a drink and some food."

"He was breaking the law."

"Yeah, but the look on his face when they carted him away stuck with me."

"You wanted to be a hero, didn't you?"

"She was dehydrated. She'd passed out."

"It's her own fault for trying to walk through the desert."

"She's not illegal. She had a passport."

Slocum laughed. "Yeah, right. I'll bet she whipped it out and showed you, didn't she. Or was it one of those passports you can show on your iPad?"

J. D. grabbed another carton and lugged it under the tent. This one was filled with onions twice the size of his fist. All golden brown with the husks. "She's *not* illegal. She's in trouble. I tried to help."

"Yeah, that plan went real well. Look what happened to the doctor in Benson. I'll bet he's real glad you helped. And that she has a passport."

J. D. leaned against the cart and crossed his arms. "Mr. Slocum, I'm sorry. I came here this morning to tell you that and give you a hand. I didn't mean to leave you hanging. I'm a man of my word and—"

"A man of your word? You a comedian now?"

"This thing took on a life of its own. Things happened I couldn't control."

"And you didn't come back because you knew you'd get arrested at the house."

"Well, I'm not stupid."

Slocum cursed and said under his breath, "That's up for debate." The man took off his hat and wiped his forehead with a sleeve. "Can you imagine how Win feels? He's the one who suggested you see that doctor. He feels responsible for his death."

"He's not."

"Well, I'd like to see you try and convince him."

"That woman I found has a bounty on her head. She's mixed up in something."

"So now you're in over your head. You admit that."

"I could admit it from the minute I found her, but I don't just leave people." The words caught in his throat as he stared at Slocum.

"How about running from the police? Do you do that normally?"

"I didn't run from them; I ran from the guys with the guns. If she had been arrested, they would have walked into the jail and shot up the place. There would be more people dead."

"Oh, so you saved half of the Tucson police department?"

"I didn't say that."

He stepped closer. "She really got to you, didn't she? She's mixed up with drugs up to her eyeballs and you bought it hook, line, and sinker."

"I'm not saying I did everything right. I just did the best I could under the circumstances."

"Then do the best thing now and call the police. Tell them what you know. Otherwise you'll be in more trouble."

"I can't do that yet," J. D. said.

"And why not? What's so all-fired important about this wetback that you've got to risk your neck?"

"I believe her."

"Believe her about what?"

"That somebody's trying to kill her. And you can stop laughing because there's more to it than just some big drug deal. I need to find her and tell her what I found out in the desert."

"Her passport?"

"No, the case she was carrying. It was handcuffed to her. It didn't have drugs or money."

"If it was on my property, it's rightfully mine. What was it?"

"Something the people after her will want back."

Slocum shook his head and took out his cell phone. J. D. couldn't tell if he was dialing or bluffing. "If you're not calling the police, I will. They think I'm an accessory to the whole thing anyway."

"Then why did they let you come here this morning?"

Slocum rolled his eyes. "They're not going to keep me from feeding my family. The only thing that's keeping us afloat is these markets. And thanks to you, we didn't get those chickens slaughtered."

Slocum hung up. J. D. grabbed a carton of red potatoes off the truck and the two worked in silence as the heat rose. They unloaded the freezer and J. D. strung a long extension cord to the barn to keep the meat cool. Slocum had loaded the cooler with enough ground beef and brisket for the whole month, but it was better to have too much than too little.

When other vendors began to arrive, J. D. pulled Slocum aside. "I know I don't deserve it, but I need your help. I need cash."

"What are you fixing to do?"

"Find the girl. Help her get back to her home. Or some-place safe."

"Where did she run off to?"

"She got in touch with somebody who picked her up. Some people she trusted. But the way I figure it, she's better off with an unknown like me, somebody who isn't connected with her family."

"Leave it alone, J. D. You're in enough trouble."

"Twenty dollars will get me enough gas to get out of here and find her. That would be a start. And I'll pay you back. You know I will."

"How are you going to do that?"

"I got some money saved up. I just can't get to it right now."

Slocum shook his head and looked off. "I ever tell you about the guy who stayed with us before you? Kid from Oklahoma. Or maybe it was Arkansas."

J. D. had heard the story more than a few times, but he let the man talk. How the kid had gotten into pills or weed and his work suffered. Then one Friday night while Slocum had taken the family for a rare weekend camping by a lake, the kid stole some money from the cash box and hit the road.

"I would have given him the money. That's the screwy thing about it. All he had to do was ask. But instead he broke the lock and took eighty dollars and left. The animals survived. We were only gone through the weekend, but the problem was the storm that night. Lightning knocked out the breaker switch to the barn. The two big freezers were full of chickens. About two thousand dollars' worth of meat went bad by the time we got back."

"I'm not running out on you," J. D. said. "I'm not breaking the cash box. I'm just asking."

"The point is you've already run out. You made your decision when you hooked up with that wetback. And don't give me that look or talk about the passport. I don't care if she had an invitation from the president himself. This is not your fight. For the life of me, I can't figure out what kind of spell she has you under."

J. D. moved closer and lowered his voice. Something deep rose up within him, something he had held back. "I know you think humanity stops at the border. Somebody has browner skin than you and they're not worth as much. People are people. They're not wetbacks."

"You meet one pretty Mexican and you're ready to open the border. I told my wife you was a bleedin'-heart liberal the moment I laid eyes on you."

"Hate whoever you want, Slocum. I don't think a porous border is good for anybody north or south of it, but most of the people coming from their side are just trying to find a better life."

"At our expense. They're filling our emergency rooms, and it's my taxes paying for it."

"When somebody's hurt, you help them. I don't care where a man is from if he needs help."

"I got no problem helping. But break our laws and you pay the price." Slocum pointed a finger at J. D.'s chest and held it there. "I fought for people's right to come to this country legally. I fought for every long-haired, dope-smoking liberal like yourself to go traipsing up to Washington to protest. But there comes a point where a man says enough is enough, and this is where I draw that line."

The lady Slocum paid to weigh and sell produce arrived, put a tablecloth down, and grabbed a fan. Her name was Dorothy but everyone called her Dot. J. D. didn't know how she and

Slocum had gotten together but the team worked. Slocum hooked up the spritzers that would spray a mist of water on people as they walked under the tent, and J. D. gave Dot a hug.

"You doing okay?" she said. Her eyes were like an old dog's, sagging skin all around but a face full of compassion.

"Plugging along," he said.

"Didn't think you'd be here this morning from what Slocum said."

"I didn't think so either."

"What were you two bickering about?"

"A lot of things."

The fellow with rattlesnake training for dogs pulled in and began to set up away from the playground.

"I think my time at the farm is about up."

Her hair was thinning on top, so she usually wore a bandanna to cover it. Her eyes showed worry. "Is there any chance you'll stay?"

Slocum had his phone out again and was walking toward the Suburban.

"I don't think so."

"Well, there must be some way I can help."

He looked at her kind face, etched with lines and contours of age. "You've done a lot to make me feel welcome, Dot."

She moved toward the table and he noticed Karl pull in and open the hatch of his minivan to unload tortillas. Goat Milk Girl popped the back of her Prius. There were three men waiting to help when she reached the trunk.

He felt something in his hand, a folded bill, and turned to see Dot.

"Now you take this and use it however you need, you hear?"

It was a twenty-dollar bill. "I can't take this from you."

"Well, you're going to have to because you're holding it now." She held up a hand beside her as she walked back to the table. "You throw it down and Slocum will get you for littering."

A family pulled in that always came early and bought at least three hundred dollars' worth of vegetables and meat. They had several foster children, and it was like watching a rainbow to see them all get out of the car and attack the carts. The wife was a well-oiled machine, choosing the right amount of peppers, cabbage, and meat for upcoming meals, as if she could keep all the ingredients and the process spinning in her head. While she took charge, the husband pulled one of the little kids in a Radio Flyer wagon they used to transport the produce to the car. Something about the man cut J. D. to the quick.

Thoughts and memories flowed together in a stream through his sleep-deprived mind, trickling over rocks and cutting some new channel. Water flows where it will and thoughts will do the same. He knew the trick was to simply surrender to the torrent. That's when he could figure things out. If he followed his instincts, the words would come out in a song—not some paint-by-number approach to life, but something real and true and resonant.

Slocum hung up and glanced back sheepishly. J. D. knew he had only a few minutes before the police showed up. That was when he spotted a black car with tinted windows driving past the playground. A week before, he would have thought it was someone looking for a fresh burrito or just disregarded it, but now, heightened as he was to his surroundings, he knew instinctively what was on the other side of that tinted glass. He also knew if he stayed, he would endanger them all.

Seeing that car finally made the pieces fit—the reason the man had found them in Benson, how the two men had driven the road to the well on Slocum's farm, and how the black car with tinted windows had showed up here.

"How's it hanging today, J. D.?" Karl said. He flashed his normal smile and crusty laugh and shook J. D.'s hand like he was fitting pipe.

J. D. kept one eye on the car and took a step away from the barn. "I need your help, Karl."

17

THE ROAD WOUND AND PITCHED toward the mountains, and Muerte thought he had seen this setting in a movie. The saguaros grew statuesque and dotted the hillside like soldiers in their own military procession. A green militia moving in step down the rocky crags of the national park. He wanted to slow and take it in, but the prospect before him of finding the girl and eliminating her fueled him and he accelerated.

He had enlarged the program on his phone and now it pulsed and beeped as he drew closer. His mind numb from lack of sleep, he ran over the events of the previous hour and smiled. There was a certain satisfaction in knowing the trail he was leaving was untraceable, even though he had left many bodies in the wake of his movement north. The police officer was the most unfortunate and the one he wished he could have back. His death would only heighten the interest for the American law enforcement community. They held each other in high esteem and violence toward one was violence toward all. But they were soft. Their anger would lessen and they would all go back to their football games and *American Idol* or whatever television show was hottest. And he would continue his mission and slip away unnoticed. If they thought the death of a police officer was tragic, they had seen nothing.

The authorities would not make the connection between the officer and the doctor in Benson for some time, or ever, and it would probably be several days before anyone noticed the two he had left in their car in the hospital parking garage in Tucson. He was firing as he climbed into the backseat, shooting downward, taking them by surprise and diminishing the blood spray. He then arranged their bodies to make it appear they were merely sleeping. They would be seen by passersby as two more Mexicans exhausted from their day labors and trying to rest before they visited a sick loved one. He had made sure the windows were up to keep the flies away and diminish the death odor. He did not envy the investigators who would be called to the scene.

Muerte pulled into the farmers' market and slowed to a crawl on the graveled lot. Though he was not at 100 percent, he was invigorated by the fact that he would be able to sleep the rest of the day if he simply took care of business. It needed to be a clean shot, however. The last thing he wanted to do was mow down a dozen market vendors. He would if he had to, of course. But he knew it was in his best interest to provide a single shot each to the head and chest and leave. That was his goal.

He had spoken with the men before stepping into their car, receiving information about what they had seen in the desert. He had assumed they were lying or simply didn't understand how the electronic gadget worked. But the description of the desert encounter sounded plausible. Perhaps the girl had retraced her steps to find the satchel she had stolen and ditched. Perhaps she was hiding nearby and they hadn't seen her. Whatever the reason, she was now here and he would put an end to the chase.

He parked on the opposite side of a fence enclosing the parking lot, where he could see all the trucks and cars pulling in and backing up to the tent. He enlarged the phone application. She was just outside the barn, headed inside. He chambered a round in his Glock, concealed the gun in his jacket, and strode toward the building.

The area was a beehive of activity with adults and children preparing for the day's sales. The smell of freshly brewing coffee hit him as soon as he rounded the corner. He passed a booth selling tortillas, water, and soda. The young girl there didn't look up as he walked past. Maria was somewhere inside the barn, but as he stepped inside, there were too many people carrying and moving things. He struggled past a man holding deer antlers and checked his phone again. She was outside now and moving through the vendors.

In the sunlight he smelled the cooking beef brisket and bratwurst and wiped away sweat from his forehead. He shielded the phone's screen from the light, then ran through the gauntlet of vendors under the canopy. He surveyed the lot but didn't see the familiar black hair cascading down her lovely back. For the first time since he had begun his search, he had the feeling that he could be the hunted one.

"Care to try some fresh honey?" an older woman said.

Muerte glanced at her and shook his head before returning to the tracker. Maria was now stationary near the front of the barn.

He strode along the graveled road, determined, as a truck rumbled past advertising gyro sandwiches. Then an old Suburban pulled by him, dust funneling. When he reached the playground area, children were gathered around a goat tethered to a crudely fashioned climbing structure. He moved past it, then checked his phone again only to see Maria was behind him. He grasped the gun in his right hand and turned. There were only children there. He walked to the road again but there was no one.

He heard a commotion in the parking lot. Someone shouted. But Muerte could only stare at the goat. On the chain around its neck was the ring. Something gave way in his stomach.

"Mister, is that your car over by the fence?" a man said. He was older and wiry, white-haired. "That lady doesn't like people parking on her property."

A siren screamed in the distance and Muerte hurried to his car, cursing his luck. Maria had figured out the tracking device and was mocking him by using the goat. She would pay for her insolence.

He was met by a middle-aged woman wearing hospital scrubs, hands on hips, fire in her eyes.

"Is this your car?" she yelled. "This is private property—can't you see the signs?"

Muerte had his hand on the Glock and had picked out the spot above her right eyebrow where the bullet would enter her brain. Contrary to what most believed, he did not enjoy killing. It was a necessary part of his profession, like a garbage collector dealing with smelly plastic bags each day. But for a person like this, he felt an almost-irresistible urge to inflict pain along with the kill shot.

As he judged the many witnesses behind him and the

screaming siren that was approaching, he simply smiled and nodded. "I'm very sorry, ma'am," he said in his best American voice. "It's my first time to the market. I'll move right away."

"I've told you people you can't park here! I called the tow truck and he's coming."

When she said *you people,* he could tell she wasn't lumping him in with all the vendors. He had a knife in his boot and if he knelt before her, he could perhaps bring it into her chest and leave her in the dirt without anyone noticing.

A sheriff's cruiser screamed into the parking lot, throwing gravel and kicking up dust. Muerte smiled at the woman, stepped into his car, and pulled away.

18

J. D. PASSED THE SHERIFF'S cruiser as it screamed toward the market. He drove toward I-10, winding his way around the back roads, keeping his air-conditioning off to conserve fuel until he reached a Fry's. He used the entire twenty Dot had given him and then cursed himself for not saving some for food. But every drop of gas counted in propelling him forward, so better to have an empty stomach than an empty tank.

With the fog in his brain he tried to focus as the numbers whizzed by. He had to do two things. Find Maria and get his money, not necessarily in that order. Wait, three things. Stay away from the police. Four, if you counted avoiding that crazy Mexican guy. He thought of the Monty Python routine about the Spanish Inquisition. But he couldn't raise a smile.

He could go back to the gas station where he'd left her and

try to track her from there, but it felt like a dead end. Had she gone to a house or apartment nearby? Had someone picked her up behind the store?

Then another thought struck him. She had given him the ring. Had she known it would lead the killer to him? He couldn't help feeling set up, but she had kept the ring all the time they were being chased, so maybe she didn't know.

He shoved the thought from his head and tried to recall her conversation on the phone. He wished he had listened instead of buying donuts—maybe he could've picked up a few more words or even a location. But he remembered something she'd said in the car about a church that helped her village. He tried to come up with the name.

He went back inside and asked the kid at the counter if he had the yellow pages. The young man looked confused. "What are you talking about?"

"A phone book." The Internet had taken over the world. There was no doubt about it.

The kid pulled a dusty phone book from under the counter and handed it to him.

Tucson Evangel Tabernacle was a tiny building a few blocks away from Miracle Mile, in a rough section of town. The main road was lined with seedy motels and bars, and the church fit right in with the rest of the neighborhood. The building looked more like a house, and parking was limited to a few spots directly in front of the worship center and along the street. Something was going on inside when J. D. pulled up, which seemed odd for a weekday.

He walked in as a man with large tattoos on his arms was speaking to about fifty people who had spread out in the sanctuary. There were four pews and the rest of the place was filled with folding chairs.

"Come on in and have a seat, brother," the man at the front said. "Everyone is welcome."

Everyone meant street people. Some wore biker jackets. Others had eyes so red it looked like Christmas. Some of the ladies had short skirts and looked like they might have been working overnight, but they were nodding and agreeing with everything the man in front said.

"We're talking about spiritual warfare," the man said. "We're talking about the enemy of your soul who wants you to fail at life. We're talking about someone sent here to kill, steal, and destroy. That's what your enemy wants to do with you. But I want to introduce you to someone else named Jesus."

There was a smattering of applause throughout the room. "Yes, Preacher! You tell it! Speak that name."

"Jesus," he said again. "Hay-zuus. Yeshua. The name above every name."

Some in the audience yelled the name at the top of their lungs.

"He is King of kings and Lord of lords. Immanuel. God with us. Savior. Lord. Friend of sinners. Prince of Peace."

With each phrase the crescendo rose from the crowd until people were standing and clapping, encouraging the man to continue. But as soon as he finished, another man took his place and opened a Bible.

"Six of the best words in the Bible come from this passage," the man said. "Six of the most wonderful words in the English language. 'And such were some of you.'"

"Amen, Teacher."

"Preach it."

"Tell us, now."

"'And such were some of you.' Did you get that?"

"Tell it again, Teacher."

"'And such were some of you.'" The man emphasized each word and J. D. was captivated by the command he had over the small crowd.

The first speaker wandered through the sanctuary carrying a Bible heavy enough to be a ship's anchor. He made eye contact with J. D. and smiled.

"Could I have a word with you outside?" J. D. said.

"Certainly."

The man followed J. D. out of the room to the front porch, which served as a concrete vestibule.

"This your first time here?" the man said.

"It is."

"What do you think?"

"Pretty impressive turnout for this time of day," J. D. said. "But I didn't come to get religion; I came looking for somebody."

"What you're really looking for is in that room. The Bible can help you change from the inside out."

"I know about the Bible. Learned it a long time ago. But let's just say God and I don't see eye to eye on a few things."

"I can understand that. Been there myself a time or two." The man reached out a hand. "Ron Barfield. One of the pastors here. I'm the most messed-up, sobered-up, tattooed-up pastor you'll ever see, but I love Jesus. He's made all the difference in my life."

J. D. shook his hand.

"Who are you looking for?"

"A Mexican woman. Just came over the border."

"You've just described a lot of females in Tucson."

"Yeah, but this one is special. Her name is Maria." J. D. watched for any reaction from the pastor that would give him away, but he saw none. "Have you heard anything about her?"

"We have a lot of people come through the church needing help. A lot of Mexican people looking for a place to stay. And a lot of people like myself. Lost. Lonely. Meth addicts. Heroin addicts. Alcoholics. People who need God to reach down and pull them out of the sewer. What do you need?"

"I need to find this girl before the men looking for her do."

"Is she in trouble?"

"More than you can know. She met up with some people last night over on the east side. Maybe I'm grabbing at straws to come here, but it was the only thing I could remember. She talked about a church that came down to her village in Mexico."

"And how did you find out about us?"

"A friend of mine said you folks go down that way every now and then with food and clothes."

The man nodded. "We do. Who is this friend of yours?"

"I met this young lady at sunup yesterday in the desert. Tried to help her. She was half-dead. More like three-quarters. I got her to the doctor and that man got killed. You may have seen it in the news."

"I did. Terrible. The police are looking for her and you, too, I suspect."

"I guess they want to talk to me. But I don't know a whole lot more than they do. All I know is that girl is in danger."

"Have you ever thought that if you can't find her, maybe those other men can't either? Maybe she's safe." He said it with a knowing look, like he was trying to communicate with more than just words.

"I hope that's true. But I have information for her. Something I found out that she doesn't know. And my guess is she'll want to."

"Well, I haven't talked with your Maria."

"Maybe somebody else in the church has. Could you ask around?"

"I can check, but I wouldn't hold my breath. People who go underground usually stay there." The man looked hard at him. "I have a sense about people, an inner compass that tells me when somebody needs help, and my sense is that you're in as much need as Maria."

J. D. took off his hat and wiped his brow. "I'll admit I'm hungry and just about dead tired."

"We can help you. Is there anything else?"

The man's care and concern didn't surprise him. He'd had people touch his life. His mother was both the wordsmith and caretaker of the family. He had inherited her love of words and how they shaped a life. How many times in his teenage years had he been low and unsure and she had picked him up with a touch and a kind word? And there had been a teacher, early on, who seemed to free his heart to touch something bigger than the little town they called home. But to have a stranger look at him like this choked him up. Those rheumy brown eyes with dark pinpoints seemed to bore a hole through him. It was like this broken man could see through all of his calloused pain to the hurt that festered and burned and had nearly eaten him alive.

If he began talking right then, he knew the dam would burst and it would all come pouring out and he would be no good for a day or a week or maybe the rest of his life. So he held back, kept the water tight inside.

"I just need some rest and something to eat."

Ron nodded. "Do you want to bring anything in from your truck? This is not the best neighborhood."

"No, I'll take my chances."

The bread was just north of moldy and the coffee tepid, but the chicken and beans and salad filled him and he felt like he could live again. He learned that the church received several tons of food each day, which they distributed to ministries throughout southern Arizona and into New Mexico and then south of the border. Some of it was hard as granite, like the cupcakes and fruit pies, but most of it was edible. The effort fed the homeless and some battered women and children who had nowhere else to go, many of whom were on the street in the heat all day.

They served him food on a Styrofoam plate, and the plastic fork he used broke when he stuck it into a sliced carrot. The evening meal wasn't until six, but the pastor had them serve J. D. early. Then another man who knew very little English showed him to a cot in an office at the back of the building. He fell asleep as soon as he hit the pillow and descended into a black hole of questions and finally nothingness.

She came to him again through smoke and clouds, parting cobwebs before her in the attic of her youth. She was his first sweetheart and this place was where they had first kissed. They were flanked by a gathering of furniture and trunks from another country. A musty smell of old leather and cast-off clothing discarded like bad memories. Dust-covered magazines stacked in corners, marked with tracks of spiders and mice and covered again by time and the settling of a century. Wallpaper curled.

She sat before a sheet-covered couch, crisscross applesauce, wearing a skirt and long socks and penny loafers. A floral print. Grass stains from a game of tag in the field during recess. They had both made childhood promises they would never be able to keep.

She tucked her hair behind one ear like a schoolgirl ready to read her first poem, and he remembered. Her reading a speech by someone. Martin Luther King Jr.? "I Have a Dream"? It was the content of his first song, written in childhood—red hills of Georgia and free at last. Eternal themes repeated by children but not fully understood.

She let the left side of her hair hang straight like a veil, a curtain that couldn't be parted though he tried to reach it. He saw only profile, but her profile was beauty squared, and even in the muted light of memory, she made his heart ache with longing. Given all the words and music in the world, all the languages, all the notes on the scale, all the instruments ever conceived, he could never capture her. Never hope to.

I've been thinking, she said. Delicate words from delicate lips.

Thinking what?

How it will be when we're apart. What that will look like for you.

Why not what it will look like for you?

She smiled. *I already know that. It's nothing I could describe. And nothing I would want to because it would only make you long for it.*

What's it like? Is it clouds and harps and angel wings?

She giggled and closed her eyes and took a breath. Darkness sparkled on her skin like sunlight on a lake. *This is not about me; it's about you.*

Everything about me is about you. Don't you see that?

She put a hand out and he took it. Soft and supple, her skin white but her fingertips deeply calloused. Her nails were child-like, cut to the quick, and the veins in her hands stood out like tributaries to some inner world that left him an outsider. He was an illegal alien and the border was her heart.

I can't be everything any longer, she said. *I was never meant to be.*

What do you mean?

You have to move. You have to leave. You can't keep coming here and holding on.

I could never leave you.

Yes, you can. You're stronger than you think.

I'm weaker than you think.

Remember Santayana, she said.

He searched his mind. She loved quotes. She lived by words pithy and profound. Some were maudlin when he first heard them, but the longer he turned them over, the more they meant. Dredging from some well of words, he said, *"Those who don't learn from the past are condemned to repeat it"? Something like that, right?*

Not that one, she said. *Everyone knows that one. Everyone botches it.* She turned from him and pulled her hair back, the other side this time. Unveiling. *"It is not wisdom to be only wise . . ."*

I don't recall it.

Sure you do. "And on the inward vision close the eyes . . ."

He shook his head. *No, I can't.*

"But it is wisdom to believe the heart."

She touched his chest again and he said her name, soft as a whisper. *Alycia.*

And then she was gone. He reached for her but empty foot-prints filled the places where she should have walked. It was that moment he dreaded most, though he knew if she did not leave, he could not be surprised by her coming.

When he awoke, it was dark and he could taste the sleep in his mouth. The only sound was the thump, thump of a bass guitar coming from the sanctuary. He thought he should write all of that down, capture it quickly on some scrap of paper or write it on the dry-erase board. The words she had said to him, the start or finish of a song yet unwritten.

Then he thought of Maria. Was she alive? Had Muerte found her? And if he hadn't, what was the man's next move?

Maybe Maria was better off without J. D., as far away from him as she could get. Perhaps her salvation would come in the distance she kept. But he couldn't shake the feeling of connection, a bond between them. He had felt it from the moment he saw her move, from the moment he put her on his horse. Something unspoken, something spiritual. That sounded like a romantic feeling, but it was true. Had she felt it as well?

The cot creaked as he sat up, and his head and stomach swirled—a thousand thoughts and some underdone chicken combining in a perfect storm. But he had woken up feeling worse all those days on the road chasing pavement and double-yellow dreams with hangovers the size of Nebraska. A time in his life when he'd played it safe, guarding the hand he was dealt, protecting himself and listening to voices that said they had the perfect plan, the design that would lead to prosperity. People who told him who he needed to be to get his songs heard, the brand he needed in order to conform him to their view of who he was.

Alycia's illness had shown him he was searching for someone else's songs. And after her diagnosis, his career had gone into a self-imposed free fall. He poured himself into saving her and pulling her back from the brink, waking every day with the fear that he'd lost her.

The decision to come to Arizona had been irrational, impetuous, spur-of-the-moment. That was how Alycia had lived and how she compelled him now. She had said the gut and the mind were connected, that if you were sick in your stomach or intestines, there was a direct connection to your head. He had been skeptical and dismissed her out of hand, laughing at her pronouncements against the toxic lifestyle the world had embraced. The change of diet, the way she had cleaned out all the chemicals and had begun growing her own vegetables and copied verses that said you could be satisfied living on the side of a mountain growing your own food and taking care of your family. She had been connected to all of that while he had stayed aloof. Maybe that was why he had come here, to follow what he hadn't believed. Or maybe he just wanted her back and this was his way of searching.

Now the sane part of him wanted to tell the authorities what he knew and walk away. He could head back east and face what he'd walked away from, which was almost as daunting. But he could practice what he had learned on the Slocum farm. Maybe find some kind of rhythm and live out his life as part of the landscape of humanity, just moving day to day, sunlight to dusk, and beginning over.

But something deep in his heart wouldn't allow giving up. He couldn't help feeling he was on a path with destiny at the end and life and death on either side of the road. He just wasn't sure which ditch he was sliding toward.

He walked into a room with books in stacks several feet high. On the side of the wall was a crudely drawn sign that read *Libary*. Glue strips for mice lined the floor and a few had been successful but not discarded. Out the window were security lights over the front church doors. People milled about, some smoking, some staring at the sky, all of them sweating and listening to the music emanating from the sanctuary.

The sound brought back the first night he had walked to a microphone, singing words scribbled on a page in a three-ring binder. He was just a kid, so he didn't know enough to be scared of the chance he was taking. He'd spent hours working through the chords without looking at his left hand, closing his eyes or standing in front of the mirror, but no matter how much he practiced, he couldn't prepare for what happened deep inside. The strange, unexplainable mix of exhilaration and fear, like holding a loaded gun on a charging tiger or feeling the bat in your hands as a curveball hangs on the inside corner. Opportunity and chance all wrapped up in a singular moment in time before people who dared you to entertain them. That was the moment, the first time in his life when he truly felt at peace in the midst of the chaos of his own heart. He finally felt at home.

He wandered through the rest of the building and found a spartan bathroom with copies of *Our Daily Bread* and a missions magazine by the toilet. The outer door opened. Footsteps on the tiled floor. Then a flash of fluorescence under the door.

"J. D.?"

It was Pastor Ron—at least it sounded like him.

"I'm in here."

"I was just seeing if you were awake. We need to talk when you have a minute."

The room where he had slept was Ron's office. The pastor moved behind the cluttered desk with a makeshift bookshelf behind him and sat with his feet propped. There were Spanish and English volumes behind him stacked in haphazard rows. Thick Bible commentaries and books that said Tozer and Spurgeon and Lewis and Packer on the spines.

He motioned to the plastic chair in front of the desk. "Sleep okay?"

"I was out pretty fast," J. D. said. "Thanks for the food and the place to rest. I appreciate it."

"Glad you got some sleep." He shifted in the chair and crossed his legs. "Let me get to the point. Two things. First, your truck is gone."

"What?"

"I'm sorry. I told you this wasn't the best neighborhood. Was there anything of value in there?"

J. D. thought of all he had just lost. "Just a rifle."

"Where did you get it?"

"I found it."

"Did you find the truck, too? Because from the looks of it, I'm afraid it wouldn't have gotten you much farther anyway."

J. D. rubbed his face and stared at the wall.

"The second thing is, I talked with a couple of people about your friend, Maria. Word's out on the street about her. She must be pretty important."

J. D. nodded. "A bunch of people want her dead."

Ron scratched stubble on his chin. "Yeah, and there's big money that wants her back. If you keep looking, I'm not sure you'll be with us much longer. The police are looking for her *and* you. There are people from Mexico on her trail. Rumors that the Zetas are involved."

"She mentioned them."

Ron winced. "Did she tell you who she thought was after her?"

"His name is Muerte."

Ron's mouth dropped and he raised his eyebrows. "Gabriel Muerte? He's here? Are you sure?"

"I don't know his first name, just that he wasn't a real nice guy and wanted her dead for some reason."

"Madre mía," he said, holding up both hands and putting his feet on the floor. "If I were you, I would walk away. No, run as fast as you can. If you don't value your life, keep looking for her."

"I'm not the kind who . . . gives up."

"J. D., there's not a police officer below the border who would sneeze in the direction of Gabriel Muerte. You know what his name means in Spanish, right?"

"I can't help what a man's name means in another language. Doesn't matter to me if it's Smith or Jones or if it means liverwurst. That girl needs help."

"There was an officer killed last night in Tucson. The police are looking for anyone with information."

"I don't know anything about that."

"They think it may be related to the doctor's death and a man found dead on the road near La Pena."

J. D. knew about that but didn't say anything.

Ron stood and looked out the small window that faced an alley. The reflection of the streetlight showed the tattoos like a signpost to his past. "I've been with this church since it began and I've always said the day we put our protection over our mission is the day we give up on being who we're supposed to be. Greater is he who is in us than he who is in the world. The Lord has protected us. We've placed our complete faith in him."

"You got a family?"

Ron took out his wallet and tossed it to J. D. In the front flap was a photo of him behind his wife and five smiling children around them.

"I've never worried about my back or my family or what might be coming down the road."

"That's good."

"Until now."

J. D. nodded. "Those are beautiful kids." He put the wallet on the desk.

"The church is growing. There are people getting saved every day. And then we go to the people south of the border and take the love of God right to them. Right through the cartel, with the guys with M16s standing guard. We go there in plain sight and distribute food and clothes and coloring books and Bibles. Some have been talking with cartel members themselves. They're listening; they're interested. There's so much going on down there."

"I understand. But why are you telling me this?"

"I don't want it to stop."

"How is my finding Maria going to stop any of that?"

Ron sat heavily in the chair on the other side of the desk. "We know Muerte is after her. Maybe the Zetas. Her own family. Maybe she stole something. Maybe someone's upset about her involvement in the work we're doing. I don't know—"

"Wait," J. D. said. "You do know her. You lied to me."

"No, I didn't lie. Maria . . . showed up at a couple of our events down there. Some of the townspeople saw her and became afraid."

"Why would they be afraid? She said she wants to help people."

"They thought she was with the cartel. That she was trying to infiltrate us and harm the work."

"Do you believe that?"

"I don't know. But I do believe there are forces at work here a lot bigger than her. And her motivation may not be as pure as you hope."

"What do you mean?"

Ron sat forward. "I have family members in that town. My wife is from there. We have tried to get as many out as we can. Muerte is personally responsible for many deaths. Beheadings. The people are terrified. You can cut the fear in that town with a knife."

"And a few throats, it sounds like."

"Muerte is only one evil you face. I made some calls. Maria has a bounty on her head. Dead or alive, it doesn't matter. One million dollars."

"Who's putting it up?"

He shook his head. "I don't know. But you can imagine how many are trying to find her. If you are working for next to nothing and you are offered a million dollars, what would you do? Add the police to that, and the Border Patrol, who seem to think she had something to do with the death of one of their agents, and you have a powder keg. One spark will set the whole thing off."

"I'm not trying to ignite anything, Pastor. I just found a girl out in the cactus. And for some reason I'm drawn to her. Call it God if you want. I guess I'll find her again if it's meant to be."

Ron interlaced his fingers. "Is there something you're not telling me?"

"About what?"

"About anything. About why she is so important to you."

It was an open gate to a field J. D. wasn't sure he should enter. He studied his fingernails for a moment, figuring and calculating. Thinking about what his voice would sound like if he spilled more. Finally he said, "I don't have a real good track record with preachers."

"Why's that?"

He shrugged. "I just don't."

"Did you grow up in the church?"

"I went because my parents made me. And then I went because the pretty girls were there."

The man laughed and J. D. thought it was a good sound to hear a preacher chuckle. But Ron turned serious when J. D. said, "Then I got in trouble for hitting a pastor. Knocked him out cold."

"What for?"

"He said something I didn't like. He wound up not pressing charges but it kind of soured me on people of the cloth."

"What did he say?"

The next logical question. The next bread crumb along the path. Should he keep dropping them?

"It was at a funeral. I'd rather not talk about it."

Ron studied him. "Where was this?"

"Nashville."

"That's where you're from?"

"Near there."

"And why did you move here?"

"To learn farming. Pick up some pointers on how to do it without all the pesticides and chemical engineering they do to food. This situation has gotten me sidetracked."

"Well, there's a purpose in everything."

J. D. closed his eyes and bit the inside of his cheek. The magic words. "That's what the preacher said just before I hit him."

"Seriously?"

"He meant it to give comfort, I guess. To give hope that God is up there and in control. I don't want a God in control who lets all this happen."

The man stared at him.

"The other thing people are fond of saying," J. D. continued, "is that he works all of this for our good. You've probably said that one, too."

"Romans 8:28. It's an important verse but it gets taken out of context."

"Well, if you'll forgive me, I'll skip the context and the sermon."

"I understand." A long pause. "Whose funeral were you attending? Someone close?"

"My wife."

"I'm sorry. How long had you been married?"

"Six years. Almost seven."

"What happened?"

"Are you asking me this because you care or because you're trying to figure out if you can trust me? Because if you're going to tell me what I need to know, I'll keep talking. But if not, I'll leave."

"What if it's both? I care and I want to know if I can trust you."

J. D. nodded and peered at the low ceiling tiles with brown water stains. "She had a growth in her brain. Everybody assumed it was cancer and kept calling it that. I didn't have the energy to correct them."

"What happened?"

He spoke unlike any preacher J. D. had ever known. Most of them he had met as a child and even those who had helped his wife had treated him with something akin to polite indifference. As if there might be someone behind him they'd like to talk with a little more. Some better opportunity they didn't want to miss. And he couldn't blame them because they probably sensed he was a closed door.

But this man was different.

"It was something growing inside her head they couldn't get to," he said after a while.

"Did they do surgery?" Ron said.

"They tried. Sliced her open to have a look. Then they pieced her together and the stitches made her look like Frankenstein. If the tumor hadn't grown, she'd have been okay."

"But it did."

"Yes, sir. Grew like a weed."

"Did she go through radiation?"

How much to tell. He could tell her whole life story. All the particulars if the man wanted to hear it. Somehow speaking the words made him feel better, like he was still connected with her—which he was, all the way from head to toe.

"She believed in doing everything natural—no antibiotics, no medicine except if she really needed it, which was pretty much never. Didn't take Tylenol or Advil or NyQuil. But when the headaches and the dizziness got worse, and then her vision blurred, she got a prescription. Then . . . Well, it was downhill pretty fast from there."

"So no radiation."

"Right. Even the thought of it killed her. I don't mean literally—it was just a sense of giving up, you know? Admitting that she couldn't fix herself naturally. Her body couldn't heal what was wrong. She always believed the body could repair itself, that left to its own was better. But when she couldn't stop the sickness, it shattered her."

"It sounds like there was nothing anyone could do."

"Yeah, but it kind of blew apart her theory on life."

"She lost her faith?"

"No. That actually got stronger."

"Then it didn't blow her theory apart. Maybe it blew yours apart."

J. D. didn't answer.

"And that's why you moved here?"

He nodded. "Maybe it was partly guilt for not listening to her. I guess I wanted to honor her, to carry on the legacy. See if I could live what she believed. Show people she was right."

"Which put you on a collision course with Maria."

"Yeah, Hurricane Maria."

The pastor came around to sit on the edge of the desk, and the closeness unnerved J. D. at first. Ron's phone buzzed and he tried to ignore it but couldn't help looking at the screen. He placed it on the desk beside him as if that would keep it from interrupting them.

"J. D., this is not a scenario where good wins over evil. You know that, don't you?"

"I don't understand."

"I'm sorry for your loss. And you're doing an admirable thing. But you can't take on this girl and her troubles. This is not how you make up for the loss of your wife."

"I'm not trying to make up for her."

"The man on the white horse does not win this battle. You can't fix her life by helping her find safety. Do you understand? This is pure evil. More evil than you can imagine in a lifetime. In a situation like this, good can only hope to survive. The best you can do is outlive the evil."

He let the words sink in and tried to discern the man's motivation. Maybe he knew where Maria was and didn't want her found. Maybe he didn't know where she was and wanted to find her himself. A million dollars was a lot of money for anybody.

"What do I lose by trying to help?"

"Your life."

J. D. blinked. "So nothing, really."

The man smiled painfully. "Your life is a precious thing. A wonderful gift. Don't throw it away."

"Isn't *her* life precious?"

The pastor looked away and suddenly something didn't feel right. The man had drawn him out as if this were a counseling session, and J. D. had opened up, but at what cost?

"You're quite persistent, aren't you? Like a man who plants a garden every year and hopes the crop will grow."

J. D. didn't answer. He heard voices outside.

"Farming is a hard life full of faith."

Someone knocked at the door and the pastor rose, not looking at J. D. A man opened the outer door and signaled Ron. He turned to J. D. "I'll be right back."

When the door closed, J. D. went to the window and saw the reflection of blue and red light on a concrete wall in the alley. He grabbed the pastor's cell phone and wallet and found the back door.

19

J. D. CURSED AS HE WALKED the alley behind the church. Ron had kept him busy while the police arrived. He had been pulled in by this seller of God. Maybe the man felt he was protecting J. D. That calling the police was the best thing for him. But it wasn't about what the tattooed pastor thought.

He wanted to search the neighborhood for the Suburban but there was too much activity. He had lost it, the gun in the glove compartment, the Uzi, and the case from the desert.

It had taken a while for the cops to arrive, though. Maybe Ron had wrestled with the decision, whether or not to get them involved. Maybe he had prayed. Maybe he flipped a coin. It didn't matter. The gun had probably pushed him over the edge.

The heat of the night hit full force and his pores opened. The concrete room had been hot, but compared with the heat outside, it was an ice chest. With the water trickling down his face came thoughts, one leading to another, flowing and coursing.

A siren behind him. *Stay away from the main road.* They would look there first. But the side streets were dark. Gang-infested. A white guy in cowboy boots and sweats wouldn't blend.

When the blue and red lights passed a few streets over, he took the chance. Streetlights were dark. The only light came from flat-screen TVs through barred windows.

He passed a house where cigarette smoke wafted from the front porch. He counted five orange glows and let his eyes focus on several men in wife-beater T-shirts. He tried not to make eye contact but his boots clip-clopping along the uneven concrete sidewalk gave him away.

"Órale, el cowboy se ha extraviado," someone said from the porch.

J. D. picked up his pace, trying to put some distance between himself and the voices. He balled his fists and wondered how long he would last in a fistfight. One-on-one he might have a chance, but with several of them . . . He wished he had taken the pistol into the church. At least he would have some protection until the bullets ran out.

His father had taught him not to run from danger. As a child, his brother had taken that instruction to heart and faced everything with abandon. Once when they'd seen a movie, they encountered several men standing near their father's car in the parking lot.

"Whatever you do, don't stop swinging," Tyler had said.

J. D. smiled at the memory. There had been no fight that night. The men backed away, partly because of what they could no doubt see in his brother. J. D. wished he could live that way, with the same recklessness and abandon his father had tried to instill. Perhaps that was part of the reason he was in this arid wasteland. Somewhere deep inside he wanted to please his father, though the decision to come here had put them at odds. And with that thought came the growing feeling of being alone in the world. He was hunted by shadows and his chances of finding Maria were growing slim.

J. D. was convinced that she was the key. A girl carrying a weapon like that and stalked by animals like Muerte was the key to a lot of things. The town in Mexico. The drug trade there. And something else—something more, but he wasn't sure what. And it didn't matter because she was probably already dead.

But what if she wasn't?

"¡Ey! ¡Alto ahí!"

He knew enough Spanish and enough from the tone of the speaker to run. The voice had come from behind him, back where the orange glow congregated.

"Quieto, muchacho."

An engine fired. Something deep and resonant that reverberated off the one-story brick houses. What would his father do in this situation? He would turn and face them. Take his chances. What if they would help him? What if they were looking for Maria?

This was what being alone did. It played with his mind. It clouded his thinking and made him even more desperate.

He came to a stop sign and ran left, crossing the high beams of whatever car was closing on him. Music boomed from the speakers—thumping bass over the squeal of metal on metal brakes.

"¡Ven acá, cowboy! Queremos hablar contigo."

"Mejor que no vayas por allá. Te arrepentirás."

"Ya lo tenemos."

He could feel his underarms swimming, sweat pouring from his brow. The car followed but the street was a dead end, which seemed fitting.

He turned as both car doors opened. Finally a working streetlight overhead. They were in a souped-up Honda with an oversize muffler that made it sound like a 747. A paint job that looked like it was done in a backyard. J. D. chose the yard that seemed least likely to house a pit bull and sprinted toward it, vaulting onto the chain-link fence and steadying himself with his left hand on the wobbly metal rail.

Shouts behind him. As he jumped down, he felt a buzzing in his right hand and was surprised at the phone's light. He hadn't remembered grabbing it. Running through the rock-filled back-yard toward the next fence, he flipped it open.

"Yeah," he said, masking his fear and shortness of breath.

It was a woman's voice, but he couldn't make out what she said because there was a dog barking, almost as deep as the car's rumble and closer. Just a black streak behind him, then a flash of light at the house and he saw the six-foot fence rising ahead. The men were laughing as the dog caught him. Not a pit bull, but a wide mouth. Maybe a boxer. J. D. wished he had tucked his sweats into his boots. White teeth and clenched jaws and a rip-ping and pulling at his pant leg. He closed the phone andhung on as he lunged toward the fence, but his jump was like a toddler's, only about a foot onto the structure with his right leg trailing.

The dog had torn a hole in the bottom of his sweats and was pulling, down on its haunches, grunting like a linebacker huff-ing toward a quarterback, backing up through the stones, trying to get a foothold in a place where J. D. could tell the thing went to the bathroom. He released his hold on the fence and went down on the ground, struggling to keep the sweats on.

He kicked with his left boot and landed one to the dog's jaw. It was like kicking concrete. The dog held its grip and stared, growling. Like staring down a clench-toothed devil. J. D. was kind to animals, but he made a distinction between something defenseless and a snapping turtle. He didn't blame the dog— J. D. was the intruder—but a man had to do what he had to do. J. D. saw a man standing in the doorway of the house holding a gun. He shouted something in Spanish, which seemed to be directed at the dog.

The man didn't care about J. D.; he didn't want to shoot the dog.

Perhaps it was the click that made a mixture of anger, fear, and determination to live rise up and aim the toe of his boot for the dog's eye. When he connected, the animal turned and yelped in pain, releasing the sweats long enough for J. D. to scramble up the fence.

With a renewed vigor, the dog leaped, but J. D. had made it to the top. A siren wailed and lights flashed in front of the house. He hit the ground and felt pain shoot through his left ankle. Then came the gunfire. Birdshot ticked against the metal fence and through tree branches above. He didn't stop to see if he was hit.

He staggered through the parking lot of a single-story hotel. People in doorways smoking, watching him stumble. These were his enemies, able to describe him to police that were sure to follow.

He crossed the street quickly, four lanes of fast traffic that had thinned because of the hour, and came to a graveyard walled with concrete and iron, as if it were needed to keep the people inside. He found an entrance and stole in, walking past tombstones and crypts and rose-scented flower arrangements dotting the walkway. It was a huge cemetery, and he wondered how many people lay quietly under the earth.

The phone buzzed again. He flipped it open and said, "Hello."

"Ron?" A woman. A frightened voice. Trembling.

"Yeah, what's up?"

"Why haven't you called? I've been waiting. What do you want me to do?"

Think fast. Get information. "Just calm down. Relax."

"Don't tell me to relax. We're in danger."

Deep breath. Take a chance. "How is she?"

"I told you, she's fine. Bruised and scared, but she slept. When do we move her?"

He tried to sound as much like Ron as he could. Keep his sentences short. "We've got police here now."

"Police? Are they picking up the cowboy?"

"Exactly." A squad car screamed by, siren blaring. *Think.* "Let me call you right back. I'll tell you where to meet."

Silence. As the police car got farther away, he heard something in the background on the phone. Music. Maybe a television.

"You're not Ron," she said.

The phone clicked and J. D. felt more than the connection die. In the distance were more sirens and lights. Probably crime scene tape going up and the guys with the Honda on steroids giving their version of events. He found an exit at the other end of the cemetery and sat in the darkness behind a Pollo Feliz restaurant.

He hit Redial and the phone rang. Someone picked up but didn't speak. Like the chain-link fencing he had vaulted, this felt like a last chance, a once-in-a-lifetime risk.

"Listen to me. You're right; I'm not Ron. He gave—no, I took his phone from his office. I'm the cowboy you were talking about. I need you to get a message to Maria. Are you listening?"

A long pause. Still a tremble in the voice. "Yes."

"Tell her J. D. is looking for her. I need to tell her something about what she left in the desert. I found the case. I think she needs to know what was in there."

He paused to listen. Heavy breathing on the other end of the line. Fear and uncertainty.

"You are just like the rest of them," the woman said slowly. "You want the money."

"I understand you being scared. I'm scared too. I've never been mixed up in anything like this. But you ask her how I treated her. If it wasn't for me, she'd be dead."

Another long pause.

"Tell her I need to talk to her."

He searched for more to say, something to reassure her he was trying to protect the golden goose, not snatch her. The phone's screen switched to a picture of a young girl, probably one of Ron's daughters. The woman had hung up.

He took a deep breath and the odor of the nearby trash bins sickened him, but he couldn't move. Couldn't do anything but rub at the sweat stains on the curvature and contours of his hat and think. How different his life would be but for a few choices. If he hadn't come to Arizona. If he hadn't fallen in love. If he hadn't been born. Little things.

In the time between his run from the dog and his escape through the graveyard, he realized that with each blip of the police cruisers and swirling lights, with each new danger and lifeless move toward existence, he *felt* again. The energy had coursed through him with Maria's first movement. His heart had jump-started. He was alive. Prepared for something more instead of marking time and waiting for the next bad thing.

He'd always feared being too simple—feared his music and life would be judged irrelevant or clichéd. An untalented man grasping for the unattainable. However, on a deeper level, beyond the definitions of success that caused him to stay in the shallow end of life, the bigger terror that seized him and chased him through the night watches was that there *was* something great inside, something powerful, and failure would be to let that atrophy. Death would not be the cessation of life, as it had been for his wife, but allowing the life inside to remain paralyzed when it longed to bubble and gurgle from his soul until it reached the surface.

Maybe he was being called to something bigger, something higher, and the strength to accomplish it wasn't his own.

Then again, maybe he *was* a failure. Maybe he was inadequate and the thoughts of strength were just some positive-thinking charade.

The phone vibrated and he nearly dropped it. He answered without looking at the number.

"J. D., it's Ron. Are you all right?"

"Why did you lie to me?" J. D. said.

"I didn't lie to you. I'm trying to help you."

Risk. Go ahead. "Did you tell them you have information about the officer who was killed?"

"What are you talking about?" Ron said.

"Did you tell them your connection with Maria? Do they know about that?"

"He's making this up," Ron said away from the phone. "I don't know nothing about the officer killed."

"Tell them the truth, Ron. I'm not the one they're look-ing for."

A noise on the phone as if it were passed to someone else. Then, "J. D., this is Detective—"

He pushed the red button and ended the call, then walked across Oracle Road, dragging the chewed-up pant leg and passing a used-car lot surrounded by a fence with razor wire at the top. Neon windshield stickers glowed in the fluores-cent light. He continued down a side street, looking over his shoulder at the cemetery that seemed to stretch forever, pass-ing more homes with barred windows. Mexican music played in a bar.

He knew he had to toss the phone and had wandered toward a Dumpster when it buzzed again.

"It's me," Maria said softly.

That voice. He closed his eyes as he spoke. "You okay?"

"Yes."

"Well, I'm not sure how long that's going to last. A lot of people are looking for you. Not just Muerte."

"My friend said you found the case."

"Yeah. I'll tell you all about it when you come get me."

"I can't do that."

"Maria, the people you're with are going to turn you in. To the police or to Muerte. You're not safe with either. You have to get away."

"These are good people."

"Maybe so, but they're getting pressure from all sides. Can you get a car and meet me?"

"What happened to your truck?"

"I donated it. I'm sure Win won't have a problem with that. I'm on foot."

She was quiet a moment. "I appreciate all you did. But I can't leave. These people have risked their lives."

"Did you know it was your ring?" he said.

"What?"

"Your ring led Muerte straight to me. Did you know you were setting me up?"

She said something under her breath. "My mother gave me that ring. It couldn't have been used to track me."

"Then those guys are part bloodhound. It had to be the ring. I haven't seen anybody since I got rid of it. So if you can get here, you'll be safe. We can get out of Dodge and figure out what to do."

"I swear I didn't know about the ring."

"All right, I believe you."

A big sigh. "But I can't let these people down."

"All the more reason to get away. Don't endanger them. You know what's going to happen if Muerte finds them, and you know he will."

"These are people of prayer. They believe God is going to protect them."

"Prayer is one thing. Bullets are another."

A pause. "Good-bye, J. D."

Last chance. Last shot to convince her. "Wait, Maria. Are you still there?"

"Yes."

"The case I found in the well. Do you know what was in it?"

"I assumed it was money or drugs."

"That's what I thought. Until I opened it and found a high-powered rifle. I've never seen one like it."

Maria gasped. "A gun?"

"Fancy thing with a scope and enough ammunition to take out a regiment down at Fort Huachuca."

Silence on the other end.

He weighed his options. Speak or just let her think? He chose to wait. To sit with the night sounds.

"Why you?" she said, and the way she said it made him feel like the camel's nose was under the tent. Like there was a longing in her that went past survival.

"I can help you, Maria. We can see this through. Together. I'll get you to your people or some other place that's safe." With all the passion he could muster, he added, "For some reason I found you out there. For some reason this has worked out between us. I can feel it."

A car passed slowly at the end of the block, then backed up.

"I don't know. Even if I could get a car, I'm lost. I don't know the city."

"Find someone you can trust and bring them. But hurry. Tell them Ron called. Tell them anything you have to." He glanced down the street. "There's a Denny's restaurant on the corner of Oracle and River. I'll be waiting."

"I don't think I can—"

"I have to get rid of this phone now. Just get there, Maria."

20

J. D. WALKED THROUGH the heat toward the Denny's. Night
sounds of cars passing and the headlines he saw on newsstands
made him think about how the world spins on small choices
made in darkness. Hidden drones drop payloads on unsuspect-
ing targets. Men in dark corners of the world illumine similar
dark corners with explosions. Lives are taken behind closed
doors. Others are spared because of mistaken coordinates.
Locked up in the human heart are decisions, thousands every
second, of life and death.

It felt like chance that moved J. D. along, but he knew it was
more, even if in his heart he did not want to admit it. Chance
meant that everything in his life was of his own doing, his own
striving. It meant he was making his own story, writing it on
some cheap napkin he took from a dispenser at a diner. He
carried the weight of his choices, paid his own tab, made his

own breaks, and if he was lucky, lived with the consequences. It was all on him.

This was frightening, but not as daunting as believing he was being drawn on his current path, heading toward an eventual confrontation with destiny, an enemy, and even himself. If this unchained melody had already been playing when he stepped behind the guitar, then his life had a point, a purpose, and was shaped and guided by something bigger than himself. The light and dark, life and death, verses and choruses, no matter how well or poorly they rhymed, were all part of the bigger picture he couldn't see as he moved in the oppressive heat.

He had memorized the 520 number of Maria's call in case he needed it later and then tossed the phone over the fence at the used-car lot. As sirens split the night, he opened Ron's wallet. No cash. When he made it to the Denny's parking lot, hunger pangs hit and he could taste the coffee and chicken-fried steak. The sign in front of a bank across the street said it was still 102 degrees. The old saying about Tucson was that it was a dry heat. Say what you will about the lack of humidity, but it was still an oven.

A homeless man pushed a Safeway cart filled with empty cans and bottles. He wore a dirty Diamondbacks hat and a tattered white T-shirt stained with what looked like chewing tobacco. Shoes that were barely attached to the soles. Thin, hairy arms.

"Excuse me, sir. Do you think you could spare some change? Just to get a cup of coffee."

"Wish I had it to give you," J. D. said.

"Aw, come on, man. Just fifty cents?"

J. D. pointed at the shopping cart. "You got more in there than I have. Just lost my truck and everything in it."

"Sad story. Sorry to hear it. You must have a credit card or something."

"Yeah, I got one, but I can't use it."

"That don't make no sense. How could you not be able to use a credit card? You go over your limit?"

He shook his head and looked at the special on the sign above the restaurant. He could go for some scrambled eggs, biscuits, and gravy. So what if the cops saw the transaction. He could think of it as his last supper. Wait to pay until Maria showed up. If she showed up.

And then he got the plan. Beautifully laid out in front of him like a five-course meal.

"You want to eat?" J. D. said.

"I thought you didn't have no money."

"Park your vehicle and let's go."

The man's eyes widened and he ran the cart into some gravel beyond the pavement and followed J. D. inside the freezer of a restaurant. They waited to be seated like the sign at the front said. The waitress took one look at the homeless man and then at J. D.

"He's with me."

She stared slack-jawed at him, like he was speaking in an unknown tongue, then grabbed two menus and placed them at a table in the back where no one could smell them. At least that's what he figured.

J. D. ordered the special with coffee and the man asked for a burger and fries with a milk shake, looking at J. D. for the okay. He nodded and said, "Whatever you want."

The man's name was Freddy and he had come from St. Louis ten years earlier searching for a construction job that didn't pan out. Life had been difficult growing up in the Midwest and had only gotten worse once he headed west.

"It's all the illegals here, man. Why is somebody going to pay me when they can hire somebody across the border for half of that? If I owned a business, I'd hire 'em too."

Freddy spoke as if he were hard of hearing, loudly and over the table. When J. D. talked, the man leaned forward and squinted, concentrating on J. D.'s mouth and working his tongue.

"How long have you been on the street?"

"Last three years. No, four. I had me a girlfriend when I first moved out here. Lived off of Ruthrauff. Nice girl but she got tired of me not having a job. I was just as tired of it as she was, but I couldn't convince her."

He laughed and coughed something from his lungs. When his drink came, he opened the straw with filthy fingers, then sucked down the thick shake and smiled. "Not as good as Mr. Jack, but it's close. Makes you cool down deep on the inside. Wish I could have one of these every day when the sun comes up."

J. D. kept an eye on the parking lot. He asked the waitress for a pen when she returned with the food, and she rolled her eyes and unhooked a Bic from her apron. He pulled out a credit card from the wallet and wrote something on a napkin, Freddy watching like a dog would study a man opening a can of Purina.

"Why are you giving me something to eat like this?" the man said. "You religious?"

"Do I look like it?"

"I don't know. You act like it. There's three kinds of people in the world. There's the no-looks, the guilty givers, and religious people. The no-looks turn away from you and hope you don't talk to them. They don't want nothing to do with you. The guilty give you change or a couple of dollars because it makes them feel better. You tell them 'God bless you,' and they smile real big. But the religious, those are the ones you gotta watch out for."

"How so?"

"They want to give you food, not money. Never give you money because they figure you're going to drink it away. Which is true, but still, it's my choice."

"They bring you into restaurants?"

"Sometimes. Most of the time it's fast food. The Lord seems to be partial to the dollar menu. Egg McMuffins and double cheeseburgers. I'd rather he was partial to Mr. Jack."

Freddy laughed again and the milk shake rattled. He hardly had teeth to chew the burger, but he made a valiant effort. He doused the whole plate with enough ketchup for a regiment and doused it again when half his fries were gone. He used enough salt to make Lot's wife jealous.

"I have an ulterior motive for bringing you with me," J. D. said.

"You have a what?" Freddy said, cocking his head.

"I'm waiting on someone." J. D. slid the credit card toward him. "When they pull in, I'm going outside. And I'm leaving this with you."

The man took the card and squinted. "Yeah, like they gonna believe I'm you."

"It's not my card either."

Freddy pulled his head back like a turtle receding into its shell. "This don't make no sense."

"Denny's wants to get paid." He showed him the napkin. "That's the guy's signature. Just do it like that and you'll be fine."

"They gonna want a picture ID."

"They're not going to get one, are they?"

He rattled again. "No, that's sure the truth." He said his *th*'s as *f*'s. "What am I supposed to do with the card after I pay?"

"Is there a liquor store still open around here?"

The man licked his lips and tried to wipe some ketchup from his mustache. "You can't buy after 2 a.m. What time is it?"

J. D. checked his watch. "It's 1:45."

"If I leave now, I can probably make it to the Albertsons at La Cañada. If not, you have to wait until 6 a.m. That's when they start selling again."

"It's not for me. It's for you. Here's what I want you to do. After I leave, wait as long as you can. Order something else. A piece of pie if you want."

"I was just looking at that lemon meringue in the case up front," Freddy said.

"Get a whole one. You can put the rest in your cart and take it with you."

"Yeah, maybe they'll give me a box."

"After you pay and sign the slip like I did, take off. And when the grocery store starts selling, go and buy whatever you want."

"With the card?"

"Yeah, that's the point. I want you to use it."

His eyes grew big. "I could get me a room for the night."

"There you go. Get two double beds. One for you and one for the pie."

"Now you're talking." A cloud came over him and he put down his burger, licking a black finger. "Why are you doing this? You're getting me in trouble with this card, aren't you?"

"You'll be fine."

"You're in trouble, aren't you?"

"You could say that." He glanced out the window. Was Maria on her way? Had Muerte reached her?

The man sat deep in thought. "If I get caught with this, they're going to throw me in jail."

"No, just tell them what I'm about to tell you. Are you listening?"

He nodded and picked up his burger again.

"I found someone in the desert, half-dead. I tried to help, but this person is wanted. Not just by the police. Some bad people want her dead."

"Her? You found a woman in the desert?" Freddy cursed. "I wish I had me some of that luck."

"No, I don't think you do. I'm having you use this card to throw them off until I can help her again. You tell them that when they find you."

"I don't know, man. Last time I was in jail, it didn't go well."

"Then just skip out. Rent the room and sleep for a while and hit the street. Leave the card on the dresser. You don't have much to lose, and you'll be helping me."

"Helping you by spending somebody else's money. Never heard of such a thing."

"Think of yourself as the government. They do the same."

He laughed again and rattled the cup. "I suppose you're right."

The waitress came back and refilled J. D.'s coffee three times before he said he was okay. He wished he had used the restroom after the second cup. A silver Toyota Camry pulled up in front of the restaurant at 3:15 and sat with a window rolled down. J. D. felt something in his chest. Something like hope.

"That's my ride, Freddy. You okay with the plan?"

"Sure thing, but my name's not Freddy. It's Ron. Ron Barfield." He smiled and laughed/coughed and reached to shake J. D.'s hand. "You stay safe with that desert lady of yours." He looked through the window to try to see Maria. "Whoo, I wish I had some of that luck."

"Instead of buying some Mr. Jack, maybe you can check into a detox," J. D. said.

"I knew you was religious."

"Might help you."

"Been there a few times. Didn't take."

"I hope we meet again, Freddy."

He waited until the waitress headed to the kitchen for an order and quickly exited, climbing into the backseat of the Camry. Maria sat in the passenger seat and a woman who looked like she could be her younger sister drove. The girl looked in the rearview mirror with frightened eyes.

"This is Rosana," Maria said.

J. D. glanced at the restaurant and saw the waitress at the table talking with Freddy. "If you don't mind, let's get away from here, Rosana."

The car chugged onto River Road and moved across three lanes to make a left on Oracle. The engine misfired and the sharp left turn brought a clacking sound from the front wheel. The cloth seats were worn and there was an old-car smell that brought back memories from his childhood. They passed the used-car lot where several squad cars huddled. He told Rosana to drive toward the interstate.

"Do the people who helped you know where you are?" J. D. said.

"No," Maria said. "Rosana is the only one."

"Mis padres me van a matar."

Something about her parents. "Do you have a phone?" J. D. said.

"Yes, she has a cell phone," Maria said.

J. D. directed her to the interstate, then south on I-19 to Valencia. She stopped in the mostly empty parking lot of a twenty-four-hour Walmart and the car idled like a purring cat.

Rosana looked at Maria, then got out. The girl was tiny and wore skinny jeans. Legs like matchsticks. Maria hugged her and spoke in Spanish. Rosana was in tears when she walked into the store.

"I hate leaving her here, but it's probably the best way to protect her," J. D. said.

"Where are we going?" Maria said.

"Someplace they won't expect."

"Which is where?"

"I don't know."

SATURDAY

21

MUERTE SAT IN A METAL OFFICE CHAIR with his feet on the windowsill, watching the gathering light pool in the cloudless sky. He had rested fitfully through the day and finally felt a breakthrough with a phone call after midnight.

His contacts were working, as well they should with the amount of money he was offering. The woman he had spoken with had new information about J. D.'s past, but it didn't help him find the man. As Muerte suspected, the girl had been tracked to the religious group that had been a thorn in his side for many months. They had invaded Herida with their food and games for children and evangelistic events, but because of a directive from on high, he and his men had let them continue. Religion, it had been said, was the opiate of the masses. If talk of faith and Jesus calmed the residents and kept them docile, he would allow it. Their religion made them more sheep-like and easier to direct. Still, there was something dangerous about the group. He could sense it in his gut. Strength and determination in the face of poverty and ignorance.

With this much time, Maria could have gone anywhere, but something told him she was nearby, waiting. She couldn't get back into Mexico without her passport, and the Border Patrol had recovered that. She was on their radar, or so his contacts inside the Border Patrol had told him. He did not want her in their hands, revealing what she might know of his plan, if anything. The faster he could eliminate her, the better.

He had seen the strength in her, even as a young girl. But he could never have foreseen this trouble. If he had simply taken care of her in Mexico . . . But he hadn't wanted to tip his hand.

The best news of the night came from a phone call about a mysterious rifle that was suddenly available. It had been recovered from an abandoned SUV on the city's west side, and when he heard its description, he knew. Muerte had arranged for the delivery and the payment to be made. He would have the rifle later in the afternoon, and everyone would be happy.

A squad car pulled up to the church and someone got out. Muerte watched the man pause at the car parked in the lot and pull a note from the window. He glanced at the church and came through the office door and stopped abruptly when he saw Muerte. A look of shock covered his face like the tattoos on his arms and neck.

"Hello, Pastor. I assumed that was your car in front."

The man's eyes shifted toward the rear door. Muerte revealed his gun and told him to sit.

"I was admiring your library. Very impressive. Quite a variety of theological treatises, though you could use some help with organization."

"What do you want?" He said it abruptly, without deference or respect.

Muerte pushed the slight aside. "Do you know who I am?"

The pastor nodded.

"Good. Then we can dispense with the introductions and with convincing you I mean what I say. I have watched your group from afar. I'm sure the work you do south of the border is rewarding for you and your congregation."

"The people need help. They need hope."

"Yes, but hope can be dangerous, can't it? It makes people do things they were not meant to do. Hope can cause people to think they're more powerful than they actually are. To do things contrary to their nature."

"Hope in God is the only thing that will last."

Muerte paused a moment and noticed a trickle of sweat running down the pastor's forehead. "Why do you do this?" He put his hand out to the cluttered desk and bookshelf. "Why do you spend your time here? Studying. Talking. And then you travel across the border to people who cannot repay you. What's in it for you? Do you have another wife in that town?"

"I don't do it for money or anything else. It's a call on my life. A mission."

"From God."

"Yes."

"You believe the Almighty put you here, right in this dusty office in the armpit of America. You are here for a purpose. To help people run back to a sovereign, all-loving, all-knowing God."

"Yes."

Muerte cocked his head. "But if he is sovereign, if he controls everything, why would he create evil? Why would there be suffering and death?"

"Why would he allow people like you to flourish? That's your question."

"Yes, in a way, I guess you're right. I'm asking you to justify my existence. Why would he allow me on the planet?"

"This is a game to you, but it won't be someday. You'll be called to give an account."

"Yes, judgment is coming. One group even gives a date. Jesus will come in the clouds." He chuckled. "Your days of preaching are over, Pastor. You've fulfilled your mission. Well done."

The pastor lifted his shirt and wiped the sweat from his head. "The answer to your question is love."

"Pardon me?"

"Without a choice, there can't be love. I get the question a lot. It's tiring, in a way, to have to explain it again and again. I've talked about it in our services, and some of the great minds of the faith have addressed it as well. You should come or read one of my library books."

"I'm intrigued with your message. Continue."

"Someone asks why their brother died of an overdose or their child is going blind or why children across the border suffer because they can't pay for a vaccination or medicine that will heal a cough."

"And the answer is love?"

"Yes. In a way. If God had created a world without the possibility of choosing evil, there would have been no possibility of choosing love."

Muerte pondered for a moment. "So in order to have peace and tranquility, you must have hurricanes and mass murders. Is that it? That seems a little too convenient for him, don't you think?"

"No, sin was not convenient at all. It cost a great deal

to redeem humanity. He did not create us to sin; he created us to enjoy and follow and obey him. But he gave people a chance to choose. Without that freedom, we would not be human. There would be peace and tranquility and obedience, but no love."

"Love," Muerte laughed. "It sounds overrated, don't you think?"

"Real love can't be forced. You have the choice right now. Pick good or evil in this office."

Muerte held up a hand and smiled. "I'm afraid it's too late for me to choose a different path. Besides, let's not get to the application of the sermon until you've given the Scripture reference and a poem. Isn't that how it works? Perhaps an emotional story from your childhood or something from the news to make things more pertinent and relevant to the congregation?"

"First John, chapter 4. 'Dear friends, let us continue to love one another, for love comes from God. Anyone who loves is a child of God and knows God. But anyone who does not love does not know God, for God is love.'"

"And the God who loves lets little girls get shot. And big girls, like Maria. Missing daughters of drug lords."

The pastor paused and searched Muerte's eyes. Then he continued. "'God is love, and all who live in love live in God, and God lives in them.'"

"Yes, I heard you. But you have sidestepped the issue, Pastor."

"God allows us to choose our path, a path of love or hate. The path of self-gratification and sin or the path of sacrifice and giving." Something came over the man's face and he sat forward, elbows on knees. "The plan of God, from the beginning, was to have relationship with his creation. We chose to leave him. And the answer to our rebellion was the cross. The crucifixion was the way God chose to reconcile us to himself. It was not an afterthought. That's how he chose to love us."

"Why? Why would God sacrifice himself? It makes no sense."

"It makes no sense unless he was motivated by love. 'We love each other because he loved us first.' Before we were reconciled to him, while we were sinners, God loved us and gave himself for us." He sat back and stared, unblinking. "You can have that kind of love in your heart, Mr. Muerte."

Muerte ran his index finger along the Glock's slide. "Yes, I have heard of this love. I'm sure it is reassuring to you, but I am not compelled to follow your God. I am not convinced of this love."

Unmoving, the pastor said, "'Such love has no fear, because perfect love expels all fear.'"

"Well, there are times when you should be afraid, don't you think? And here is the reason: You have one chance to survive this meeting. One path leads to life. The other leads to destruction. You get to choose."

"You do not have the power to take my life."

"Really?"

"He has protected us as we've gone across the border. He can protect me now."

"Or he can allow evil to take your life. Isn't that what you've just explained? And allowing this evil will show his love, will it not?"

"Greater is he who is in me than he who is in the world."

Muerte stood. "Time for the benediction. Or is it Communion? I can't remember the sequence. Yes, Communion, I think. 'This is my body broken for you. This is my blood poured out.' Something like that?"

The pastor stared at the floor.

"I will ask you a question and I will not ask you twice," Muerte said. "One question and the freedom to answer in truth. A real choice."

He stepped behind the pastor and placed the gun against the back of the man's skull. "Where . . . is . . . she?"

Unflinching, unmoving, the pastor took a breath and let it out. "Father, into your hands I commit my spirit."

Muerte pulled the trigger. He pushed the body to the floor and shoved the chair in place at the desk and left.

22

ALYCIA WALKED IN FADING MOONLIGHT, hair shimmering, her body vaguely visible beneath the nightgown. He studied her contours as she led him farther into the woods. They were behind the house of her youth, ascending a knoll that rose like pregnant earth. She lay on the freshly mowed grass, bathed in crescent shadows, hands behind her head, elbows out, gazing at the stars, soaking in the galaxy.

This is my favorite place in the whole world, she said.

I know. J. D. sat beside her, fresh denim creaking and settling in the early morning dew.

She closed her eyes. *This would be a good spot for a tombstone, don't you think?*

He shook his head. *I thought you wanted to be buried at sea. Or have your ashes spread on an amusement park.*

Right over the midway from the Ferris wheel. She smiled. *No,*

I wouldn't want to rain down on someone's corn dog or funnel cake. I think I want to be buried right here, where you can come and lie like this beside me. Think of the good times. Stare at the sky. Think of what we had. You'll write a song about this, you know.

I don't want a song. I want you.

You don't always get what you want, bucko. And getting what you want is not always what's best anyway.

How could not having you be good? It's the worst thing that could happen.

If I left you for another man, would you go on? Let's say I had a thing for Kenny Chesney or Tim McGraw and I left. Would you survive?

Yeah, but they might not.

She laughed. *You'd hunt us down, wouldn't you?*

It'd be like the first day of squirrel season.

Well, my point is, you'd survive and find a way to thrive. You'd probably write the best song ever about losing me.

I'd write it from jail.

Listen. Losing me is not the worst thing that could happen. Losing yourself is worse.

Why can't I have regular dreams? Why can't you just come to me and kiss me?

She laughed again and rose, scampering off into the dew-laden grass, skipping and bouncing away.

Why do you have to do that? Why do you have to run just when we're getting started?

She turned as she ran and called back, *And why is death so hard for you?*

He caught up. *Why is it so easy for you?*

She stopped and faced him, the scar on her head visible in the moonlit shadows. *Easy? You think it's easy?*

You talk about it. You make jokes.

You don't talk about it at all. It's taboo. The more you talk about it and twist it and turn it, the less afraid you'll be.

Easy for you to say. You're not the one who will be staring at a tombstone.

John David.

When she spoke his name, every time, something magical happened. It was a herald of something wonderful or terrible, but he could never tell which.

You're afraid. You're a little boy afraid of the dark. Afraid of being alone. Afraid to go back or move forward. Afraid you're going to make a mistake no matter which way you go. She touched his hands and brought them close to her chest. *You have to grow up.*

What?

Little boys who fear are paralyzed. Men who are afraid don't let the fear hold them back. They use it to propel them. And it's your time, J. D. This is your opportunity.

You mean with Maria? With Muerte?

There was a look of sadness in her eyes. *You know what I mean.*

She turned and walked toward the grove of trees, the dew collecting on the soles of her feet and dripping, staining the hem of her gown with a thin line of water. Every movement was beauty, every sway of her hair, every chosen footstep perfect in its economy.

Don't go, he whispered.

She put out a hand and touched the first tree at the edge of the thicket, then, without looking back, disappeared.

J. D. awoke to a hint of light and a sharp, stabbing pain in his neck from sleeping at an angle against the headrest. He grabbed his head with one hand and pulled his body forward like he would guide a sick animal toward water. Raising the seat back, he tried to remember where they had stopped. He could smell the old Camry, a mix of mildew and perfumes from the previous owner. Maria wasn't in the passenger seat.

He found her down the hill from the parking lot. She sat on a stump at the edge of a burned-out area overlooking the lake. Fire had ravaged the hillside and left only charred remains. She looked like the last person left on some desolate planet.

They had passed a checkpoint several miles before winding their way to the lake. Going south wasn't the problem because they weren't stopped. It was getting through on their way back that worried him, if they ever went back. He had no driver's license or wallet. She had no ID. They were vagabonds. But as far as he could tell, they were safe for the moment.

Though the fire had been months earlier, he could still smell it. The charred, smoky remains left a visible reminder of the power of nature, though the initial spark was believed to have come from a group of illegals who had simply been trying to keep warm or heat something over a campfire.

"Did you sleep?" he said, coming up behind her.

Maria had her chin on one knee with both arms wrapped around her leg. "I was okay until you talked in your sleep."

"What did I say?"

She shrugged. "Just moaning. You sounded upset. What were you dreaming?"

"I don't know," he lied. "I can never remember much."

She looked up at him, then back at the lake. "It's peaceful here."

"Yeah. I didn't think of it until we hit the exit off I-19. Nobody's going to look for you here. At least not for a while.

But the bad news is we've got no way to get back through the checkpoint and we have nothing to eat."

She stood and wiped soot from the seat of her pants. It didn't help much and he watched the black stain move back and forth as she climbed through the loose gravel to the car. She held a hand out for balance as she walked and he noticed how each footstep was calculated. Even when she slipped, it looked graceful.

She popped the trunk and pulled out a gallon jug of water and a paper bag marked *Food City*. "Rosana put this in the car before we left."

"If Rosana had found you in the desert, this whole thing would have gone a lot better."

Maria pulled out lunch meat and cheese in a ziplock bag and half a loaf of bread. In another bag were vegetables—cooked onions and peppers and lettuce. She opened the bread and made two sandwiches. When she'd put everything away, they sat at a picnic table under the shell of a black pine tree and stared at the rippling water made by a slight breeze from the south. Tucked between two hills and mountains beyond, it had the look of a secluded oasis. It felt like something primal they were doing, like living off the land, only it was out of the back of an aging Toyota.

"How did you know this was here?" she said.

"Curiosity. Found it one Sunday when I had the day off. Just drove around and saw the sign for the lake."

"It's beautiful."

"Yeah, you don't find water this clear and clean just anywhere. Not bad for fishing." He told her the elevation and a little about the history of the people and as much as he could remember about the area. "I could catch a fish or two, but the park service would be on a campfire out here like a duck on a june bug."

She looked at the sun peeking over the hill behind them and pointed south. "Mexico is that way."

He nodded and bit into the sandwich.

Seeing her, being with Maria again, felt like catching his breath after having it knocked out. That had happened once in a JV football game when he finally got playing time. The coach put him in to replace an injured linebacker. When the running back came through, J. D. stood his ground and planted his feet for the tackle. Instead of going low, he stood up, and the next thing he knew, he was looking at the lights of the stadium and little stars swirling inside the helmet. His dreams of being a sports star were over and he concentrated on music.

He also had a feeling about Maria akin to a dog chasing a car. If the dog catches up to the thing, what's he going to do? That was his question. What should he do?

"They're searching for us," she said.

"That's an understatement. But I'm not the main draw. They only want me because I'm connected with you. You've got a price on your head."

"What do you mean?"

"Somebody offered a reward."

"The police?"

He shook his head and her face showed pain.

"My guess is it's your friend from south of the border. And it's dead or alive."

"How do you know?"

"The pastor at the church that helped you told me. Ron something or other. He's how I located you."

"I didn't think I'd ever see you again," she said.

"I was worried. I know you trust those people, but a million dollars can turn even ones who believe in Jesus."

"A million dollars?" She shook her head. "I would have thought $2 million, easy."

He laughed and opened the jug of water, trying not to touch his lips as he tipped it to drink. He offered her some and she opened her mouth and leaned forward. He poured a little too much and she laughed, the water dripping down her shirt and onto the sweatpants and table. They both went back to their sandwiches and it felt almost like a movie trailer, some rapturous moment of humanity in the midst of the inhumanity. A tender moment before the death knell.

"Why are you doing this for me? Why don't you want the money?"

"Maybe I do."

"No. I don't believe it."

"You're right. There's no amount of money on earth that can make a person happy. Look at the people who win the lottery only to go broke or kill themselves. Millionaires always want more. Same with billionaires. I used to think like that. Used to chase hundred-dollar bills."

"You made a lot of money?"

"No, I've always pretty much scraped by, but I've made enough to know that wasn't going to make me happy."

"What changed you?"

"Life, I guess. Losing. When what you love the most dies, it resets your iPod."

She gave him a bit of a smile mixed with sadness as if she understood.

"Money can't give me anything I don't already have. Took a long time to figure that out."

"What do you think will give you happiness?"

"You don't think I'm happy?"

"I think you are a tortured soul."

"Well, so much for trying to be the strong, silent type. You read me like a book."

"It's not hard to read you, J. D."

"I guess you could say I've been trying to answer that question for a while and the jury is still out. If I come up with something, I'll let you know."

She looked over the lake, her hair sweeping across her face in the empty breeze, and he thought it was the most beautiful morning since Eden. Her face was thin and he imagined her in better times with makeup and without the hungry animal look.

"I really didn't know the ring had a tracking device. That was a gift from my mother when I was a girl. I've only taken it off a few times. A couple of years ago we had it cleaned and restored. Perhaps that is when the device was inserted."

When she looked at him again, it felt like her eyes were boring a hole through his head.

"Who would have done it?"

"Maybe my father. He is very protective. He never let me date the boys from the neighborhood."

"If I had a daughter, I'd probably do the same thing. I was one of those neighborhood boys once."

She smiled. "What I mean is, I didn't try to get you harmed. I would never do that to someone who helped me. I was hurt that you thought I had done it on purpose."

"Well, I was holding the ring and that fellow came knocking. It seemed strange you'd hand me the very thing that drew him." He explained what had happened at the farmers' market. "I didn't mean to hurt your feelings."

"I understand," she said.

He moved to the other side of the picnic table and sat facing her. "Maria, I think it's time you and I had a heart-to-heart. If I'm going to help you survive, I need to know more. I need to know everything."

"What do you want to know?"

"Who is Muerte?"

"I told you, he's an evil—"

"No," he interrupted. "Who is he to *you*? Why would he care about one girl from Mexico, unless you're mixed up with him? And how would you get sent north with a gun that could kill an elephant? If your daddy would put a locator in your ring, surely he wouldn't want you doing something like that. And don't tell me it's a long story. We got lots of time. Were you and Muerte lovers?"

She rolled her eyes. "Muerte does not love anything but himself. He does not have the ability. He and I only had a working relationship."

"Meaning what?"

She paused, choosing her words carefully. "In the last few months, I was able to get closer. To discover more of what he was planning."

"Don't tap-dance."

"Muerte is the reason my brothers are dead. I think he had a great deal to do with my mother's death as well. But my story is no different from most in the little town where I am from. There are many grieving women there."

"And Muerte was the one who pulled the trigger."

"No. You would have to understand the culture. The setting. The fear. He was the man who ordered my brothers killed, but I discovered this by accident. It's different there."

"Doesn't sound too much different from what's happened the last couple of days. So you got on the inside? Is that why you were carrying that weapon?"

"I did not know what was in the package, just that it was important. To the cartel. Then I learned Muerte had other plans and I convinced him to allow me to deliver the package."

J. D. rubbed his forehead and found dirt and sweat and salt mixed in a gritty mess on his fingertips. "You had no idea what was inside?"

"No. When you told me it was a weapon . . ." She leaned forward. "That makes sense. J. D., he's planning something. It's part of why he wants me dead. He knows that I know. Or thinks I do."

"You know what?"

She stared at him with furrowed brow. "I'm not sure. No, listen to me. I overheard him speaking. He didn't know I was there. He was talking to a man . . . I believe it was one of the Zetas. They are at work here, recruiting young people, those who are illegal and can't find jobs. I don't know what he has planned, but it's happening soon."

"So he wants you dead because you might know something? Seems like he's going to an awful lot of trouble and expense."

"There are other reasons. Revenge is one. You have to understand Muerte, and I'm not sure anyone can. Who can understand evil? The expense doesn't matter. He will do what he has planned."

"Which makes it a miracle you've survived."

"Yes. That's exactly what it is—a miracle."

"When you first crossed the border . . . the agent who was killed—how did that go down?"

As she spoke, she scratched at a spot on her arm as if she

were allergic to the past. "The driver of my car . . . I didn't trust him. I knew he was loyal to Muerte. And when we stopped after the crossing . . . he made advances."

"He jumped you?"

"He came to the backseat. We struggled. He tried to subdue me and put one of the cuffs on my wrist, but I secured the other end to the case. He got very angry. He jumped from the car and fumbled for the key. That's when the other car arrived."

"The guy picking up the package."

"Yes. It was a Border Patrol agent. At least that is how he was dressed. I don't know if he was an agent or just posing."

"So you struggle with Muerte's driver and hook yourself to the case out of desperation. Then what happened?"

"The American approached our car and called my name. The driver said something, and before I got out, another car pulled in. Gunfire erupted and the driver and the border agent dove for cover, but I think they both were hit."

"And you got away?"

She nodded. "We were on the side of a narrow dirt road. The car behind us got close, blocking the view of the other car. I simply opened the back door and slipped into the desert. I heard them cursing behind me, looking for me."

"That explains the flip-flops and skirt when I found you."

"And all of the cactus stickers. I had no light, no way of seeing."

J. D. let the image sweep over him. He cringed when he thought of the bullet wound. How frightened she must have been. So close to death, close to becoming another body on the side of the road.

"If the border agent was after this case, were the other guys after it too?"

She shrugged. "I heard them use my name. They knew I was there."

"So the whole thing was a setup. Why didn't they follow you?"

"I don't know. I was praying that God would protect me. They were firing into the desert even after I escaped. I heard an explosion minutes later—they burned the car. I don't know what happened after that."

J. D. heard a noise that didn't sound like it fit in the pristine wild and finally recognized the helicopter overhead. He cursed and told Maria to get under a burned-out tree. "I have to move the car."

When he had the Toyota hidden beneath a copse of pine trees above the parking area, he made his way back down the hillside. As far as he could tell, the chopper hadn't seen them. It was on the other side of the valley, searching near some hills.

The sun was up and the temperature too. He had no idea what the thermometer read, but it felt above ninety before the rays hit his back.

"Let's get closer to the water."

Maria followed him down the incline, shuffling through black pinecones, rocks, needles, and the occasional mesquite beans that had blown across the landscape. The ground was a tinderbox, ready for any spark. Lightning fires were common here, a cruel twist of irony. They needed rain to wet the earth but with the storms came lightning that could cause the whole region to smoke and burn.

They sat under a cottonwood tree at the edge of the water. The ground beneath the tree showed children's and small animals' footprints to the water's edge. J. D. had seen paddleboats and children swimming at the tiny pier when he had walked the perimeter of the lake weeks earlier. The gift shop was closed and the lake deserted at this hour, but families would head for this oasis soon.

"Want to go in?" Maria said.

He shook his head and watched her take off her shoes and socks and wade into the water. There could be broken glass at the bottom or snakes or any number of things, but he knew she wouldn't listen. She rolled up her sweatpants, then tossed caution aside until water was up to her waist, splashing her arms and face.

"It's really cool," she said.

She found a rock and sat in the water up to her armpits, and it looked so inviting he couldn't resist. He kept his boots on but sat, letting the water envelop him. It felt unnatural, water seeping through his clothes and flooding his boots, but as he let the coolness seduce him, he closed his eyes and listened to the birds and the gentle lapping of water. He pulled his hat lower to absorb the sun's rays and felt his arms go weightless.

"My father would take our family to the beach when I was a little girl," Maria said. "Bahia Kino. It's on the Sea of Cortez. We would leave for a week in the summer. The three of us were in the sand at sunup building castles and digging tunnels, searching for seashells and buried treasure. We would laugh and play in the surf until dark. We never stopped. Not even hunger could bring us inside. My mother would bring us sandwiches and Coca-Cola and we would play in the water and get burnt by the sun. Then in the evening we'd smell my mother's cooking coming from the little house we rented, or my father would be cooking meat on the grill in the back, and we'd race each other for the table."

"Sounds like a great memory."

"It was the happiest time of my life."

He thought of his own family and the handful of times they had taken a vacation when he was little. J. D. had vowed things would change if he ever became a father. But what was learned stuck.

A memory of his brother at the beach flashed through his mind. Tyler laughing at him for thinking he could spend a sand dollar at the store. Their father had spoken with the manager, explaining the innocent childhood perspective, and J. D. triumphantly exchanged the worthless debris for a pack of gum. This infuriated his brother but gave his parents something to laugh about all the way home. Plus, it was fodder for one of the few songs J. D. had written that actually made it onto the charts.

"Tell me more about your father," J. D. said. "Were you raised on a farm?"

She scooped a handful of water and doused her head. "He inherited it. Many acres of land. He was considered wealthy by local standards."

"So it was big."

"Yes. There is a vineyard. We have horses. Gardens and fruit trees and flowers." Her eyes sparkled as if she were describing the Magic Kingdom. "It was peaceful when I was little, but so was the whole town. Things changed with the coming of the cartel."

"And your brothers were killed."

She nodded. "They were caught up in the violence like others. So many have lost their lives. And the ones left are shells, just making it day to day. My greatest hope is to help rid them of this evil."

"That's a big job for one person. You're not getting much help from the authorities down there."

"Poverty is rampant. Turning to the drug trade makes sense

to young people because you can make a lot of money in a short time. You can provide for your family. Sadly, you can also get hooked."

"Did that happen with your brothers?"

She looked away, toward the west end of the lake. "One of them, yes. The other was innocent and young. A follower. He was my twin."

He couldn't think of anything to say.

"The sad part is it doesn't have to be this way. But this kind of change doesn't happen with new laws or a bomb or even a fence. There are ways around fences and under them. This change must happen inside."

"Well, I don't know if the whole 'love your enemies' thing is going to work with the cartel."

"When God is at work, it doesn't matter how big the problem is. He can do mighty things. He can move mountains."

J. D. nodded and held back but finally blurted out, "I asked God to move a mountain for me once and he didn't seem to be able."

"Your wife?"

He nodded. "I could write a song: 'God moves other people's mountains but not mine.'"

"What happened to her?"

"She passed away."

"I'm sorry. You should write a song about her. I'm sure it would be wonderful."

"I don't write songs anymore."

"Why not? Some of the best songs—some of the best art—come from pain, don't you think?"

"Well, if that's true, I ought to be a country music da Vinci. But I'm not even close."

"What kind of songs do you sing? What are they about?"

"It doesn't matter because I don't sing anymore."

Maria thought a moment, watching the water drip from her hand above the surface of the lake. "And you came to the Slocum farm to get away? To escape the memories?"

"No, I wasn't really escaping. I can see that now. I don't think I'll ever escape what happened. I think I was trying to keep something alive." A bass surfaced near them and struck at an insect.

"Before your wife died, were you happy?"

"Yeah. I was the happiest I'd ever been. Doing something I loved, sharing my life with someone. Working toward something together instead of being alone. It wasn't a perfect relationship because I was part of it, but we were good together. She loved me for who I was and not who she wanted me to be. That's unusual, from what I can tell."

"So what now?" she said.

The chopper returned, the rotor beating at the air from a distance, and the two stayed still until it went out of sight.

"I don't make plans anymore," J. D. said. "I don't think about what I want because it doesn't really matter."

"Because no matter what you want, if you get it, it will be taken?"

"Something like that. It'll either be taken or it'll be an illusion. Not what was advertised on the outside of the box." He studied the algae in the water and tried to see to the bottom of the lake, but they had stirred it too much. "What about you? What do you want from life?"

She looked toward the cottonwood tree, into the sun, and the light hit her face just right. J. D. thought if he had a camera, he could take a picture that would fit on the wall of the farmhouse in his mind, the place where he'd eventually settle. If he could capture this moment, freeze her beauty for a split second, it would be enough.

"I don't want to be afraid."

"Okay, kill Muerte and all the members of the cartel and you won't have to be afraid."

She shook her head. "Have you ever thought of what the opposite of fear is? What would you say?"

"Bravery. Courage. Something like that."

"That's what I used to think. I would have said that to be courageous and brave meant you put fear away and run ahead into danger. Like a firefighter running into a burning building. The head says to run from, but the heart says you must go toward it."

"I didn't know they grew philosophers down there in Herida."

She laughed. "I am not a philosopher. I am a woman with a heart and a desire to live."

"So what's the opposite of fear, in your mind?"

Maria ran her hand in the water back and forth, making ripples on the surface that spread out around her. "There is a verse in the Bible that talks about love that is perfect. It's the kind of love that helps people do the impossible. That kind of love is not afraid because you cannot love and fear at the same time. They cancel each other. Do you understand?"

"I hear you, but I'm not sure I understand."

"For love to be real, for it to grow deep inside, it must not give in to fear. It is not afraid to give, to risk, to chance, even if it hurts. Love believes. It is faith moving forward. Fear holds us back. It makes us stop or turn and run. It blocks us from doing what would bring life and health. Fear keeps us overwhelmed.

It makes us look at the problem rather than the answers that lie asleep inside."

He took a deep breath and tried not to let her see what was going on inside him. "Sounds like you heard a sermon or two. You said it well."

"I have been reading," she said. "And I'm captured by the man in the book."

"Which man is that?"

"Jesus. In every situation he is moved by love. He has great reason to fear. Great reason to be moved by anger at injustice and disease and the hatred of those around him. He could have been overwhelmed with everything the world had become. It was so far from the plan. And yet he had love for the woman who came for water who was not holy. For the adulterer, he did not condemn. He beckoned children and showed compassion and kindness and mercy."

"You should have married some Mexican preacher," he said. "Maybe changed the mind of a priest down there at some mission."

She blushed and shook her head.

"Those are good thoughts," J. D. said, "but you can dump out all the love in the world and it won't keep people from getting hooked on drugs. It won't make them stop selling or running it across the border. It's not going to keep Muerte from killing."

"You don't understand love, then. You think it is just some kind of mushy feeling."

He set his jaw. "Don't start in on me about what I think about love."

"Love is not just a feeling couples have. It's not just a mother cradling her baby. It's so much more powerful." Her eyes flashed fire and something came over her he didn't like.

"I never said it was just a feeling," he snapped. "And don't tell me it's powerful—I know that already." J. D. watched a long-legged egret fly to an inlet near a dry stream that fed into the lake. It pecked at some insects on the surface of the water, then stuck its head underneath and pulled up a struggling fish and flew away.

Maria stayed silent, taking it in with him.

"I can hear the words, Maria, but I can't hear the music. You know what I mean?"

She nodded and crossed her arms. "I don't know if I can do anything to help my people, my town, but I'm not going to let the fear hold me back. Perhaps I will fail. Worse things could happen."

"Such as . . . ?"

"I could do nothing. I could try to live a safe life."

"I admire your pluck."

"Excuse me?"

"Your attitude, your courage. And your faith. I wish I had it."

"But you can have it."

"No. I'd only be pretending. Kidding myself that there's something bigger out there that wants to be involved in this mess."

She slipped from the rock and stood facing him, planting a foot between his boots and leaning close enough that he could feel her breath on his neck. Close enough to see the part in her hair and his reflection in her eyes.

"There was a reason *you* found me, J. D. Not Slocum. Not the Border Patrol. Not the cartel. *You* found me. God is up to something in your life."

Whether God was working was up for grabs. The stirring inside him wasn't. That was real. He searched her face and tried to think of something to say but nothing came. All he could do was stare at her eyes and lips and try to dredge up something that might make sense.

She spoke in a whisper now. "What if you were to give love a chance instead of fear?"

"I'm not afraid of love." His voice cracked.

"Yes, you are."

"I think my ability to love died with my wife."

She pulled her hair back over one ear, then gently touched his chest. "It's not dead. It's dormant. Waiting. You will know it when it comes because it will not act out of fear of what might happen. It will compel you to do what is right, what is best for the other person no matter what the consequences. That's real love."

"So you're saying I'm a coward. Because I won't take a chance at love, I'm—"

"I'm calling you to something bigger than your own vision. Something better than protection. Instead of running from what you fear, instead of turning from the things that could change you, what if you embraced them willingly?"

He was distracted for a moment by movement at the far end of the lake. When he looked back, she had moved away and he saw a child stumbling toward the water with something white.

"Come on," he said.

23

ERNESTO WAS THE BOY'S NAME, and when he saw them, his face
had shown horror and relief. He tried to run, but Maria called
to him and J. D. was too quick. The child hung his head like a
trapped animal. His lips were chapped and his face marked with
dried sweat. His shoes were held together with strips of duct
tape, his hair filled with dust and stickers. When he leaned out
over the lake to fill the plastic jug he carried, his ratty backpack
dipped into the water.

"He got separated from his family when they came upon
border agents," Maria said, translating some of what the boy
gasped between gulps. He was drinking way too fast, with
algae running down the side of his mouth, and J. D. took the
jug from him. Ernesto leaned over the water and drank from
cupped hands.

J. D. studied the boy. A child should not look so hardened. What had he been through? And what was his family thinking bringing him here? His eyes were brown like Maria's, and behind them were years of hardscrabble poverty and want. His face was gaunt from dehydration. He seemed almost hollow.

Children take much more than they give, J. D. thought. *And this one will take too.*

Another traveler was not what they needed. Or perhaps it was. J. D. had been looking for an out, a way to get caught. When the store opened at the lake, they could wander into the bathroom and he could ask someone to call the police. But that felt like running from life and their shared destinies.

"Has he had anything to eat?" J. D. said.

When Maria repeated the question in Spanish, the boy shook his head.

They led him into the trees. Once he felt comfortable, Ernesto was a fire hydrant, talking nonstop. J. D. let them speak. He couldn't pick up much, but he got the impression the kid knew Maria or had heard of her.

J. D. slapped a sandwich together as Ernesto continued. The boy grabbed the food and ate like a hungry wolf, which quieted him for a moment, but when he finished, he began again. J. D. made him another sandwich.

"He talks like he knows you," J. D. said.

Maria shook her head, but Ernesto spoke with his mouth full. "She famous lady."

"What do you mean, famous?"

"He's not thinking correctly," Maria said. She turned to him. *"Ocúpate no más de tu comida."*

"No, go on," J. D. said. "What do you mean she's famous?"

"Everyone know her. In Herida and *por todos lados. Es la hija del hombre más poderoso de la región. Y nos dijeron que cualquiera que la encuentre será rico. Es la gallina de los huevos de oro. Es lo que dice mi padre."*

Maria glared at the boy, her lips pursed.

"What's he saying?" J. D. said. "Something about a rich man who has gold?"

"He's mixed up," Maria said. "The sun has gotten to him." She grabbed the boy, shaking a finger in his face. *"Si no dejas de soplar, te llevaremos derecho a la migra para que te echen de aquí."*

Tears came to Ernesto's eyes and J. D. didn't know what to make of the confrontation. He wanted to reach out and comfort the boy, but something held him back.

"Maybe if you didn't yell at him, he wouldn't cry."

"He's talking crazy. We have to help him get back to reality."

"Well, reality is, if they've caught his family, they're going to send the posse."

"We should move, then," she said.

"I think it's best we let him go. Give him some fresh water and point him toward the Border Patrol."

"He could die out here. He could get turned around and lost."

"They'll find him. And they'll get him back with his family. If he stays with us, they'll be worried sick."

Maria turned to him and her face changed. No longer the beauty, she was an angry mama bear. "What are you thinking? He is a child. We have to help him."

"Fine, hop in the car and we'll drive straight up the road to the checkpoint. They'll probably have his family there, don't you think?"

"That's not what I mean. We should take him with us."

"Great. It'll be a big reunion." He put his hand on the boy. "Come on, Ernesto, hop in the car and we'll go for a ride."

"Stop it," Maria said. "We're not turning him in and we're not giving up."

"Then what do you suggest?" J. D. said.

She asked the boy another question and he fired back an answer.

"He has family members in Tucson," she said. "His father sent money so they could make the journey. The father is waiting for them near some highway; he doesn't know which. His mother had the map."

"Good. Then let his daddy come out here and find him."

"How can you be so cruel?" she said.

J. D. looked at the sun climbing through the trees. Even his sweat drops were sweating. He couldn't imagine what walking through the open desert would be like. Who would risk it? Only the desperate or crazy or those without a choice.

"Maria, let's face facts. About him. About us. We're cornered. The only road out of here leads straight to the authorities."

"You did that on purpose. You knew we would be trapped."

"I was exhausted. It felt like a good plan. I thought we could regroup and figure out the next move. I'm sorry. I think we're out of options, but I don't think this Muerte will mess with us—"

"It's not about him messing with us now," she yelled. "How can I get you to understand?" She said something to Ernesto and he backed up to the car, fear on his face. Then she grabbed J. D. by an arm and pulled him farther into the thicket.

"I won't give up," she said. "I've been given something to do. And you are part of this. You were the one who asked me to return to you."

"I wanted to keep you safe from Muerte. I've done that."

"It's not just about keeping me safe. It's about what I must do."

"What do you mean? A mission from God?"

She didn't answer, but it was clear that was it.

"When did you realize you were on this mission?"

"Last night. In the car. I had a dream."

J. D. closed his eyes and muttered, "Oh, for crying out loud."

"You can make fun if you want, but it's true. I know what I'm supposed to do."

"Well, Joan of Arc, if you want to get burned at the stake, that's your choice, but the rest of us are running from the flames."

"I'm not Joan of Arc. I'm not trying to get us killed. I'm trying to follow the path laid out for me. The task God has given us."

"Given *you*, not me. I haven't seen him looking out for anybody but himself. You can't drag me into that."

"That little boy over there depends on us. The people of my village are depending on us. You can't quit."

"Depending on us? I can't even get my own life together, let alone help your village."

"There is more life in you than you think, J. D."

"Listen, Maria. I like you. You're beautiful. You're intelligent. You've got more spunk than anybody I've ever met. In some other situation we might have . . . I don't know, but you're talking crazy."

"You think I would be interested in making a life with you?"

J. D. looked away. "No, I doubt you would. And I wouldn't blame you. I'd get in the way of you and God."

"Well, I would be interested," she said.

He blushed.

She reached out a hand and took his chin, turning his face toward her. "There is strength in you. And wisdom. And kindness. I have seen that from the beginning. You make me smile, even when I am afraid. And you haven't given up, even though the one hunting me is a madman."

He couldn't speak, couldn't do anything but watch her lips. There was a softness around her eyes he hadn't noticed.

"Whether you realize it or not, you are a handsome man." She placed an open palm on his chest. "The world needs the strength of good men right now."

"If the cause is right, I'm not afraid to die."

She nodded. "I know. Your fear is much greater than death. You are afraid to live. And that's what I'm asking you to do. Help me. And by helping me, you will help yourself."

"Help you do what?"

"Stop him. Stop his plan. It is evil."

"I got the evil part. Exactly what are we supposed to stop?"

"He wants to take lives."

"How?"

She looked away for a moment, then back at him. "You will think I'm *loca*."

"I'm leaning that way already. Go ahead and push me over the cliff."

"In my dream there was a sea of people. My people. Faces I know from my town. They were stretched from one side of a gathering place to another. Perhaps a stadium or on some city street, I'm not sure. And they were all in danger and didn't know it. They didn't understand. They were like cattle being led to slaughter. I tried to get them to see; I screamed, but no one would turn. And Muerte was there, preparing to kill."

"With that rifle?"

"I don't know. I believe God was telling me I am the one to stop him. And it will be soon."

J. D. took off his hat and ran a hand through his hair. "Maria, if there are people in danger in your town, we have to alert the police."

"It was not my town. I knew these faces, but it was here. In America."

She was crazy. That was all there was to it. She believed her dream was reality. That there was a connection between the real world, God, and what was in her head.

J. D. had run into this before at concerts. People shoving crumpled sheets of paper toward him. God had given them a song. And J. D. was divinely appointed as the conduit. He had read the words, at least the first few verses, every time it happened. His observation was that God had a spelling problem. And lots of relationship issues with women. He had felt it bad luck to toss someone's song in the trash without at least reading it, but that was usually the end of it.

"If people are really in danger, we need to tell the authorities. What can two people and a kid do against some big plot to kill hundreds?"

She dipped her head and said something in Spanish.

"What?" he said.

"You know what they're capable of and I can't even convince you. How can I convince the authorities? Who will believe me if you don't?"

She had a point. As soon as she was taken into custody, there would begin a long succession of questions. Her insight would be tossed away like a scribbled song.

Fire in her eyes now. "Instead of him hunting us, we will hunt him. He'll never see us coming. And if God is for us, who can be against us?"

"The devil, I suppose," J. D. said.

"You believe in the devil?"

"I don't know what I believe."

She smiled and something inside J. D. melted. "If you cannot believe yourself, then hold on to my belief," she said.

Before he could figure out a comeback to put her in her place, the boy called to them.

"*¡Maria! ¡Alguien viene!*"

They moved to the edge of the thicket and saw four riders on horseback coming through the cienega. Noise of the chopper sounded in the distance but it was too low to see.

"You must choose," Maria said.

J. D. studied the landscape and set his jaw. "Get him in the car."

24

THE WIND PICKED UP as J. D. drove away from the lake on the main road. Mesquite trees and cottonwoods flailed at them as he veered toward a dirt lane that led past driveways of houses and farms. J. D. didn't know where it ended, but he was sure it got them closer to the Slocum farm and his stash of cash, which was where they were headed. They couldn't go back toward the Border Patrol.

He drove slowly so they wouldn't trail a plume of dust. The end of the road wasn't more than a path with ruts and rocks worn by the wind and cattle, an open range. J. D. parked behind a wooden Dead End sign.

"That's not the best omen I've had all day," he said, pointing.

"How far is it from here?" Maria said as she grabbed the water.

J. D. squinted into the sun. "I'd say about ten miles as the crow flies."

"I wish I were a crow right now," she said.

"You and me both."

J. D. put the remaining food in Ernesto's backpack and took the water from Maria.

"How long will it take?" she said.

"Never tried to walk it before."

"Guess."

"I'm hoping we make it by sundown."

She looked at the sun.

"What's wrong? Want to go back for sunscreen?"

Maria smiled, then put her head down and walked into the cactus and flat grassland.

"Watch for snakes. And tell Ernesto to follow close behind, right in our tracks."

"I hear," the boy said.

They had walked less than twenty minutes when J. D. felt the air change. The days were filled with sun and blue skies, but there had been something different about that morning. A scattering of clouds had formed and warned anyone willing to look that there was something on the way.

When he glanced in the direction of the car, a dust devil had kicked up. It was a thin tornado, a line of dust and dirt that rose in the air and swirled. He couldn't see the car or houses behind them, just the mountains in the distance. There wasn't a bird in the sky.

"I don't like the looks of this," J. D. said. Already the sleeves of his shirt were flapping and he had to turn from the sand as it stung his face. He pulled his hat down.

"Keep moving," Maria said.

J. D. waved Ernesto in front of him, guiding the boy with the jug of water pressed between his shoulder blades. He was so thin they stuck out through the shirt he wore. He was skin and bones and eyeballs. A desert rat. But he knew how to walk through the desert.

"Ever heard of a haboob?"

"No," Maria said.

"Big windstorm that picks up the dust and covers everything."

"Is that what's coming?"

"Doesn't happen here because the mountains block it. At least, that's what I've heard."

The wind didn't lower the temperature; it just made the walk more unbearable. Like walking against a fan turned outward from a blowtorch. The farther they went, the harder it blew. J. D. leaned into Ernesto, bending forward as he kept the boy going.

"I think we should go back to the car," J. D. said.

"It's too far," Maria said.

"We have to find shelter, then." J. D. shouted now, the wind whistling.

"No," Maria said. "Keep going."

Sand whipped at them and J. D. pulled Ernesto behind him. He wished they had stayed in the car. At least they would be safe from the debris.

Without warning, the wind became violent. It was so hot and filled with dirt he couldn't breathe, couldn't look into the maw of rising dust that settled in the lines and sinews of his face and tore at his eyes. He turned his head sideways, letting his hat take the brunt of the spray as he reached for Ernesto and pulled him closer. He could hear Maria struggling behind. Each step was like another foothold up Everest.

And then it struck. Rippling through the canyon behind them, through the arroyos and gulches, the wind worked like an unseen hand gathering and lifting. There was no time to look for shelter because they were inside the maelstrom, dots on the landscape. The saguaros stood sentinel-like as they dug in.

He gathered the boy in and unzipped the backpack. Ernesto whimpered and held on, burying his face in J. D.'s chest. He dumped the contents and pulled the backpack over the boy's head, zipping it so it wouldn't fly away. Then he planted his knees and pulled Maria close, creating a shelter for the boy with their bodies. She hugged J. D., not romantically but of pure necessity. Even so, he felt a stirring from being so close.

He took off his hat and placed it over Maria's face so she could breathe. He buried his face in her hair, and soon he was sitting back on his haunches with her in his arms and Ernesto between them.

"I'd like to see Muerte find us in this," he shouted.

I'd like to see God find us in this, he thought.

Maria didn't move or try to speak. Once you found a position where you could exist, you didn't look for a better one. What he wouldn't give for goggles and a mask. If they had stayed in the car, they could have driven rings around the Border Patrol checkpoint.

J. D. thought of her words about purpose and meaning and things happening for a reason. His whole existence felt like wandering in a sandstorm.

He kept his eyes and mouth shut, but the sand was everywhere. When he clenched his teeth, there was grit between them, sand like seeds in his mouth.

"You okay, Ernesto?" he shouted.

The backpack nodded against his chest.

"How about you, Maria?"

"I am okay."

"Try to breathe and hang on," he said. "This can't last long."

But he was wrong. The storm continued and he retreated to a winter in his childhood. His father had taken his brother and him looking for a Christmas tree, parking on an icy road near the mouth of a logging trail. Each of them armed with a hatchet, they trudged through knee-deep snow toward a ridge of evergreens. Snow fell as they left the house but it picked up intensity near the mountain. J. D.'s face stung and snow worked its way into his boots and down his shins. Icy cold.

They hunted a good half hour before finding a tree. Tyler and their father chopped as J. D. huddled underneath the boughs. Tyler kept working while his father picked J. D. up and carried him to the car. It was the closest he remembered being to his father's beating heart. Their footprints in the snow were gone by the time they reached the road and there was a thick coat of sleet and snow on both of them. They must have looked like a snow monster moving down the hillside, but his father carried him through the blinding drifts, started the car, and placed him in the front seat. He stripped J. D. down, then pulled off his boots and shook them free of snow and shoved his feet under the heater to thaw. The car was tomb-like, dark and covered.

"Your job is to stay here and get warm," his father had said. "Don't get out. Understand?"

Teeth chattering, he nodded, then watched the snow fall from the driver's door as it closed and his father climbed back into the storm and disappeared.

Minutes seemed like hours. First his fingers began to move, blood coursing and stinging his toes. He rubbed the windshield, searching the landscape for his father and brother. He closed his eyes and prayed that if God would answer and save them from this bitter wind, he would never say bad words again and wouldn't stick his gum under the seat at school or try to look up a girl's dress and a thousand other promises.

Just this once, he prayed. *Listen to me and answer me.*

How long would it last? How long could he hold out? What if the car died? What if his father froze and his brother lost his way? What if some car came with mean people? What if no car ever came? He couldn't decide which was worse. There was no sound but the whir of the heater and the soft tick, tick of ice.

His father had climbed back to find a tree stump and no Tyler. He followed the track to a gully and found his oldest son near a frozen creek bed, pulled both back to the car, tied the trunk closed around the tree, and got in.

"You didn't think I'd make it back, did you?"

J. D. stared at him, not knowing what to say.

"Going to take more than a little snow to kill us." He looked in the rearview mirror. "Isn't that right, Tyler?"

Looking at a Christmas tree sent a shiver through J. D. after that. His father would cradle a coffee mug in his big hands and smile, knowing how close they had been to not coming back.

The first day of school after Christmas break, his pencil had rolled off the desk—it really had—and when he bent over and saw the flowers on Karen Lohr's underwear, he remembered his promise and at the same instant a word slipped out. He sat up straight, knowing he had just broken two of his promises. It felt like the spell had broken. He would be punished the rest of his life.

"I thought you said this couldn't happen here," Maria said in his ear. She was shouting but it sounded like a whisper.

"There are a bunch of things I never thought would happen," he said.

"It's okay. This is protecting us. What is meant to harm us is helping."

"Always looking at the positives, aren't you? Does that run in your family?"

She spit out some sand and burrowed deeper into his chest. "Our family does not know the concept of positive thinking. We are realists."

He tried to speak again but got so much sand in his mouth he coughed and spit. Every time J. D. looked up, he had to retreat like a turtle into its shell. In fact, he wished he were a tortoise right then and could burrow back into himself.

Maria spoke gently to the boy and patted his back. J. D. listened to her voice through the howling wind and it reminded him of Alycia. Maria would make a wonderful mother someday, if she made it through. If she gave up her illusion of hunting down Muerte.

She was right. Maybe this windstorm gave them a chance.

"Tengo miedo," Ernesto said through the backpack.

"Todos tenemos miedo," Maria said. "But God will take care of us."

A half hour later the cloud moved north. The three of them were a sight. Sand and dust everywhere—their hair, down their backs. Sand piled around J. D.'s legs and the same with Maria. Sweat popped out and ran down J. D.'s cheek. Maria's jet-black hair was filled with bits of sand and debris, and her face had a layer of dust that made her look clown-like. Ernesto took off the backpack and laughed.

"I could use a shower," J. D. said. "Either that or the two of us can put on rubber noses and apply to Ringling Brothers."

She was busy helping Ernesto get sand out of his shoes. "How much farther?"

"A long way just to the edge of the Slocum property," he said. "Let's go back to the car."

"No," she said, picking up the plastic water jug. "We can do this. We must do this."

"Maria, you don't have to prove anything."

She grabbed Ernesto's hand and turned, bewildered. "You go back and get the car. We will meet you at the Slocum ranch. Or leave. If you can't do this, I understand."

Ernesto looked at him with eyes as big as Texas. They were the sorriest-looking bunch he had ever seen, but something inside said this was the way to go, the way to life. He grabbed the boy's other hand and they walked behind the dust cloud as if it were leading them to the Promised Land.

25

THE THREE OF THEM were dusty shells of humanity when they came in sight of the Slocum ranch. They had gotten water from the back line—not by puncturing it but by turning the spigot, like anyone could if they bothered to find it. Or could wait long enough for water. They filled the empty gallon jug and kept walking.

J. D. could see why people would discard much of what they carried. They had only been going a few hours and he could hardly stand to hold anything, though he had picked up Ernesto several times when the boy couldn't go farther. They crossed dry washes where clothes and backpacks lay. Plastic jugs. Empty bottles of formula. Diapers. He'd seen the e-mails Slocum sent out with pictures of this debris and figured it was lazy people not caring about litter. But when you were so tired you could hardly pick up one foot and so hot your brain basted, he could understand discarding things that weighed you down. Didn't make it right, but he could understand.

They didn't spend much time in the wash because of the rattlers. The boy was scared of snakes and held on to Maria's hand until the cactus became too thick and they had to walk single file. When they made it onto the cattle trail, J. D. began to have some hope. He pointed out where he had found Maria in the distance, and if they hadn't been so hot and tired, he would have walked to it. It was a sacred place now, where their story had begun.

J. D. knew Red would see them and bark when they neared the farmhouse, so he found a cottonwood and planted Maria and Ernesto beneath it and neither protested. Her feet were blistered.

"I'll be back as soon as I can," he said but they were too exhausted to respond.

He managed to make it to the schoolhouse before Red barked. He knelt and patted his leg and called him. The tail wagged and he growled, but soon the dog recognized him and came with his tail and head down.

J. D. watched the farmhouse closely for any movement and hoped they were eating dinner. He scratched the dog's ear and the thing rolled over in the dirt in surrender. It only takes a little love to make something innocent believe.

Yellow police tape surrounded the schoolhouse but the door hadn't been locked. He walked inside the darkened room and wondered how he'd ever slept in such a place. There was no air to speak of. He went straight to the spot on the wall behind the rickety bed where he'd stashed his cash. As he moved the bed, he noticed a bloody bandage by the sink, but most of the evidence that Maria had been there was gone. The money was there and he stuffed it in his pocket and replaced the wood over the hiding place.

As he pulled the bed into place, the door opened and light flooded. A silhouette trailed by the dog.

"Is that you, Mr. Jessup?"

The boy, Cooper. "You've got a lot in common with lizards, you know that?"

"How's that?"

"Creeping up on people. You ought to get a job with the CIA."

"What's the CIA?"

"It doesn't matter. How's your family?"

The boy shrugged.

"Your daddy get the water pump fixed?"

Cooper was wearing the same frayed, dirty jeans but he had a shirt on. All that was left of the Adidas iron-on was a little of the first *A* and slivers of the *i* and the *s*. "No, he's been busy with the police."

"I'm sure they needed his help."

"Did you see that big cloud of dust?" Cooper said. He seemed overcome by the fact that J. D. was talking to him, paying attention for once. "It came over the house and we had to get inside. I thought we were going to get blown away."

"I can see it messed up your mama's clean windows. You'll be sweeping the front porch for a week. Maybe your allowance will go up."

"Were you out in it?"

J. D. nodded. "Right in the middle. And I don't recommend it."

Cooper stared at his dust-covered clothes and the dirt streaking his face. The kid's eyes were moon pies and his face showed an uncommon level of concern for his age. Finally he said, "People in town are talking about you and that Mexican woman."

"People will do that."

"Where'd she go?"

"She's still around. What are the people in town saying?"

"That they knowed you were trouble when you first got here."

"Is that from people in town or is that what your daddy's saying?"

The boy looked at the floor. "The police say you've done a bad thing. People are dead because of you."

J. D. sat on the bed and the springs creaked loudly. "And what do you think?"

"I don't think they care what a little kid thinks."

"I do."

Cooper looked up. "They must have some reason to think you've done something bad."

"The police can make mistakes. They don't know everything. But I don't blame them for thinking I'm part of the problem. Sometimes I think it's my fault too, and I know different."

"You didn't kill anybody?"

"No. Well, not directly. I tried to protect somebody and hit a guy with my truck. He was shooting at the girl."

"And you ran him over?"

"I wanted to stop him from shooting."

"I guess if somebody was shooting at me, I'd want you to try and help."

"I'm glad you understand."

"But then you ran."

"Do you think it's wrong to help people in trouble?"

"It's wrong to help illegals."

"Why's that?"

"Because they don't obey the laws."

"I can't argue with you there. But illegals are people too."

"I guess so. But they're taking our jobs. And my dad says there are too many at the hospital."

"He may be right," J. D. said. He wanted to say more but he didn't want to come between the boy and his father, so he just sat there.

"Are you leaving us, Mr. Jessup?"

"I believe I am, Cooper."

"Why?"

"It's not something I planned. Things have just worked out this way."

"You told me you were going to take me to the county fair."

The fair had been in April, when he first arrived, and wouldn't be back until next year, but kids Cooper's age didn't understand the ebb and flow of time nor the seasons of traveling fairs.

"Your dad will do that. Or your mom. Wouldn't be any fun with me—I'd upchuck on the tilt-a-whirl."

Cooper didn't smile. "You said we'd have cotton candy and caramel apples with nuts on 'em. And drink lemonade."

"I had good intentions, Cooper. But good intentions don't always get you to the county fair. I'm sorry."

The look on the boy's face was worse than the windstorm, at least in what it did to J. D.'s heart. He dug in his pocket and pulled out a twenty-dollar bill from his stash. "I want you to take this and tell your mom I said to take you to the movies. And get the biggest tub of popcorn you can find, okay?"

Cooper looked at the bill like he had never seen so much money in one place. "Do they sell cotton candy there?"

"They just might. Tell her to get you some of that, too."

Cooper fell onto J. D.'s neck and the dust on his shirt flew in the air like Pigpen's on Charlie Brown. While they hugged, Cooper whimpered, "I wish you'd stay with us. It's not the same without you. You're the best WWOOFer we've ever had. Mama said that the other day. The very best. She couldn't believe you were in so much trouble."

J. D. pulled the boy back so he could look at him. "You've got a good mama and a real nice family, Cooper. I wish I could stay longer, but it doesn't look like that's in the cards."

A tear leaked from one eye and J. D. nearly had to look away. "If you could do me a favor, I'd appreciate it."

The boy wiped his face with the bottom of his T-shirt. Freckles and red eyes and teeth sticking straight out that should have been growing down. You don't get orthodontia on a farmer's salary. "What is it?"

"Wait a little while before you tell your dad I was here. Can you do that?"

Cooper's eyes showed fear. "He already knows. He seen you coming."

"Did he call the police?"

Cooper shook his head and looked at the floor. "He called somebody else."

"Who?"

Before the boy could answer, the door opened and Slocum stood there, his face clouded by his hat brim. "Get back in the house."

"But, Dad, he didn't kill anybody. He just hit somebody with the truck."

The man grabbed his son by the arm and slung him out the door. Cooper tumbled into the dirt and the twenty-dollar bill fluttered away. He was crying when he gathered it in and ran, but not toward the house.

"It's not enough for you to bring the law down on us? You have to corrupt our kids, too? Why did you give him money, to keep him quiet that you're here?"

"Mr. Slocum, I'm not here to make excuses. I chose to help somebody and it didn't turn out."

"There's an understatement. Bodies are strewn from here to the border. I got a call from Win before noon saying one of his best friends was dead and they think it's because of this."

"Who?"

"I don't know, some reverend at a church. A bullet in the head. Secretary found him this morning."

"Was his name Ron?"

"Yeah, I think so. That sounds like him."

J. D.'s mind spun. He had been sitting with the man, face-to-face, only last night. Speaking heart-to-heart. And he had no doubt been questioned by the police after what he had said on the telephone. Had J. D. gotten him killed?

Maria. This would be crushing to her. And Win.

"Where's the girl?" Slocum said.

"She's not here."

"I can see that. Where is she?"

J. D. looked at the man. Reading his face was like trying to decipher a newspaper through the plastic bag thrown on your driveway.

"She's safe. That's all that's important."

"Well, I'm glad she is, because everywhere else you go, oxygen and blood flow stop. How do I know you're not here to take me and my family out?"

"I would never harm your family, Mr. Slocum."

"You can stop with the mister business. You don't have to put on airs."

"I'm not putting on airs. It's how I was raised. It's how I've always treated you. I came here—"

"Yeah, just why did you come here, J. D.? You came here and worked, but you told us nothing about your past. That you were some kind of entertainer."

"How'd you find out?"

"The police."

"My past isn't important. I came here to work hard and learn as much as I could from you and your wife."

"You didn't learn much about how to treat illegals." There was disgust on his face as he spat the words. "If you'd have done what I said, you wouldn't be in this mess and people wouldn't be dead."

"I couldn't leave her to die. You wouldn't have done it either."

"We make our choices, don't we?"

J. D. stood from the bed and nodded. "We do. And for what it's worth, I'm grateful. You've taught me a lot. I'll take that with me. You've got a wonderful family. Your kids are smarter than whips."

Slocum ignored J. D.'s outstretched hand. "I don't know why you came here. I don't know why you lied to us—"

"I never lied."

"You lied every time you ate with us and didn't tell us who you were. You lied every time you slept in this little bungalow. You lied when you got on that horse and took off in the morning. You're not a farmer; you're a pretender."

J. D. shook his head. "I guess we'll have to agree to disagree about that. Which reminds me—there's a heifer pulled up lame back near the water line. Didn't get close enough to find out why."

Slocum stared at him. "Is that the way you came? You walked through there?" The light went on for the man, something swirling around in his head. J. D. searched hard for something to say and didn't recognize the rumble of tires until brakes squeaked and dust rolled through cracks in the wall.

When J. D. moved to the door, Slocum put a hand on his chest. "I wouldn't go out there yet."

"Who is it? Who did you call?"

"I saw you when you first came up, heading toward the schoolhouse. I called friends. Welcoming party."

Something deep in the well rose. Slocum had always represented something J. D. didn't want to be, even though he knew a lot about planting and how to raise cauliflower without spraying pesticides. He also represented the easy way out, the shortcut across the mountain, a man who judged by skin color and language.

"You don't know what you're doing," J. D. said. He pushed past Slocum and walked out. Dust hung in the air from the truck that had approached and there were two others coming up the driveway at a fast clip. Two men J. D. recognized as farmers he'd met at the feed store got out of the first truck.

"I know exactly what I'm doing," Slocum said behind him.

Dust billowed and floated across the field. The old tom turkey clucked and ran from one end of its pen to the other. Slocum's kids pressed their faces against a dirty window and Mrs. Slocum stood behind them.

"Tell us where she is, J. D.," Slocum said.

"What are you talking about?"

A man from the first truck spoke, a short guy with stained armpits and a gray beard that stretched from his neck to his cheekbones. He looked like Kris Kristofferson in the face, but only enough to scare you. Part of Slocum's good-old-boy posse. "Maria, the little cash cow. Where is she?"

J. D. turned to Slocum. "What are you doing?"

"Nothing I shouldn't have done a long time ago. Don't worry; we're not going to take her to the police."

J. D. walked up to Slocum and stood an inch from his face, his jaw tight and a fire broiling. Now his words were a statement, not a question. "What are you doing."

"I got back taxes I owe on this place. You know that solar company wanted to buy the whole farm? They bought up just about everything close to here. I'm hurting, J. D. We all are."

"Word is out," Kristofferson said. His voice was gravelly and he grunted and whined through his nose. "That little woman of yours is a prize to somebody. And we aim to collect the finder's fee."

The other two trucks came to a stop amid more dust.

"He was on foot when he got here," Slocum yelled. "Said he came from that direction."

When J. D. moved toward the driveway, Kristofferson grabbed an arm and J. D. swung at him and connected just below one of his beady eyes. His knuckle split and blood coursed from the wound. He'd never hit a man in the face before and the pain of bone on bone surprised him. Then they were on him, and as soon as Kristofferson got to his feet, he was trying out his pointed boots on J. D.'s rib cage. Somewhere the Slocum kids were yelling and crying.

When the dust and pain settled, he opened his eyes and saw dirt and three pairs of boots. Slocum bent down on one knee and pushed his Stetson back. To keep Maria safe from Muerte and lose her to this bunch felt beyond irony. Beyond sadness.

"We need the girl. Tell us where you left her. We'll take care of her."

J. D. tried to lift his head and felt swelling under his eye and cheek. His ribs felt like he'd been run over by a truck, and he tasted blood. "You don't have any idea what you're doing," he mumbled.

"I think we do. A million dollars split five ways will pay a lot of bills."

"And who's giving you the money? Have you thought of that? The guy who's offering this is the one leaving a string of bodies. He'll kill her. That's what he's going to do."

"It's none of my business what a man wants with an illegal."

"You think he won't kill you like he did the pastor? He's not giving you a million dollars. He'll gun you down like a dog and laugh on his way back to the hole he crawled out of."

"Where is she?" another man said. "Was she on foot with you?"

The questions meant they were clueless. That was good. Had Maria seen the commotion and taken Ernesto back into the desert?

Another kick to the ribs. He rolled his face into the dirt and struggled to breathe. He wasn't afraid of lying and had no moral objection to it; he just wanted to make it convincing.

"She's headed to the border," he said, gasping. "She's probably past it by now. Somebody from her family picked her up in Tucson late last night."

"Then why'd you come here?" Slocum said.

"My stuff is here."

"He's lying," Kristofferson said. Another kick.

"We ought to call the sheriff," the third man said.

"No sheriff," Slocum said. "Cops get involved and we'll never get the money. We'll handle this."

"Who told you about the reward for her?" J. D. mumbled.

"Carl heard about it from one of his day workers," Slocum said. "Word spreads fast among 'em."

J. D. pushed himself up to a sitting position, trying to breathe through the pain. "Where are you supposed to take her if you find her?"

"We find her first," Kristofferson said, cursing him and angling for another kick.

Slocum held up a hand. "You want in on it? Is that it, J. D.? We'll cut you in fair and square. A million six ways is still a lot of money."

J. D. wobbled and stood, spitting blood in the dust. "How much would it be?"

Slocum looked at the others. "It was two hundred thousand split five ways, so I guess it would be a little less than that. Maybe one seventy-five?"

"One sixty and change," said another man who had better computing skills.

"He ain't going to give her to us. He wants the million for himself," Kristofferson said.

"I'm just now hearing about it," J. D. said. "If I'd have known she was worth that much, I'd have hired a limo and driven her myself."

A couple of them laughed.

"It makes no difference now—she's gone," J. D. said. "She's probably home by now. Back down to the farm where she grew up."

"Farm?" Kristofferson said. "What are you talking about? She doesn't live on a farm."

"That's what she told me."

Kristofferson cursed and laughed. "Boy, she took you for a

ride, didn't she? She told you she lived on a farm? That girl is the daughter of a drug lord down there in Mexico. Probably up here running some of her daddy's contraband. I say the more of them we get rid of, the better."

J. D.'s head spun. The story about coming across the border, slipping into the desert—had it been a lie?

"Time's wasting," Kristofferson said. "Gonna be dark soon, and once it gets dark, there'll be no finding her."

"What's your answer, J. D.?" Slocum said. "You in or out?"

"I'm in."

26

THEY DROVE AS FAR as they could into the desert, then continued on foot a little way.

"This is where I left her," J. D. said.

"Carl's our best tracker," Slocum said, motioning to the man.

Carl knelt in the dirt. "Looks like two people went this way, toward the road."

"Two?" Slocum said.

"Maybe three. Her and a couple of kids, judging from the footprints."

They looked at J. D.

"We picked up a straggler a few miles back. Boy who got separated from his family. I left them here. But it was just Maria and the boy."

"Where were you headed?" Carl said.

"I'm not sure. No, I'm telling the truth. We'd lost our wheels

255

and had no money. We were taking it a day at a time, trying to stay away from the police and that other guy."

"So you were going to steal a car from me?" Slocum said.

"No."

"He ain't telling the truth," Kristofferson said. "I say we duct tape his hands and feet and stick him in my truck. I'll get my dog and we'll track her and the other wetback and turn her in for the money. The kid goes to the Border Patrol."

"I don't think we can trust him, Larry," Carl said.

In the distance, more dust. One man thought it was the police. Another said it was Border Patrol. J. D. recognized the truck as Win's.

"Carl, see if you can follow those tracks. The rest of you get in your vehicles and head to the road."

"What about him?" Kristofferson said, pointing at J. D.

"I'll take care of him," Slocum said.

Win got out of the truck and Cooper hopped out as well and headed for the house. Slocum yelled after the boy but he had more sense than to stop.

Win shook J. D.'s hand and gave him a warm hug. When he pulled back, his eyes said there was something he wanted to say but couldn't.

"Sorry about your farm truck," J. D. said.

"That's the least of my worries. I've been worried about you."

"Don't waste your time being worried about him," Slocum interrupted. "He's the reason people have died."

"Nonsense," Win said. "He was trying to help. He was a Good Samaritan."

"He's a good-for-nothing," Slocum muttered. "Get in the truck and we'll hunt."

"J. D. can't stay here," Win said. "The police are on their way."

Slocum scowled.

"If I'm arrested, I can't help find her," J. D. said. "I'm no good to you behind bars."

Slocum took off his hat and slapped it against his leg. J. D. saw him then, a small man with a dream that had been handed down like a secondhand pair of boots, worn and fitted by someone bigger than he was.

Slocum looked at Win. "Take him. I'll deal with the boys and the law." Then, to J. D., "If we find her, you don't get your share."

J. D. didn't argue. Win put an arm around him and pulled him toward his truck. The engine fired and they pulled away. "Maria and the boy are safe. They're at the house."

"How did you find her?"

"Cooper led them to the road."

How had the boy known?

"What about you? How did you get here?"

"Carl's wife called Iliana and said something was happening at Slocum's farm. I came as fast as I could. I stumbled onto them by the roadside."

"Did you call the police?"

"I didn't."

"So you lied to Slocum?"

"I didn't know what else to do. I had to get you away. God forgive me."

"Slocum's going to tan Cooper's hide when he finds out he helped her escape," J. D. said. He told Win what he'd heard about Maria's connection with the cartel. "Do you think she's the daughter of a drug lord?"

"You'd be a better judge than me. You've spent more time with her. But deception can be alluring, especially from a beautiful face. I was afraid we weren't getting the entire story."

"Yeah, I know. But she talked about that town like it was her own people. Like she really cared. She threw in God, too. Talked about the pastor from the church . . ."

Win's voice lowered and with sadness he said, "You heard Ron Barfield was killed."

J. D. nodded. "I was with him last night."

"So it's true. You were there."

"Yeah, my fingerprints are all over the place. He let me sleep in his office. I sat across from him and he told me about the church and what they were trying to do. The trips they took across the border. I think I got him in trouble."

Win shook his head. "I can't believe he's gone. With all the violence, all the chances he and his men took traveling south, to be killed in his own church . . . They'll think you had something to do with it."

"Just another part I hope I'll have the chance to explain."

"There'll be a big hole left by Ron. He was a leader of men."

"Who'll take his place?"

"God will provide. Someone will step up to fill the gap."

They pulled up to Win's house and saw Ernesto on a tire swing in the backyard. He still wore the same dirty shirt from the desert, pant legs frayed, but he was holding a soda bottle in one hand and a squirt gun in the other, swinging like he owned the place.

"I put it up for the grandkids," Win said.

"You don't have grandkids."

He smiled. "I'm a man of faith. I can dream." He turned off the ignition and pointed at Ernesto. "I'm glad you didn't send him back to the desert."

"You should thank Maria." J. D. cursed. "I don't know what I'm doing anymore. Nothing's what it appears."

"You mean, like you?"

J. D. stared at him.

"You are not what you appeared to be either. We are just now learning things. The police gave us information you never gave. Why didn't you tell us?"

"Didn't know you wanted a press release. I didn't know I had to tell my life story for you to be my friend."

"We are your friends. What happened in your past does not define you. We knew you were a good man. But you didn't trust us."

"Maybe I would have told you after some time."

"Perhaps," Win said. "But how long were you going to wait?"

The two of them got out and walked toward the house. Win stopped and turned to J. D. "No one can accuse you of having a hard heart. I know you care about Maria. Your heart is good. And you are our friend."

Maria sat at the kitchen table eating something Iliana had made for her and Ernesto. When she saw him, her smile brightened the room. She hugged him but he went limp at the embrace.

"What's wrong?" she said.

"I think you know." He took off his hat. "Why didn't you tell me?"

"Tell you what?"

"Who you are. The reason you came up here."

She studied him, then glanced at Win. "I've told you everything that happened when I came across the border."

"Really? What about growing up on a farm and going to the beach?"

"That is true. Our family lived on a farm, and we traveled—"

"I don't recall the point where you mentioned your dad was

a drug dealer. You left that part out. Unless you were farming marijuana and cocaine."

She stared at the floor and her hair covered her face.

"That's how you came to know Muerte, isn't it?" he said. "That's why your brothers died. The Zetas or some other cartel got them."

She nodded. "Their bodies were discovered by local police. We were told it was the Zetas, but I think it was Muerte. I know it was."

"Still doesn't make sense you'd lie to me."

"Please, don't be angry."

"Excuse me if I get testy, but that seems like important information. It would have helped while we were dodging bullets."

"It would have made no difference. I never lied to you. I told you who he was."

"But you didn't tell me who *you* are. Who your father is. That changes everything."

She spoke vacantly as if her heart wasn't in it. "I don't agree with what my father does."

"But you lived with him. You enjoyed the fruits of his labor."

"I told you that I want to help the town—"

"Right. All the people in shallow graves, beheaded, hands cut off, the violence and shootings. You're for the people. You want to change things. Seems strange you couldn't divulge who Daddy's little girl was, the one with the secret decoder ring."

She said something under her breath and he wanted to slap her, shake her, anything to wake her up. Instead, he walked to the door.

"I thought if I told you, you wouldn't help me," she said to his back, her voice strained. "I thought you would leave. I didn't think you would understand."

"Well, now I understand," he said, turning back. "You used me to get what you wanted. Safety. And if I had died, you would have found some other schlub, wouldn't you?"

She wiped a tear away, like swatting a fly, and sat at the table, putting her head in her hands. "I thought you helped because you cared."

"I did. I helped because I believed you. That you were a farm girl who cared about her people. Little Miss 'Save my town from the bad drug guys. My brothers were killed and I don't want that to happen again.' The good girl fighting the evil cartel."

"I'm not a good girl, but the rest is true."

"Then you added all that Jesus talk. 'God gave me a dream.' I bought it. And your scheme is getting more costly for *real* people of faith like that pastor."

Maria looked at Win.

"Pastor Ron was killed early this morning. He had been with the police most of the night, evidently."

She turned and held J. D.'s gaze as something welled in her eyes. "Is that what you think? That I tried to trick you and get the pastor killed?"

"I don't know what to think. Who knows what else you're holding back."

"I was afraid you would judge me like all the others in your town. You call us names. Illegals. Wetbacks. We are not human to you, just animals crawling through the desert."

He gritted his teeth. "I never treated you that way!"

"No, you were kind to me. You risked your life." Her voice softened and it did something to his anger, though not much. "But I was afraid you would turn on me if you found out. The further we went, the more time we spent together, the more I wanted to tell you. I felt bad that you didn't know. When I went with the church people, I was glad I did not have to deceive you. . . ."

"So you admit it—you were deceiving me."

"I was letting you think what you wanted. But I was also sad that you would learn the truth from someone else. Or from some newspaper report after I died."

"You didn't trust me. That's what it comes down to. Did you ever really talk to your father on the phone? When we stopped at the gas station, was that real or a ruse?"

"It wasn't my father. I called the pastor. He connected me with the others. I'm sorry."

He moved to the table and knelt on the floor. Her clothes were still dust-covered but her eyes were moist and pleading. "Are you mixed up in your father's business? Are you dealing, transporting? Is that why you came here?"

"No."

"But you used to?" J. D. said. "You were part of the business."

"I helped my father. It was mostly behind the scenes, setting up meetings, making phone calls. I took the place of my brothers. And the deeper I moved into that world, the more troubled I became. I was just as caught as my father and Muerte."

"What happened?" Win said.

"I heard the truth," she said. "Ron and the others came and spoke of God's love, how we can be forgiven and find freedom in the power of Jesus' name. Their love was real. It was what I had been looking for all my life."

The room fell silent except for the running water in the sink and the clink of porcelain as Iliana moved dishes.

Win stepped forward and put his hands on Maria's chair. "Instead of a daughter of a criminal, you became a child of the King."

"Yes. But I couldn't tell my father. I couldn't reveal this to Muerte and the others. I had to keep working until I could find a way to tell the truth. I wanted him to have a new heart. If my father and the others experience forgiveness, what it feels like, how it can change a hardened heart, there is no way they could resist."

"They can resist if they're blinded by the enemy," Win said. "But you're right, this kind of love has the power to change anybody."

"I discovered Muerte was trying to take over," she continued. "He was planning something with another cartel. I told you this, J. D."

"So you coming here, volunteering for that job, was really about protecting your father?" J. D. said.

She shook her head. "No, I was a new person, but trying to escape. I wanted to break free from the business. When Muerte organized a shipment, I discovered it was part of the plan with the other cartel, and I volunteered. I asked my father to intervene. He ordered Muerte to let me go."

"Then Muerte organized a welcome party for you."

"Yes. He must have believed I knew his plan. That's why he wanted me dead."

"You're sure you don't know the plan?" J. D. said.

"No. And my fear is he will act before anyone can stop him."

J. D. glanced at Win and saw worry. His face was a map of deep lines cut and drawn in his sun-darkened skin.

"You both have the same story," Win said.

"How's that?"

"You've withheld information from people who care most. That's why you're upset. You see yourself in how she treated you."

"I didn't know you'd taken up psychology."

BORDERS OF THE HEART

Win ignored him and kept plowing through his soul. "Your lives are a mirror. Until you trust, it'll be hard to move forward."

"This is different," J. D. said.

"Is it?" Win said. "You are not the son of a drug lord, but you have secrets. Things that would have helped us understand. Maybe we could have helped you."

"Fine, I'll tell you my life story. Does that make you feel better?"

"J. D., don't get upset."

"My wife died in my arms. Afterward I came here to learn to farm so I could honor her memory and live what she didn't get a chance to. And try to forget. I'm sorry I didn't spill all that when I first met you."

"You don't have to apologize—"

"No, obviously I do. You want me to keep going and tell you the name of the hospital where she died and the type of radiation she turned down?"

Win didn't speak, didn't acknowledge the emotion in J. D.'s voice. He just stared at the floor and grasped the chair back until the blue-green veins in his hands surfaced. Maria had a frightened look, like she was watching a beheading.

"I could tell you more, but I don't see what any of that has to do with Maria. I don't see how our situations are even remotely similar."

"What about your son?"

Silence in the room. Then Win said, "Iliana, don't."

"No, I think he should explain," the woman said, drying her hands on a dish towel. She spoke something in Spanish J. D. didn't catch, then lifted her head to him. "How could you leave your son?"

264

She stood beside Win now, and the man put his arm around her and pulled her close.

"You have a son?" Maria said.

J. D. nodded. Memories flooded like a swollen wash. The child's cries. The tears and embrace of a dying mother. J. D. tried to stem the tide but couldn't.

"I can't go there," he said.

"What about your music?" Iliana said. "That must still be a part of your heart."

"My music isn't anybody's business."

"Do you think your wife wanted you to throw that away? To become a farmer? Why would you abandon a gift God has given?"

J. D.'s face flushed as the three studied him. They must have discovered the information online or from the police like Win had said. It didn't matter how they found out; they knew, and they would never look at him the same again, just like he would never see Maria the same. Drifting like the wind was one thing, but abandoning your son was another. Throw in a few songs and you've committed the unpardonable.

"Not everybody thought it was a gift. I wasn't really popular."

"But you were becoming who you were meant to be," Iliana said.

"My music is something I had to put away after Alycia passed. It was too painful to keep going. Every song brought her back. I can't even stand to listen to music on the radio anymore."

Iliana wiped her eyes with her apron. She put a hand on his shoulder and he glanced up to see her trembling lips. "Let me get you something to eat," she said.

"Tell us about your son," Maria said. "Where is he?"

"I left him with my parents. And Alycia's mom is still living. She watches him some, I expect."

"What is his name?"

He shook his head. "You can judge me for what I've done, but you don't know the full story."

"Tell us," she said. "How old is he?"

Before J. D. could respond, Ernesto burst through the back door running full tilt. Soda fizzed through the loose cap on the bottle.

"*¡Aguas, alguien viene!*"

"Someone is coming," Maria said.

27

DUSK DESCENDED LIKE A BLANKET on the landscape, and the mountains turned red in the haze. Four trucks rumbled up the dirt road, headlights dipping and bobbing over the uneven path. J. D.'s first instinct was to run. Win quickly tried to usher Maria toward the shop, but she wouldn't go.

J. D. and Win walked onto the front porch as Slocum and his friends parked near the house, blocking Win's truck. If they were going to get out, it would be on foot.

"I figured something was up with you two," Slocum said. He spit a stream of tobacco at the ground and rolled the chaw in his mouth. "You and that girl are as thick as thieves."

"Thought you could collect on her all by yourself, didn't you?" Kristofferson said to J. D. "She in there?"

"Bring her out, Win," Slocum said. "We got no trouble with you."

"Gentlemen, don't do this," Win said.

Kristofferson pulled a handgun from the back of his jeans. Another took a shotgun from his truck. J. D. couldn't believe what he was seeing. He looked hard at Slocum. "I've never questioned anything you've done on the farm. But you know this is not right. You're going to get her killed."

"Why do you care so much about one illegal?"

"What did you do, taste the goods?" Kristofferson said. "Maybe that's what happened. He sampled the Mexican merchandise."

The men laughed.

Win stepped off the porch, moving toward them. "There's a verse in Proverbs. 'Rescue those who are unjustly sentenced to die; save them as they stagger to their death.' You don't want this woman's blood on your hands."

"No, we don't. We just want the money in our pockets," Kristofferson said, laughing. "Save your preaching for Sunday morning."

"All your do-gooding is not going to change our minds, Win," Slocum said. "Bring her out here or we'll go in and get her."

Win lowered his voice and a look came over the man's face that J. D. had never seen. "Leave my farm now."

"Or what?"

"Put your guns away and we'll forget this happened," Win said. "Go home."

Slocum took a step forward. "You're not listening. I said you either go in and bring her out or we're going inside. Don't make me hurt you."

Win reached for his cell phone, and Slocum's pistol cocked. "Keep your phone holstered, big boy."

"Doesn't surprise me he'd take her side," Kristofferson said. "His wife's one of them."

Win kept his eyes on Slocum. "Larry, you know me. Your family has known me all my life. I've helped you at the farm. Who took Cooper to the hospital? Who bought medicine for your oldest? Don't you see this is wrong?"

"We're getting nowhere fast," Kristofferson said. "For all we know she might be hightailing it across the desert. Let's go in."

Before the two could move, the screen door opened and Iliana walked onto the porch carrying a shotgun almost as tall as she was. And by the way she held it, it looked like she knew how to use it.

"Leave now, Mr. Slocum."

Win rushed to the porch and J. D. watched Slocum's face turn pale.

"Guess she must be inside," Kristofferson said.

The men spread out, moving away from Slocum. J. D. stepped in front of Slocum and raised his hands toward Iliana. "This is crazy."

Evidently Win felt the same way. He wrestled the gun out of his wife's hands and pointed it at the ground. The group stood looking at each other until the screen door opened and Maria appeared.

"Stop," she said to the men. "I will go with you."

"Maria, no," Iliana said.

Maria walked down the stairs, her hair pulled back, each footstep sure and steady. She glanced at the guns and moved toward J. D.

"Thank you for what you have done," she said. She had a folded piece of paper in her hand and pressed it into his.

"You can't do this," he said.

"I knew someday it might come to this. I don't want you to get hurt. And this may lead me to Muerte."

"It'll lead you to your grave."

"Then I am ready."

J. D. turned to Slocum. "You don't want to meet up with Muerte's friends. Trust me, you'll die."

"We'll take our chances," Slocum said. He stepped toward Maria.

She kept looking at J. D., staring into his eyes, and the look gave him an ache he couldn't shake from his mind or heart. He knew it would haunt him, just like the images of Alycia.

"This is the direct line to my father," she whispered. "If Muerte has not killed him, would you call and tell him what happened?" Her eyes searched as if she was asking something else.

"Maria, don't do this. You can't go with them."

"As long as I'm here, these good people will be in danger. That's what I can't do any longer."

He knew it was good-bye. He knew it was the last time he would see her. And something about the prospect froze his heart, seized his will.

"You can stop him, J. D. I know you have the strength."

"What about God's will? What about saving the little town and the people you love?"

"Heaven moves with small steps. The enemy attacks with great force and tries to shift the ground beneath us. But God moves one stony heart. A heart that seems dead."

She put a hand on his chest and closed her eyes. "Good-bye, John David."

As she turned to leave, he grabbed her arm so hard it had to cut the circulation.

"I'm not going to let you leave again." His voice cracked. "I *won't* let you go with them."

"It's not your choice," she said. "There are some things you can't control. Some things have never been in your control. And you can choose to fear or let go."

Maria took his hand from her arm and leaned forward, pulling him to her. They had never been closer but it still felt like she was a million miles away.

"Let's get this show on the road," Slocum yelled.

She pulled back, her eyes full, and smiled. Then she walked toward Slocum's truck. The men followed. They didn't grab or shove her because they didn't have to. She scooted to the middle of the seat between Slocum and Kristofferson. The sight turned J. D.'s stomach.

Ernesto came onto the porch as the trucks pulled away.

"¿Por qué no la ayudó? ¿Por qué la dejó ir con ellos?"

"He wants to know why you didn't rescue her," Iliana said. "I want to know as well." She looked hard at them and then guided the boy inside and slammed the door behind her.

As the dust settled on the darkening landscape, J. D. opened the paper and stared at the phone number. Underneath the number was a short message. Her handwriting was flowery and flowing, like a subterranean stream that had found the surface.

You are a good man, J. D. And good is much stronger than evil. I pray your heart will heal. Stop Muerte. You can do this. Tell my father I love him in spite of what he has done. And I long for him to know the truth.

A heart was drawn underneath. The kind of drawing a teenager would make to show love to some boyfriend.

"What do we do now?" Win said.

"We?"

"Nothing worth doing should be done alone." Win handed the shotgun to J. D. and hurried inside. He returned wearing his hat and carrying a handgun and a box of shells.

He tossed the truck keys to J. D. "You drive."

J. D. drove fast and finally caught the convoy heading into town. He kept his lights off for a stretch, using the horizon to navigate.

All four trucks parked in front of the Mustang Bar, a local hangout where farmers and ranch hands found respite at the end of a day. Win said there was a back room where card games went well into the night. J. D. had never gone past the front room.

"How do you know that? You have a gambling ministry?"

"I've been here to pick up friends who've had one too many. They'll take her to the back and call their contact."

"Slocum thinks they'll just drop a million dollars through the mail slot."

"Slocum would take a personal check."

J. D. smiled at that. "When whoever they're calling gets in touch with Muerte, he'll come down here and take care of the whole bunch."

"Which means we have to get her now."

"Either that or call the police," J. D. said. "She said they couldn't protect her, but they're better than these guys."

Win asked about the note and J. D. held the paper out for him in the light from the street. With the ignition switched off, the truck became unbearably hot. They rolled down their windows but there wasn't much breeze.

"That wife of yours looks like she knows how to handle a gun," J. D. said.

"She could have gotten all of us killed."

"Maybe we should have shot Slocum in the leg."

Win shook his head. "There's a reason Maria gave herself up. There is a purpose in this."

"Why do you Christians see God behind every bad decision? I can understand a quarterback thanking Jesus for the touchdown and a preacher praising God for some lost soul who wants to be baptized, but a pastor gets gunned down or Maria is taken hostage and you have to believe it's God's will?"

"God's behind everything, J. D. You can't take him out of this world any more than you can take oxygen away. He's even working in your heart. I can tell."

"Well, I think there's somebody else at work here."

"True. You have an enemy who doesn't want you to succeed. But think of it this way. A lot of people don't believe in God because bad things happen. A follower of Jesus can hope in spite of the bad things. Look at the crucifixion. That didn't look like a good outcome for his followers. But God gained his most glorious victory on that cross."

"So you're saying that Maria being held in there, waiting for some madman to get her, is a victory?"

"Not necessarily. I'm saying God can use this situation for her good and his glory. It's the same with you. And your wife. And your son."

"Don't drag my family into this."

"Think about it, J. D. What if God's calling you to something more? Something deeper than you've ever known?"

The words were familiar. Maria had said something like it, but he heard another echo that went farther back. J. D. paused, taking in some hot air. They had parked next to a trash bin that smelled horrible, hid them, but allowed them to see the entrance and rear of the bar.

"My wife said those same words in the hospital."

"She was a woman of faith?"

"She believed like you do. God is good and doesn't give us more than we can handle and all that."

"I believe God gives us more than we can handle to make us turn to him." Win unbuckled and turned in his seat. "What's your son's name?"

"Alycia wanted to call him Jonathan. She said it means 'gift of God.' And she's the one who made a sacrifice to have him."

"Sacrifice?"

"We'd been talking about having a baby. She didn't care that we were scraping by. I guess she believed God would provide. I was just trying to get established. After we found out about the tumor, I convinced her to have radiation. Before they could start, she got a funny feeling. She had a pregnancy test and it came back positive.

"The doctor told her she had to begin the treatment, but the baby would never survive. She had to choose between her life and the baby."

"And she chose Jonathan."

"Yeah. You should have seen her face when they put that little thing on her chest. She just glowed. It was like watching the sun rise on the most beautiful spot on the globe. She got to be there for his first birthday, but the tumor grew and grew. It was too late."

"It doesn't seem possible that you would leave that boy. How old is he now?"

"He's two. Turns three next February."

Win winced.

"Every time I saw him, I saw her. I saw the pain she went through. I saw her choice and the peace she had about the decision to leave us."

"She didn't decide to leave you. She chose life. I think that's a wonderful gift. No wonder she named him Jonathan."

"You can look at it any way you want. All I know is, she's in a casket in the ground back in Tennessee and she's never coming back."

Win's voice was full of care and compassion. "Oh, nothing could be further from the truth. She's more alive now than ever."

"That's what the preacher said at her funeral. That and all that 'she lives in our hearts' stuff. I don't want her to live in my heart or my memory. I want her here. I want to grow old with her."

"Is that why you gave up on the music? It reminded you of her?"

"Every song. Every melody. Everything I wrote had a hole in the ground or a hole in my heart."

Win shook his head. "I understand. I don't mean to minimize your pain. But the truth is she lives in eternity. And what a joy it would be if she knew you would meet her there."

"I can't love my son, Win. I can't love him because I keep seeing him as the reason for her death. And if God is the one who is in control of all this, pulling the strings, how could I buy into that? What would be next? Jonathan? How could I follow some being who would choose this pain to work out his plan?"

"God understands," Win whispered. "This same God you blame was nailed to a tree. His hands and feet were pierced, and he was beaten to a pulp. He was everything good and innocent and holy. He walked through the desert like you, experienced hunger and pain, loss and shame and betrayal. And all that was to show his love."

J. D. took off his hat and wiped his brow. "I want to love my son. I swear I don't know how."

"God'll help you. He can create a new heart that can love again. You are moving toward something here, J. D. Like a caterpillar spinning into a chrysalis."

J. D. gave him a look. "What?"

"You ever heard about the monarch butterfly? The caterpillar can't reproduce. It has no reproductive organs."

"Bummer."

"Yeah. But when it becomes a chrysalis, it shuts itself up and most of its body is dissolved. Gets new eyes, new digestive tract, a set of legs, and wings. A creature that was never able to do anything but crawl spreads its wings and flies."

"And it gets new plumbing?"

Win laughed. "Yeah, that too. It can make little butterflies. But the most interesting part is that they hatch in the US or way up in Canada, and late in the summer when the milkweed dries up, millions of 'em head for Mexico and wind up on a volcanic mountain range down there."

"Like salmon swimming upstream," J. D. said.

"Exactly. They fly to a place they've never been on wings they never had." Win smiled at him. "That's your life. You're a chrysalis. Your wife has already flown. But you're becoming who you were meant to be."

J. D. studied the phone number on the page. "And while we're talking about this, Maria is waiting for her death sentence. I can't see how any of this will work out."

"It's not by might nor by power, but by God's Spirit that this will work out. God has a plan and a purpose for Maria. The question for you is, can you trust her?"

"I want to believe that she cares about the people in her town. And the reason she came here was to face down something her father never could. But I don't know."

A car pulled into the parking lot of the Mustang Bar and a man sauntered inside.

"Know him?" J. D. said.

Win nodded and sighed. "He goes to my church. Struggles with alcohol."

"Doesn't look like he's struggling enough."

"Maybe he's a caterpillar too."

"Hand me your phone."

Win gave him his cell.

J. D. dialed the number, then closed the phone. Indecision. Questions. He couldn't see a future for anyone. He could imagine death and strewn bodies. He could see police cars surrounding the place and Maria in cuffs.

He felt a hand on his shoulder. "Would you mind if I prayed?"

J. D. didn't answer, just nodded and stared at the floor. Win kept his hand on J. D.'s shoulder and squeezed. "Gracious Father, you know our hearts. You know this situation. And I ask for your direction. Keep Maria safe from this man who wants to kill her. We need your insight, Lord. We need your wisdom. Show us what to do, and we will give you the glory and thanks and praise for what you accomplish tonight."

"Thanks," J. D. said. He opened the phone again.

28

"SANCHEZ," THE MAN SAID. His voice was gravelly and distant.
A cell phone with wind noise. J. D. pictured him driving on a
dirt road through a vineyard in some lonely stretch of Mexican
farmland.

"Mr. Sanchez, I'm calling about your daughter."

"Who is this?"

"I'm a friend of Maria's."

"Where are you?"

"Arizona."

Silence, then, "She knows no one in Arizona."

"Maybe that was true a few days ago, but not now."

"How do you know her?"

"I found her in the desert. Dehydrated, almost dead. I tried
to help her."

"What is your name?"

"It's J. D., but my name doesn't matter. It's your daughter we need to talk about."

"Do you know where she is?"

"Yes. I'm close to her right now."

"Get her on the phone."

"Can't. She's not in a real safe place, if you know what I mean."

"Tell me where she is. I will send a man to get her."

He was forceful. Used to getting what he wanted. J. D. had to check himself and not give too much away. "Is your man named Muerte?"

A pause on the other end and the wind noise died. He either rolled up his window or pulled to the roadside. "Tell me where she is."

"Not if you're sending Muerte. He's part of the problem, not the solution to this mess. And it's a real mess."

"How do you know Muerte?"

"I told you, I've been trying to help your daughter. But at every turn Muerte and his men have tried to kill her. Ever since she came across the border."

"Nonsense. Muerte was with me when she crossed. Did she tell you this?"

"She didn't have to tell me; I was there. We were in a hotel when he came for her."

"A hotel?"

"It's not like it sounds. Muerte was tracking Maria. We barely got out before he sprayed bullets like it was air freshener."

The man laughed and the rattle shook J. D. to the core. Callous and uncaring. Derisive. Dismissive.

"My daughter has a tendency to . . . overreact. To believe

something she has created in her mind. You said you found her in the desert. Was she pretending to be an illegal immigrant?"

"No, she said she had a passport but lost it. There was no pretending about her wounds. She was as close to dead as you get."

"She is a master at this. She gets what she wants by manipulation. A chameleon. You are in more danger from her than Muerte."

"So you don't think Muerte was tracking her with the ring from her mother? The black one?"

Another pause. "Tell me where she is, J. D., and we will take care of her."

"Yeah, that's what I'm afraid of." He glanced at Win, who shook his head and stared at the bar. "There's a big reward out for Maria. You wouldn't have anything to do with that, would you?"

"Is that what you want? Name your price."

"I don't want anything from you but the truth," J. D. said. "And maybe some help."

"Truth about what?"

"About her. She gave me this phone number. I figured you might help."

"I want her to safely return. That's why I'm asking you to tell me where she is. I'll send someone."

"You don't understand. The guy you're sending is working against you. He wants to take over your business. He's working with the Zetas. Your daughter discovered that. He's trying to kill her."

"Gabriel Muerte is my most loyal employee. I met him before Maria was born. I trust him with everything."

"Well, if Maria's right, he's going to get everything."

"That's preposterous."

"Maybe some of those Zetas are on their way to use you as target practice."

"Is that a threat?"

J. D. cursed. "I'm not threatening you. I'm trying to get you to see what you're blind to. What if Muerte is your enemy and wants to kill your daughter?"

"Why should I believe J. D. from Arizona over someone I've worked with most of my life?"

"I don't know, Mr. Sanchez. Maybe because it's the truth. Maybe because I don't have any reason to get involved other than I care about your daughter. Maybe more than you do."

"How dare you talk to me that way. I have given her everything."

"Yeah, I bet you have, except for what she needed."

The man said something in Spanish, and J. D. couldn't tell if he was talking to himself or someone else. "All right, I'll send someone other than Muerte. Give me the location."

Something wasn't right. Like a bad egg in the chicken coop. J. D. closed his eyes and tried to picture him. Had Maria gotten his eyes and mouth? Or was her beauty from her mother? What had caused him to sell drugs and ruin lives? J. D. punched the End button on the phone and held it there, thinking he had just made a big mistake.

"I don't even know why I called him."

"Yes, you do. If a father won't protect his child, who will? You were hoping he'd respond."

"He says Maria makes stuff up. That she manipulates. What if he's right? What if Maria's the one with the plan?"

"You question her belief in God? That she has been changed?"

"I don't know."

Win stretched his legs and wiped sweat from his forehead.

"Maybe she manipulates and makes up stories. She doesn't make up dead bodies and bullet holes."

"Yeah." J. D. nodded. "Maybe I'm bothered by the irony."

"Say again?"

"The fact that this guy is abandoning his daughter makes me look in the mirror."

"You mean your son?"

"Right. I'm not a drug dealer with a hit man, but I'm about as good as Sanchez as far as my boy's concerned. He didn't do anything to deserve me leaving."

"And why did you leave?"

"I couldn't handle the pain."

"Leaving isn't final. You don't have to stay gone forever. And children are resilient. I have heard they are like wet cement. You can mold them because they are pliable. They forgive."

"What about me, Win? My heart feels like thirty-year-old asphalt."

The man chuckled. "If the cement can't be molded, it gets smashed. Torn up and poured out again. Maybe that's what God is doing to your life. I know it's painful, but it's worth it."

J. D. turned in the seat and spoke with a grunt. "You people won't let up on God smacking people around, will you?"

Win smiled. "There's blessing in the struggle. The community of brokenness. Nobody wants to belong, but once you're in the club, there's freedom."

"Freedom?"

"You don't try to make everything look nice. You don't have to clean up your life. You're accepted as you are. Broken. And when you embrace the broken places, you get strength you didn't know you had. Because you didn't have it. That kind of strength comes from somewhere else."

"I think I'm in over my head."

"No you're not. There's a verse that says God chooses things the world thinks are foolish in order to shame the wise. He chooses the powerless to shame the powerful. God chooses things despised by the world, things counted as nothing."

"So he *can* use a country singer," J. D. said.

Another laugh.

J. D. stared at the bar and thought of all the nights he had spent inside places just like it. Ramshackle buildings and people cocooning with pain and alcohol. He had tried to tap the overflow of his heart with each song that bubbled and foamed in the night hours. He struggled with words and chords the tunes left. He sang into beer-soaked microphones and strummed a guitar that was the most expensive thing he owned. People watched him like a cold animal would soak in sunshine.

He played with a coin in the tray by the steering column. "Christians always have a lot more words to say than the rest of us."

"What do you mean?"

"People I've known. They have the answers to questions I haven't asked. And they won't slow down to hear the real ones. You're not like that, Win."

"I appreciate that. Your wife sounds like she listened."

J. D. nodded. "But none of this answers our problem right now."

"You can make a decision that will bring life. That will move you forward. A decision about your heart and your son. You can live again. Not the life you wanted or dreamed, but one with purpose and hope."

"What about her?" he said, pointing toward the bar. "What kind of hope does she have?"

"From what I gather, she's on a good path. A little misguided here and there, but still a good path."

"Do you think Slocum and the others are hurting her?"

Win shook his head. "I think they're protecting their investment."

J. D. stuck his arm out the window and wondered what it was like in November or December. It couldn't stay this hot all year-round.

"So you're not promising me cotton candy and Disneyland? Come to Jesus and he makes everything better?"

"Nope. The gospel doesn't promise comfort and ease and all of your dreams coming true," Win said, opening the door and stepping into the darkness. He closed the door and stuck his head through the open window. "The good news is redemption. The mending of broken places. God'll pick up your life and use you. But you have to let him in. It's up to you."

"Where are you going?"

"Check on my friend."

"The boys will see you."

"Probably."

"It'll spoil our surprise."

"Yeah, but I care about my friend. One drink may send him over an edge. Maybe I'll check the back room, too."

"Stay here. Let me go."

Win sighed. "I've spent a good deal of my life being afraid, J. D. Afraid of my wife. Afraid she might pull her love away. Afraid of the enemy. Afraid of what might happen if I stumble and fall. But you can't have power when you're always afraid.

That's part of the good news too. You do things not by your own power and might, but by his."

Win walked toward the yellow light of the building. He waved at J. D., then walked through the door, the music enveloping him. As he entered, the cell phone buzzed. J. D.'s stomach seized.

29

MUERTE KILLED THE OBESE SECURITY GUARD quickly and stashed
the body in a storage closet with the help of the guard replacing
the man. The new guard was younger and came from a pool of
men supplied by the Zetas. This man would die as well, though
he didn't know it. After hiding the body, the guard went to
work behind the circular desk in the marble-walled entryway
and erased the surveillance video.

Muerte rode the elevator to the twenty-third floor and
stepped onto thick, dark carpeting that led to medical and
dental offices. He used the guard's key card to enter the chosen office with the perfect view. The office would be closed
on Sunday, but Muerte was prepared for a cleaning person or
an assistant who might arrive. By the time anyone found the
bodies, he would be gone and the media would have his message pointing out who was responsible for the trail of bodies.

There would be an outcry for action on both sides of the border. It was the perfect plan for the assumption of his throne.

The call from Sanchez came just as he began cutting a hole in the outer window. Sanchez sounded more annoyed than concerned. He had received a call from someone in Arizona about his daughter. He wanted her back. He berated Muerte for not communicating about his progress in locating her. Muerte apologized and assured Sanchez he had been working diligently, even offering a reward. This pleased the man.

"Your daughter has eluded everyone so far," Muerte said. "You should be proud."

"I would be much more proud if I were able to hear the story from her own lips."

"Yes. And you shall."

The phone call brought relief and difficulty. It was a relief that *someone* knew the girl's location, but a difficulty because Muerte was stuck where he was, unable to leave. He couldn't ignore her. She had to die. Her survival would present much bigger problems down the road.

"I'll take care of it right away, sir," Muerte said. "Thank you for trusting me."

"Why did you say that?"

"Because I honor your trust. It is the only thing we have that is given freely. The only thing of value between employer and employee."

"We have known each other a long time, Gabriel."

"Yes. A very long time, sir."

"You have never failed me."

"And I won't now."

There was a pause on the other end, then the silence of

an ended call. Muerte scrolled through his list of contacts in Tucson. There were several who would be able to handle this.

He dialed the number Sanchez had given and someone picked up without a word. He could hear nothing but a man breathing.

"Hello, J. D.," Muerte said.

Silence.

"Please, let me hear your voice."

"Muerte. Is that your name?"

"Very good. You deduced correctly. You are a formidable opponent. Many great men have not been able to elude me as you have."

"Survival comes naturally. Unlike that police officer you killed. And the others."

Did he have the authorities on the line listening? It seemed unlikely. "Let me assure you: many have fallen and there will be many more. But for now, I congratulate you."

"Forgive me if I don't celebrate."

Muerte chuckled. The man had a sense of humor. He wouldn't if Muerte were looking him in the eye, of course.

"I understand you know the whereabouts of a mutual friend of ours."

"She's no friend of yours."

"That is debatable. She has been quite—how should I say it?—*cooperative* in our business and personal dealings. She is lovely, isn't she?"

J. D. didn't answer.

"Have you become infatuated by this Mexican beauty?"

"I've become infatuated with drawing another breath. Which is why I don't want to talk to you."

"Then you are in a good place because you understand my power. Most do not until it is too late."

"You'll come to an end soon, Muerte. I just hope I'm there to see it."

"How vindictive. You must not be like your friend at the church. He tried to save my soul, you know—not return evil for evil. But I think he was trying to save his own life. Convert me and he wouldn't have to die."

"You'll pay for what you did to the pastor."

"Yes, I suppose, if there is any cosmic justice. But I've decided to take life by the horns. Go for the gusto, as they say. And you strike me as a similar man, not wanting to waste an opportunity."

Silence again.

"I am giving you an opportunity of a lifetime, J. D. You have heard that there is a reward for Maria."

"I heard you were offering a million dollars dead or alive."

"Yes, but I am willing to make it an even better deal for you."

Muerte let that sink in. He knew the man would think he meant more money. Money was king.

"I'm listening," J. D. said.

"Bring her to me and I will give you the money *and* allow you to live."

"Doesn't sound like a good deal. How do I know you'll deliver?"

"I am a man of my word. Not everyone who kills is bereft of scruples. I am not a madman. There is purpose behind my actions."

"Heartwarming."

"I will give this opportunity once, and then you are on your own."

"I don't have her."

"Did she run away?"

"You could say that."

"Then find her. I can arrange a meeting."

"I think I'll take my chances."

Muerte felt something slipping from him as he examined the glass cutter. "Retrieve her. I will call again. But one thing more. Where are you?"

"You're funny. I tell you that and you'll send people with lots of bullets."

He was still in the area. Perfect. Muerte shuddered with delight. "This could work out nicely for you, J. D. You could see a handsome payday."

The phone clicked and Muerte went back to his work.

30

HIS HEART BEATING WILDLY, J. D. checked the phone but Muerte's number was blocked. Hearing the man's voice unnerved him, but he tried to push down the emotion. Sanchez had probably called him. Or Slocum could have contacted him. It was only a matter of time before Muerte received the message. Were others competing for Maria? Her life had so many tentacles.

If Muerte could locate Maria by her ring, he could find J. D. through the cell. But running down that track made him feel foolish for calling Sanchez. Muerte could get Win's information, and if that was true, Iliana and Ernesto were in danger. The tentacles increased. The stakes had just been raised for all of them.

One of Slocum's men walked out the front door for a smoke. He stayed as if on duty. A van passed the bar and slowed, its muffler rumbling. It was a nondescript, off-white color, and through the flickering streetlight, J. D. saw the outline of several men inside. Perhaps six? He struggled to breathe as the van pulled forward. J. D. opened the door and turned back for the shotgun. No, that would only complicate things. He had never done well with guns. To please his father, he had tried, but even shooting at circular targets on hay bales felt violent.

"Where you think you're going?" the man at the door yelled.

J. D. ignored him and hurried inside. Music screamed. Smoke so thick he had to part it like a veil. There was more light outside than in but it was cooler. He counted three window air conditioners recycling the stale air.

"Win!" J. D. called out. His voice was lost in the noise, a crying in the wilderness. A few people nearby looked up and went back to their drinks. He noticed a couple of Slocum's men at the bar.

J. D. ripped the jukebox's power cord out of the wall and the room fell silent.

A drunk in the corner stood. "What are you doing? That was my song!"

The bartender was large with curly blonde hair and looked like she could handle any disturbance that didn't include bullets, but she might have been able to handle those, too. She leaned on the bar with one hand and braced her hip with the other. Was she former military? Former cop?

"I'm looking for Win," J. D. said. "You seen him?" He looked at Slocum's men but they kept quiet.

Without blinking, she said, "Doesn't matter who you're looking for. Plug the music back in."

When J. D. didn't budge, someone in the corner lifted a hand. It was the man Win had pointed out slipping into the bar. The one from his church. "I seen him a few minutes ago.

He went to the back room." He was pointing to a hallway that had *Restrooms* over it.

The bartender picked up a phone.

"Turn the music on!" the drunk yelled. "I paid for four more after that one!" He was standing again, but he had to brace himself against the wall.

The bartender hung up and came out from behind the bar, headed straight for J. D. Behind him, from the direction of the street, came a rumble that grew in intensity. Like a volcano ready to spew lava.

J. D. held up his hands and stepped toward the woman. "You need to know, there are dangerous people heading this way. They're after the girl in the back room."

"Take it up with Slocum and the boys," the bartender said, plugging the jukebox back into the wall socket. The lights came on but no music. The drunk yelled again.

"Pay him for the songs," she said.

"You don't understand. These people aren't going to mess around."

The rumbling grew louder and brakes squeaked.

"Everybody needs to get out, now!" J. D. yelled.

"You're the one who needs to get out," the bartender said, jabbing a fat finger into his chest. The whole room clapped.

Two of Slocum's men walked past him and positioned themselves between him and the front door.

"Don't say I didn't warn you," J. D. muttered as he walked toward the hall. He heard a car door slam as he reached the door to the back room and jiggled the ancient knob. It was locked.

"Win? Maria? You in there?"

"J. D.!" Maria shouted.

Hearing her voice surfaced some inner strength. With all the force he could muster, he put his shoulder against the door and the frame splintered. The door opened a few inches, still held by a flimsy chain. Through the opening he saw Slocum and Kristofferson with their guns aimed.

"It's me!" J. D. said. "Don't shoot."

Maria sat in a chair near a card table, her hands duct taped to the armrests. Win stood in front of Slocum, his face drawn and worried. J. D. planted a boot in the middle of the door and the chain clattered to the floor.

"You're gonna be sorry you did that," Kristofferson said.

J. D. glared at Slocum. "Trouble's on the way. Get out!"

"Muerte?" Maria said.

J. D. shook his head. "Somebody else." He glared at Slocum. "Who did you call?"

Kristofferson raised his gun toward J. D. and smiled with yellowing teeth. "We're close to the biggest payday we've ever had."

"You're closer to losing your life than—"

Something crashed in the other room and a semiautomatic fired several rounds. Screaming and yelling and glass breaking. A husky voice yelled, *"¡Todos al suelo!"*

Shouts and cries and tables and chairs crashing. Then more gunfire.

Kristofferson's face turned white and he scampered to the back door. Win pulled a knife from his pocket and moved toward Maria. He sliced the duct tape that secured her and tore it off, ripping the hair from her arms in the process. Another man pushed the door closed as far as he could and turned off the light.

Kristofferson opened the back door and was met by a wall of bullets from the parking lot. The man crumpled in the doorway, dropping his weapon. Blood pooled under him and someone ran past the open door, firing a shotgun in the general direction of the parking lot.

"Get down!" Win yelled.

A second later, bullets splintered the wall above their heads and sent plaster and wood raining. J. D. fell on top of Maria and stayed there, her body shaking underneath. Someone screamed in pain. It sounded like Slocum. The noise was deafening and light from the vehicle outside shone through holes in the wall.

More yelling from the bar and the sound of a siren in the distance. The door to the hall flew open. No one fired or dared to breathe. A man flicked on the light. Short, stocky. Fat face. Just a kid, really. He glanced around the room with his finger on the trigger like he was in a video game. His eyes landed on J. D.

J. D.'s life did not flash before his eyes. He didn't lose bowel control. He simply braced for the entry of the bullets that would take his life and surely the life of Maria, who lay motionless, her hair fanned out underneath him.

Instead of a burst of gunfire, one shot rang out. J. D. closed his eyes. Had he been hit? He felt nothing. And then a weight fell on him. It was the gunman, a single hole in the man's forehead.

Slocum still held the pistol in his hand, gritting his teeth at the pain, his shirt stained with blood and a trail of smoke swirling. He slumped forward to the floor.

"*¡Policía! Lárguense,*" someone yelled in the bar.

Headlights flashed through the window and the holes in the wall, and gravel flew.

"Get up, J. D.," Win said.

Win helped roll the man off him. J. D. pulled Maria up. She was covered in dust and dirt but there was no blood.

Win felt for a pulse on Slocum and the other man but found none. They rushed for the truck as sirens pierced the night and red and blue lights lit the scene. Win started the truck and smacked into the trash bins as he threw it in reverse and retreated down an alley. He waited until he fully turned around before he switched on the headlights.

They passed an ambulance heading toward the bar and J. D. shook his head. "I tried to warn those people."

"How did you know they were coming?" Win said.

"Saw them drive past after I hung up with Muerte."

"You spoke to him?" Maria said.

"Yeah, and your dad, too."

J. D. filled them in and told them he thought it best to get Iliana and Ernesto to a safe place. Win agreed and when they reached the house, he rushed inside to retrieve them.

"You okay?" J. D. said to Maria.

She shook her head. "How can I be okay after that? When I've made you a fugitive for simply helping me?"

"I guess these guys get used to killing," J. D. said. "It's as normal as morning coffee."

Her face in silhouette was lovely, a profile of beauty. He wanted to gather her in, protect her, show his strength, and make her feel safe. But how could he give her something he didn't have?

"This will not end by taking Win and the others to safety," she said.

"This isn't going to end, period. If they find you and kill you, that won't stop it. The only way to stop a snake is to cut its head off. And even then it'll bite you."

"Another will take its place."

"Then we have to make it less comfortable for the snakes. Make them want to nest someplace else instead of our backyard."

"There is a more pressing question than that."

"What?"

"How do we keep from becoming the snake? If we kill them and the others who come behind, we become like them. Nothing changes except our hearts."

"I don't get your point. Are we supposed to sit back and do nothing? Let the snakes take over?"

"No. There has to be another way. True change only comes through the heart. You can polish the outside, but it's only clean when you reach the inside."

"Face it, Maria. Some people can't be polished. Inside or out."

She looked at him as if he had revealed something about himself. "That is not up to us to decide. If it weren't for God reaching out to me, I would be Muerte and my father."

"You're not like them."

"But I could be. Don't you see? If not for God, I would be. If he had not broken through and shown me true life and freedom, I would be exactly like them."

There was something about her words that made sense, that felt like he was being led closer to the truth. But he shoved it away. "Why not just build a fence? More border patrols? That would solve part of the problem."

She shook her head. "A fence is not the answer. It's not a political problem where you have an election and the trouble is over."

"Don't say that to the Republicans."

"Why not?"

"Their main guy is headed here. Going to come to ground zero and give people a pep talk about controlling the border."

"When?"

"Tomorrow." He looked at his watch. "No, later today."

"What is his name?"

"Chandler. He's a governor."

Maria grew agitated. "Where will he speak?"

"I don't know. Somewhere in town. It's all over the news."

Maria stared at him. "J. D., this is it."

"This is what?"

"This is what Muerte is planning. It's what he's been after all along."

"What are you talking about?"

Win hurried out of the house carrying a sleeping Ernesto. Iliana followed him with a suitcase. Maria got in the back and held Ernesto close. When J. D. tried to question her further, she put a finger to her lips.

31

THEY FOUND TWO ROOMS at a Country Inn & Suites off I-10.
J. D. followed Iliana to her room, carrying Ernesto and hoping
he'd stay asleep. He tucked the boy into one of the double beds
and touched his head gently.

Iliana tried to smile at him, but her face was a sea of sagging
lines. "We should call the police," she whispered. The two of
them stood in the dark with a sliver of light coming through
the slightly parted curtains.

J. D. turned on a light at the desk. "They're probably not
far away."

"My husband could have been killed tonight."

"But he wasn't. He was protected. And you and the boy are
safe."

She looked at Ernesto. "So peaceful. With so much going
on, he can sleep through all of this."

J. D. smiled. "That's not peace; that's exhaustion."

"Perhaps. But it looks like trust, too. He trusts us to care for him."

"Can't imagine what his parents are going through, thinking he's out in the desert."

She put a hand on his shoulder. "Take care of Maria, J. D. Don't let anything happen to her."

"That's a full-time job. I don't know that I'm up to it." He hugged Iliana and went back downstairs to join Maria and Win at a table in the breakfast area.

"I've found us something to drink," she said, pushing a glass of orange juice in front of J. D. Win had already finished his.

J. D. took a sip and looked at Maria. "Tell us your theory. What's Muerte's plan?"

She leaned forward, elbows propped on the table. "Let's start at the beginning. Muerte was setting up the transport of a package into the country."

"The rifle in the case," J. D. said.

"Yes. But there was something different about this. Phone calls where he would leave the room. I became curious and went to his office. He worked from a casita near our home. He guarded it well, but I had access."

"So you spied on him," Win said.

"Yes. I was in his office looking for information when I saw him coming, talking on his phone. I hid in his bathroom and prayed I wouldn't be discovered.

"He was talking about my father and an important shipment he needed to make across the border. I couldn't hear the other side, but it was strange. He mentioned my father and the name of a high official of the Zetas. Then his voice became lower and I thought I heard him say, 'Handler.'"

"Chandler," Win said.

She nodded.

"So you asked him to let you make the delivery?" J. D. said.

"No, I did not want Muerte making that decision. I went to my father and told him I had changed my mind. I wanted to become involved again."

"You stopped working for him?"

"Yes."

"Because of your newfound faith," Win said.

She nodded. "And my father saw my decision to return as a good thing. He thought I was coming around. It would be like old times."

"If you thought being involved was wrong, why didn't you just leave?" J. D. said.

"I considered that. At first I thought I should work with the ministry in town. I would lay aside my privilege and become a 'normal' person. But I couldn't shake an impression. God seemed to be telling me to stay. My hope was that my father would see his need for God."

She looked at Win for validation. The man raised his eyebrows and dipped his head.

"Did you and Muerte have a relationship?" J. D. said.

Maria glared. "What does that have to do with this?"

"He said something about it when he called me. That you two had something romantic going."

"J. D., let's stay with the conversation," Win said.

"It's all right," Maria said. "You have a right to know. Muerte wanted a relationship. I tried not to encourage it, but when I wanted more information . . ."

"You didn't say no all the time."

"There were times when I did not discourage him." Her face showed pain and regret.

"When you were hiding in the casita, did he find you?"

More pain on her face. "Yes. And I pretended that I was there for . . . romance. But it was only to protect myself."

Her father had spoken of manipulation. Was she telling the truth? If she could lie to Muerte, she could lie to them. But her spiritual awakening seemed genuine. J. D. pushed the thoughts away. "So you convinced your dad to let you make this delivery. How did Muerte react?"

"He was livid that anyone even knew. He wanted to keep it secret. When confronted, he said it was nothing. He was upset that my father didn't trust him."

"But he came around," J. D. said.

"When he understood I had volunteered, he seemed pleased. He encouraged me."

"Of course he did," J. D. said. "He was working it out. He wanted you dead."

"Exactly."

"So when you came across the border, he had his squad come to the rendezvous point," J. D. said.

"Yes. I'm not sure who it was, but I can see now that Muerte wanted revenge for my betrayal. Perhaps it was because I knew too much."

"Or both."

"What about the gun?" Win said. "Why go to all this trouble over a high-powered rifle?"

"I didn't put that together until now," Maria said. "It's going to happen at the political rally. There will be an assassination."

"Assassination?" Win said.

J. D. glanced at the worker who hovered near the front desk.

"That makes no sense," Win said. "What does Muerte gain? Killing a man running for president proves the point that we need tighter borders. The people of this country hate drug dealers. The authorities will smash the drug trade and Muerte and everyone like him."

Maria nodded. "That's what kept me from seeing it. It makes no sense unless you look at it from Muerte's view. This is what he wants. If he is working with the Zetas, and I'm positive he is, a tighter border means only the more organized operations get through. The smaller ones will have more difficulty. Those who depend on couriers, mules, will be wiped out. But Muerte has developed a tunnel system, with many my father has no idea about."

Win rubbed his chin. "The politicians and voters will think they're doing something good by clamping down, and it will just be making Muerte stronger."

"If he were to take over the area my father controls, he could afford to suspend activity. Wait. Others will not be able. They don't have the resources."

"Which means your father is on Muerte's hit list," J. D. said.

She looked away. "Yes. I was glad when you said you spoke to him. The only way he survives is if Muerte is caught. Or dies."

J. D. glanced at a TV in the lobby. The news anchor was setting up a reporter standing in front of an empty stage. People gathered in the background, sitting on blankets and in lawn chairs. Sweat dripped from the man's forehead. J. D. moved to turn up the volume.

". . . and already supporters of the presidential hopeful have begun to stake out their territory, as you can see behind me. They're getting as close as they can to be part of what some are calling a historic gathering."

The video switched to preparations being made in downtown Tucson. Swirling lights and yellow police tape flashed.

"The speech by Governor Chandler comes at a crisis point. In the past few days there have been multiple shootings and murders that authorities believe may be connected with drug trafficking. These kinds of killings are commonplace across the border, but when a police officer and a Border Patrol agent are killed within a day of each other, as well as a prominent doctor just east of here, residents take notice."

The screen switched to an older woman wiping away tears. "I don't know what the world is coming to. He was the most gentle man I've ever known. It's just not right."

The reporter resumed. "Investigations continue into the shootings, but there's no question that the heightened violence is the backdrop to this speech. And many feel the current administration has turned away from the reality of the violence.

"The speech later this morning will come from a candidate who says he is the political leader to finally get a handle on a fair and sensible approach to illegal immigration and the problems created by the cartels of Mexico."

J. D. turned down the sound and returned to the table.

"Do you know where that is?" Maria said to Win.

Win nodded and told her the location. "Maria, we need to tell the authorities what you think will happen. We can't keep silent."

"I agree," J. D. said. "If there's even a remote chance you're right, they need to know."

Maria shook her head. "Muerte does not just have resolve; he has resources. Do you think he would plan this without taking precautions? Without preparing a way to make it happen?"

"Are you suggesting he has people on the inside? In the police force?"

"I know he does. I've heard him speak with them."

"That's crazy," J. D. said. "That happens across the border, not here."

She said something in Spanish he didn't understand and Win grunted in agreement.

"What?" J. D. said.

Win waved him off and looked at Maria. "I know someone on the force. A man I trust. I'll call him. You can tell him what you know."

"I've come too far to be arrested," she said.

"Maria," Win said as if he were a father pleading for his daughter to come to her senses, to come home. He took her hand. "We have a chance to change the future. Lives have been lost. If we do nothing, we are complicit with this man."

"I'm not saying we do nothing. We have to stop him."

"Not alone," J. D. said. "It's time to get help."

She clenched her jaw. "Fine. Talk with your friend. Tell him what I said. You know as much as I do about Muerte's plan."

J. D. looked at the clock. His body ached and he wished he could collapse in a hotel bed like Ernesto. Just go to sleep and wake up to have this nightmare gone.

A police cruiser wound its way through the parking lot and J. D. watched it pass the front window. When Maria saw it, she stood and walked to the elevator. They followed her to the third floor. Win scrolled through the contacts on his cell phone and dialed a number. He left a message asking the man to call him about something urgent but didn't explain more.

"I'm tired," Maria said. "I want to lie down."

Win nodded and told J. D. to stay with her while he checked on Iliana. "If my friend doesn't call within the hour, I'll need to contact—"

His cell interrupted him like it knew what he was saying.

"This must be him." He answered, paused, then repeated, "Hello?" His eyes darted.

He closed the phone and handed it to J. D. "I think it was him. Muerte."

J. D. looked at Maria. "He told me he would call again."

"If he sent those men to the bar, he knows I'm still alive."

"He didn't send them. Slocum called them. They were going to bring you to Muerte for the reward. But you're safe now."

"You have no idea how many ways he can find us."

A door opened down the hall and someone stuck their head out and cursed at them. Win put a hand to his head and lowered his voice. "If my contact calls, tell him what you know. Have him meet us here."

"And if Muerte calls?"

Win shook his head. "God help us."

J. D. unlocked the room and flipped on the light while Maria slipped into the bathroom. He tossed Win's keys on the dresser and stared out the window. The view looked north toward the parking lot and I-10. Through the fluorescent lights and guardrails and concrete, cars and trucks passed, going who knew where. It all looked aimless and without purpose, like a beehive would look to someone who had no idea how it all fit together.

The police cruiser wasn't in sight. J. D. wondered if it was below them. The officers could be talking to the desk worker. That would bring a SWAT team upstairs. Men in dark clothing ready to break down the door. It might be a relief to have his hands cuffed. A bed in jail and a good lawyer. It was probably the fatigue and paranoia cocktail in his brain that made him think the worst.

J. D. closed the curtains and turned the air conditioner to

full blast. He held his hand over the vent as if calling forth cool air like an HVAC faith healer.

"Foul demon of sweltering heat, begone," he whispered and then smiled, remembering a TV preacher he and Alycia had watched. His imitation of the man always sent her into a paroxysm of laughter. Even toward the end, when it was hard for her to keep a thought in her brain and she was unable to push away the pain, she could smile.

There were two double beds, and when Maria came out of the bathroom, she collapsed on the one near the door. J. D. sat in the corner chair and put his feet on the other bed, looking at her. She was such a small thing, thin and wiry, with a beauty that felt like some ice sculpture that would melt in the sunshine and remake itself into something else equally beautiful.

They'd come a long way in the past few days and it felt like they were nearing the end. With his legs stretched out, he finally relaxed and the tension in his back began to dissipate. He took a deep breath.

"What will you do about your son?" Maria said, her voice bouncing off the bare wall.

"My plan was to learn everything I needed about running a farm and then go back."

"Did he understand that?"

"He's little. I don't know that he understands anything."

"Children understand love. They know if they have it or if they don't."

"And how do you know that?"

"There are some things you just know."

"I suppose you're right about that."

"Have your plans changed? About going back to him?"

"There might be the little inconvenience of jail time for

harboring a fugitive. I suppose if I get the chance to defend myself in court, I could tell them I was put under the spell of a beautiful woman."

She kicked off her shoes and let them fall to the floor. "You think I am beautiful?"

"There's no thinking about it."

Her arms moved inward as if she had been chilled by the air conditioner's blast.

"Does he look like you?" she said.

"My son? I think he has my nose. The rest of him is all Alycia—her eyes, her mouth, high cheekbones. That's part of my problem. Something I have to get over."

"You mean her death or seeing her in his face?"

"Both. But at this point I don't think it matters whether I'm over it or not. I just need to do what I need to do."

She turned to face him and pulled a pillow from underneath the covers, doubling it under her head. It was almost painful to look at her. Dark hair, tanned skin against the white pillowcase.

"Will you sing again? Will you start a farm?"

"I don't know." He closed his eyes. The weight of the days and nights came over him and pushed him further. He saw Slocum's face and the others. He thought of Cooper.

"Maybe I'll become a preacher," he said.

"You would be a good shepherd to the flock," she said softly, just loud enough to hear.

"I'm a lousy father. Not a very good husband either." He couldn't open his eyes. The fatigue had finally worked its way through his muscles and deep into the marrow. His arms felt numb, like they were floating, and his head was the same, just a balloon on a string floating above in the jet stream, above the world but still tethered.

"J. D., you can do this."

He tried to open his eyes but the lids were heavy. "I can do what?"

"Take care of your son. Connect with him. Know him. Not for who he reminds you of, but for who he is. Who he will become."

"Yeah. Okay."

"You are a good man, J. D."

Why was she telling him this?

His head felt heavier than a lava rock rising out of the ocean. As he put it on the back of the chair, the tether came loose, the rock fell, and he was lifted, soaring, moving among the clouds. He was free, not concentrating on the ground, just floating, buoyant on the wind.

She's right, Alycia said. *You can love him well. Even though it hurts.*

I missed my chance.

You didn't. There's always time to love well if you have it in your heart.

She was somewhere on a bed, with her legs drawn to herself, arms around them, head bent forward. A force of nature, an ingrown tide. This creature of God.

How can you say that when I don't have time to love you? That was taken from me. I'll never get it back.

That's not true. There's still time to love me.

How? You can't love something that's gone.

Your love for me is shown in a thousand ways. Rising in the morning. Living fully. Turning your heart toward our son. Opening your heart to another.

Like who?

Her.

Maria?

Yes.

I can't do it. I can't risk it again.

Why not?

Because it hurts too much. There's too much pain. It goes too deep.

The pain is to help you. The pain shows you're alive. If you can feel pain, you can feel love. And if you can love, there is a chance at life. It's right in front of you.

But you don't have that chance. You're not alive.

I am more alive than you can possibly understand.

Alycia moved from the bed and knelt before him. The light in her eyes made her face shine golden, and he closed his eyes, overwhelmed, as if it were the last sunset before the world ended.

You don't need me now, she said.

Yes, I do. I need you more than ever.

Let go, J. D. You can't move when you're looking back, when you're holding on to the past.

He stared at her face, wanting to embrace her, reaching a hand to feel her hair. *Her hair.* It had grown back and covered the scar, covered all the questions he'd never known to ask. The answers and questions slipped through the keyhole of his heart and spread.

All right. If you hate it here so much, go on. Leave.

I don't hate it here. I love it where I am, and if you knew what it was like, you would not ask me to return.

I don't want you to come back if you're happy.

I believe you. I want you to live where you are and one day join me.

I'll never be good enough.

It's not about being good enough. You know that. This is about grace. It's about releasing your need to be good enough. Do you understand?

I think so. But I don't know about . . . this woman.

Yes, you do.

That's one thing I'm not going to miss.

What's that?

You always disagreeing with me. And being right.

She smiled. *I love you, John David. I will always love you.*

He felt a hand on his chest, pushing down and down and then through him, like grains of sand through the hourglass. And then the pressure was gone. Just lifted away and closed like a healed wound that only left a scar. He took a breath and his lungs filled and there was release. Sweet release.

SUNDAY

32

GOLDEN, DUSTY SUNLIGHT streamed through a sliver in the curtains. J. D.'s arms were cold and there was a metallic taste in his mouth. He scanned the room. Both beds still made, only Maria's pillow out of place. It took him a moment to jump to his feet and check the bathroom. The door was open. Empty.

As he stood, the room swayed. His head felt like someone had hit him with a sledgehammer. Twice. A throbbing, stabbing pain above his right eye he couldn't shake. He pressed his palm to it and squeezed his eyes. The rest of him felt like the edge of some burnt parchment, ready to float away with a strong wind.

He flicked on the bathroom light and splashed water on his face, then drank from cupped hands. The mirror showed bloodshot eyes. It had been several days since he had shaved or showered. That would come soon enough. He grabbed a towel and rubbed his face dry and the white cloth came away brown from the grit and grime.

He threw open the curtains and watched waves of heat rise from the asphalt. Above the horizon and the mountains in the distance, he noticed a cloud formation. It wasn't big, but it was there. Something he hadn't seen since moving to Tucson.

He checked the clock on the nightstand and cursed. It was almost nine. How long had she been gone? And where was she? The keys to the truck weren't where he left them.

Inside he knew, but he didn't want to believe it. He grabbed Win's phone and a water bottle next to the TV and hurried downstairs. He told himself he would find her in the breakfast room, that she would be in the corner reading a newspaper and drinking coffee. She would smile and hug him and they would call the police.

She *had* to be there. He willed her to be there.

Maria wasn't in the room and Win's truck was gone.

"This crowd behind me is waiting in anticipation of the appearance, in about an hour, of the man they hope will be the next president of the United States," the reporter on TV said.

He checked the phone to see if Muerte had called. By mistake he hit the outgoing calls and noticed one he hadn't dialed. The number wasn't familiar but the time stamp said 4:45 a.m. Incoming calls included one restricted and several from an Arizona number.

He walked outside past a desk worker who had stepped out to smoke and went across the parking lot while dialing the recurring number. He got a phone message from a detective. He tried again but got the message again. He wanted to throw the phone to I-10. The sun was moving, running from the clouds from the north, and the asphalt sizzled.

"Tucson 911. Do you need police or paramedics?"

"Police. It's about the Chandler rally today."

"What's your emergency, sir?"

"They need to cancel it. There's going to be a shooting."

"Did you say there's been a shooting, sir?"

"No, there's going to be one. A man is planning to kill Chandler. Today at the rally."

"You mean Governor Chandler? Who is planning to kill him, sir?"

"Muerte is his name. He's from Mexico. Involved with the cartel."

"Are you with him now?"

"No."

"Do you know where he is?"

"No, but I figure he's close to the rally. He has a high-powered rifle."

The woman paused. Someone was saying something to her. "And where are you now, sir?"

"Just have them cancel the rally."

"What is your name, sir? Tell me your name."

"If you don't get those people out of there and the governor is killed, this will be on the police because you didn't listen." J. D. hung up.

There weren't any cabs and who knew how long he'd have to wait for one. He went inside and grabbed a business card with the hotel phone number from the front desk. As he walked out, he spotted several people wearing red, white, and blue with Chandler stickers on a rolled-up piece of cardboard. He followed them to a minivan.

"You guys aren't heading over to the rally, are you?" he said.

The people turned. A man with graying hair had his keys out.

J. D. stepped closer. "Didn't mean to scare you."

"You a Chandler supporter?" the man said. He opened the side door with his key fob but kept his eye on J. D.

"I'll probably vote for him. But to be honest with you, I just need to get to the rally."

The man pursed his lips and glanced at the van. "I'm all for an informed electorate, but it's pretty tight. Sorry."

"I understand. I don't usually look this scruffy, if it means anything. But if you'd give me a ride, I'd appreciate it."

"I wish I could, friend."

The man got in his van and J. D. heard the doors lock. He walked across the parking lot and through the bushes toward the interstate.

The van pulled over a few yards ahead on the street and the front passenger door swung open. "Your lucky day," the driver yelled. "I got outvoted. Democracy in action. Hop in."

J. D. shook his hand and thanked him. As the man introduced the others in the van, J. D. wondered if, in the coming days, they would fight over whether he'd been the man in the news reports.

"You in town for the rally?" the driver said.

"No, I work on a farm south of here. Where are you all from?"

"Prescott. We hate the direction this country's going and I think Chandler is the man to get us out of the ditch, if you know what I mean."

There were a couple of *amen*s from the backseat and J. D. nodded. They seemed sincere, but they were also walking into a buzz saw, and he wasn't sure if or when he should break the news.

Win's cell vibrated and he pulled it out.

"Is this Win?" a man said.

"No, sir, it's not."

"I'm Detective Ross. Who is this?"

"My name's J. D. I'm a friend of Win's."

"He left a message. It sounded urgent."

"Yeah, you could say that." He looked at the driver and figured this was as good a time as any. "It's about the rally. In less than an hour a guy from Mexico is going to try and kill Chandler. And I doubt he'll stop with the governor."

The driver nearly hit a fire hydrant.

"What man?" the detective said. "How do you know this?"

"Maria put it together early this morning."

"Who is Maria?"

"Maria Sanchez. Daughter of the cartel leader. You've been looking for her. I'm the one who found her."

"And Maria is the shooter?"

"No, she's trying to warn people."

"Where is she now?"

"I don't know. My guess is she's trying to stop Muerte too."

"Is he the shooter?"

"He might be. He's got the gun."

"How does Maria know Muerte?"

All J. D. could see were brake lights in front of them. When he looked to the sky, he was surprised to see clouds billowing, growing fuller and white, like cotton candy.

"Detective, I can explain this after you've cleared that area. You need to stop the rally."

"Are you serious?" someone in the back of the van said. There were gasps from the others.

"Where are you now?" the detective said.

"Headed toward the rally."

"And Muerte, you said he—"

"You're wasting time!"

"I have to convince a lot of people more powerful than I am about this, J. D. Tell me about Muerte."

"He brought a high-powered rifle across the border."

"And he's involved in the drug trade?"

"Come on, Detective, surely you know his name."

"I do, and I'm familiar with Sanchez."

"Maria thinks he's double-crossing her father, that Muerte's really involved with the Zetas."

"Why would he want to kill Chandler?"

He couldn't fault the man for the questions. He'd had them too. But he also couldn't keep the frustration down. "We could go back and forth a long time until I get you to believe me. But if you're taking this seriously, you'll get on the horn now with the Secret Service or whoever's in charge."

"I'm doing that, but I have to prove to them this is a credible threat."

"Tick off a list to them of the people killed the past three days. The Border Patrol agent, the doctor in Benson, the officer on the south side—all of those are directly connected to Muerte. Plus the shootout at the Mustang Bar last night. Body count's pretty high at this point, so I think it's credible. And if the media gets hold of the fact that the police knew ahead of time this was going down, you can kiss your jobs good-bye."

"Why'd you wait so long to make the call?"

Another good question. "Maybe I should have called you a long time ago. There'll be time to score me on all of this, but that's not now."

"What are you hiding, J. D.?"

"What do you mean?"

"What are you not telling me? About you, about the girl?"

There were many things he wasn't telling. He picked one. "She didn't want to go to the police because that would make it easier for Muerte to find her. She thinks the police are working with him. At least some of them."

"That's crazy."

"Muerte is powerful. He has contacts and lots of resources. He pays well."

"And you trust this woman?"

"I trust her a lot more than I trust Muerte or you."

The man remained calm, in control. "How do you know this man?"

"I don't know him. But every time we turned around, he was there, or some of his men, trying to kill her. Now I suggest you tell the governor and everybody who'll be on that platform to cancel the rally. Get those spectators out of there."

"We've been following your credit card transactions. We know about—"

He had been connected too long. J. D. hung up and the phone immediately buzzed. They were in thick traffic and he glanced at his watch. He was running out of time.

"How far away are we?" J. D. said.

"A few minutes if we can get around the traffic," the driver said, his face ashen. "Did you really mean what you said?"

J. D. nodded. "That was the police. I don't want to bust your balloon about this meeting, but if I were you, I wouldn't go anywhere near the rally."

"If it's so dangerous, why are you going?" someone from the back said.

"I'm looking for somebody."

Something familiar caught his eye and to his left, across four lanes, he saw Win's truck parked at the end of a Safeway lot. When the driver braked again, J. D. opened the door and stepped out.

"Much obliged for the ride. You folks take care."

The people looked dumbstruck as he closed the door and ran straight through stalled traffic. He found the truck unlocked, keys still in the ignition, but the handgun was gone. In the distance he could hear the thump of music from the band shell and the faint noise of a crowd.

He climbed into the truck and sat, staring at the phone. *Narrow your focus. Take the next step. Keep moving. You're not the hunted now.*

He dialed the mystery number in the recent calls list. The number he assumed Maria had dialed. It rang once.

"Yes?"

It was Muerte. No question. Nothing in the background, no thumping bass or clapping. Just a clean line.

"Is this you, J. D.?" Muerte said. His voice had a boxy sound to it. Like he was speaking from an empty room.

"I called to let you know the police are on their way."

"Really? You're such a good friend. And where might they be looking?"

"Maybe they're using your phone. Maybe they've got a bead on you right now. I'd take a look around."

"Oh, I have taken several precautions, my friend."

"Well, don't be surprised if they pull the trigger before you can. Unless one of the Zetas is firing the rifle."

"Is that what she told you I was doing?"

"We figured it out together."

"Why aren't you with her?"

"How do you know I'm not?"

The man smiled on the other end—J. D. could hear it in his

voice. "J. D., have you considered that the things she told you may not be the truth?"

"What do you mean?"

"How did she portray herself? Was she the pouting kitten, luring you with her beauty? The virginal damsel in distress, vulnerable? Or perhaps the religious zealot? She was trained in all these ways and more. Is this how she reeled you in?"

"You're an evil man."

He chuckled. "So quick to judge others, aren't you? You probably even gave her access to a firearm. Am I right?"

J. D. hesitated.

"So she does have a firearm. And it will be your gun that is used in this heinous crime."

J. D. couldn't speak. Couldn't breathe.

"She used you, J. D. She seduced you to believe what you wanted to believe. And now you are an accessory."

His heart rate accelerated. "What's it feel like, Muerte?"

"What does what feel like?"

"To have the tables turned. To be the hunted instead of the hunter."

The cell buzzed and J. D. held it away from his ear. It was the hotel's number. Win. J. D. ignored it.

"By the time the authorities figure out what happened, if they ever do, I will be a long way from here. And you or whoever's weapon is used will be arrested, not me."

"And Maria will be dead."

"Maria will survive. We have an agreement."

"What agreement?"

"You'll see, J. D." Another smile.

J. D. got out of the truck and glanced at his watch. Thirty

minutes until the event began unless the police intervened. *Keep him talking. Focus on anything in the background.*

"You know what, Muerte? You'd make a good song."

"What was that?"

"I said you'd make a good country-and-western song. It's what I do. Write songs. Sing. Most of them have a lot to do with losing something, having a cold, dead heart, or just wanting to get revenge. I think you'd be a good fit."

"Your homespun humor intrigues me, but I prefer the music of my native land."

"Well, you'll have plenty of time to listen to whatever they're playing at the federal pen."

The man chuckled. "If they did catch me, I would never stay locked away. Poor J. D. Taken in by a woman. Beautiful, yes, but so cunning and deceptive. And now she is going to use you to kill the candidate."

"You're a liar."

"Did you pledge your undying love? Is that why you're still chasing her?"

J. D. didn't answer.

"You should find her and prevent her from taking an innocent life."

He kept walking toward the venue, thinking.

"I'll be looking for your picture in the news accounts," Muerte said. "Good luck, J. D. You're going to need it."

33

J. D. KEPT MOVING, reaching a cordoned-off area and a security checkpoint. If Maria had a gun, she wouldn't have made it through that. He walked the perimeter, looking for a spot where she might have crawled under. Streets were closed, blocked, and the traffic around the venue snarled as crowds swelled. A stage was set up near the front of the downtown library, an imposing, window-laden building. He had to get higher than street level to find her. And maybe if he got higher, he could find Muerte. But that was a big if.

The phone buzzed and he heard Win's voice.

"J. D., I just spoke with Detective Ross. Where are you?"

"At the rally."

"Do you have my truck?" The man sounded groggy.

"I found it a few minutes ago. Maria took it." He told him where it was parked.

"I'm sorry. I checked on Iliana and I must have fallen asleep."

"It's not your fault. Maria put something in our orange juice."

"What was it?"

"Must've been the Percocet. We got it in Benson." J. D. tried a door to the library. Locked.

"But why would she do that? We're trying to help her."

The revolving door at the front of the library circled and J. D. headed for it. "I don't know. Maybe it's all an act, Win. Maybe she used us."

"What makes you think that?"

A security guard stood near the door, watching the plaza, nodding to J. D. as he came through.

"I just talked with Muerte. He says she's the one who's going after Chandler."

"That makes no sense."

"Unless she's the one angling for control of the family business."

Silence on the other end.

"Maybe she led us to believe all that stuff about Muerte and the Zetas."

"After meeting her, hearing her story, that's hard for me to believe."

J. D. agreed, but he didn't want to say that. "My other theory is she's protecting us. She went alone to find Muerte and take him out. She'll take the consequences."

"I prefer that theory."

"I hear you. What did the detective say?"

"He told me he spoke with you. He's very concerned."

"Good. He should be."

And then it came together in J. D.'s head. As he hit the

stairway to the second, then the third floor, it came to him as clearly as his reflection in the polished tile. Outside were ominous clouds and the crowd below, but inside his head swirled another storm. He hadn't figured out why she had acted as she did—he might never know that—but why *he* had been vulnerable. She had exploited, whether she meant to or not, his need. She had used his weakness, his desire to save someone. If he had not been so needy, he might have acted differently, might have stood up and involved the police instead of running.

The same thing had happened with Alycia early on in her illness, him pushing her for treatment, conventional instead of organic. He couldn't lose her. It was about him, not her.

Had Maria sensed this unfettered desire, or had they simply met each other at the right moment? It didn't matter now, of course. But following her, running toward her as she sought Muerte, meant continuing toward weakness and vulnerability. If he did it for selfish reasons, to get Maria back, to keep her safe, he would follow his life's pattern. But could there be something more? Something good in the pursuit?

"Maria called Muerte from your phone," J. D. said. "She made contact. And she has a weapon."

Win said something J. D. couldn't hear.

"That detective, did he talk to Chandler's people? Is he getting this thing canceled?"

"He said he was handling it, but I don't know how successful he'll be. J. D., we should pray for her. There is nothing left to do but pray."

"You pray, Win. Pray hard. I need to go."

He hung up and scanned the crowd.

Where would Muerte be? He had a high-powered rifle and scope. That meant distance. He was somewhere holed up in one of the buildings that surrounded the rally, but which one? Which angle would he take?

Then he saw it. As clear as the Arizona sun, he saw the building in the distance, blocks away. A perfect sight line to the stage. If Muerte were high enough in that building or especially on top of it, he would have a clear shot. J. D. focused on the roof, then on windows, but it was too far away.

He glanced at his watch. Only fifteen minutes until the rally began.

As he walked outside, the wind picked up and swept dust and grit into his face. He pulled his hat low and set himself on a straight path toward the building, skirting police officers stationed every few yards.

A siren wailed and a column of limos broke through a line in the barrier. The back of the crowd began a cheer that echoed through the throng. Their hero, the one who would lead them to their political promised land, neared the stage.

The hot air had become a swirling cauldron and he was sweating from every pore. Ahead of him, moving away from the rally, he saw a woman with long black hair and sweatpants. J. D. broke into a run.

"Maria!"

He jumped a barrier and pushed through a line going the other way. They had no idea.

She ducked into a coffee shop and he followed, seconds behind.

Every eye in the place looked at him when he burst through the door. He spotted her in the back, going into the women's room, and called again but she didn't stop.

He squeezed past the others and made it to the narrow hall leading to the restrooms.

"Maria, you in there?" J. D. said. He pounded on the door. No answer. He pushed the door open and saw the woman duck into a stall just being vacated.

"Maria!"

There were two women at the sink, incredulous that he was inside. "What do you think you're doing?" one said.

"She has a gun."

Gasps and the two headed for the door.

He knocked on the last stall. "Maria? It's me, J. D."

"Leave me alone."

The accent was right but the voice was wrong. He stood on the air conditioner and looked over the stall. The woman screamed.

"Sorry, ma'am."

A staff member was on the phone when he exited, and the two terrified women trembled with friends near the front.

"False alarm," J. D. said.

"Pervert!" one said.

The crowd noise increased. He kicked himself for following a dead end. He had wanted it to be her and it had cost him.

Straight ahead was the tall building that had looked so promising from the library. The doors were locked and a crudely written sign said there was no access until after the rally. He cupped his hand to the perfectly cleaned glass and noticed a security guard. He banged on the window and the man waved him off. J. D. moved to a side entrance closer to the guard and knocked again.

"I need to speak with you," he yelled. "Open up."

The man ignored him and J. D. felt the bile rise. He didn't need to look at his watch.

He banged again. "I need to talk to you! Open the door."

The man waved and went back to his screens. J. D. took a step back. The exterior looked like one seamless piece of glass.

The cell buzzed—Win.

"Have you found her?"

"No."

"Get out of there, J. D. Let the authorities take over."

"I don't think they're stopping it, Win. I saw limos."

"I see the rally on the television. Chandler is shaking hands behind the scenes and is walking toward the podium."

"Sir?" someone said behind him. The security guard had come to the door. He was older and stoop-shouldered. "You need to move along."

"I'll call you back, Win," J. D. said. He walked up to the guard. "I think there's a sniper in one of the offices up there. Somebody who wants to kill Chandler."

"Building's been shut down since last night. Nobody in, nobody out. You're barking up the wrong tree. Besides, nobody could make a shot from this distance."

"You don't know the gun he has."

"Secret Service did the sweep. They were back early this morning. Every one of these buildings up and down the row. And I been here since six."

J. D. ran a hand over his neck and it came back wet. "You're sure nobody's come in?"

Before the man answered, he saw her passing on the street at a dead run, hair flying, legs churning as if she'd trained as a sprinter. She had a look on her face he hadn't seen before. Determination? Abject fear?

He took off after her but she had a good half-block lead. He called to her several times before she turned slightly.

"Wait!" he yelled.

She shook her head and waved at him.

He saw the gun in her hand. "Maria, no!"

She headed for the sidewalk and hugged the buildings. When J. D. looked up, he saw an office building about the same size as the previous one, but this tower stood on a cross street. He turned to look at the venue and couldn't see it through the wind and haze, but there had to be an office with a straight shot.

He ran like his life depended on it. Like both of their lives did.

34

MUERTE HAD WORKED IT OUT with the Zetas to raid the Sanchez compound immediately following the assassination of Chandler. Muerte would take over the Sanchez operation and dispense with the farm and vineyard.

He had watched the authorities sweep the area buildings the evening prior and again that morning, stopping a block away, as he had been informed. If they had come into his building, he would have dispatched them and their animals and moved to plan B, but fortunately his contact had been correct. He was out of range for a sniper with less ability and less weapon. A weapon provided by the very government he was attacking.

Muerte had seen what this weapon could do to a barrel filled with water on a range in Mexico. The holes it produced entering and exiting were impressive and the thought of such damage to a human invigorated him. There would have been a shot at the motorcade passing, but it was riskier and he wanted this scene to be played and replayed in the 24-7 news cycle. The shock of watching something so heinous again and again would bring the feeling that no one was safe. No candidate was secure.

He checked his watch and cell phone. He knew Rafael had a knack for cutting things close, but this was unnerving. He liked being in control, and having the man play loose with something so precise gave him second thoughts.

Maria had called him earlier and he had been impressed that she had remembered the number. She offered to give herself up, playing the martyr now. The people who were helping her were innocent, she said, and they didn't deserve to die. She would come to him if he would give her his location. He had hung up on her.

He watched through the scope as the motorcade pulled to the back of the stage area. Then he glanced below and saw Rafael sauntering, as if he were window-shopping on Christmas Eve. Muerte radioed the security guard, alerting him to open the door. They already had two bodies to deal with downstairs—the watchman from the day before and the replacement who arrived early that morning.

Then Muerte spotted something that troubled him. Someone was running full speed up the sidewalk straight toward the building. He moved closer to the glass and pointed the scope down, focusing as quickly as he could.

Maria.

It was too good to be true. She must have spotted Rafael and followed. As soon as he saw her, old feelings crept in, the desire and greed for the boss's daughter. Now he was the boss. Now he would take what he wanted when he wanted it.

He radioed the guard. "There's a girl coming. This is the daughter of Sanchez. Subdue her and bring her to me."

Any other man would have been horrified at being discovered. Muerte was overjoyed. He glanced at the television monitor and saw the cameras focusing on Chandler. He raised the scope and changed the distance setting. The man was sitting; at the dais a Hollywood celebrity whipped the crowd into a frenzy.

The elevator dinged and Muerte moved to the hallway and held the door open for Rafael. He stuffed his sunglasses in his breast pocket and pulled out a pair of thin rubber gloves. Like a surgeon, he snapped them and entered the office.

"So glad you could make it on time."

"I'm always on time."

Rafael looked at the window, analyzed the hole Muerte had cut, then, satisfied, picked up the rifle as if it were an instrument that deserved obeisance. He let out a breath of air and ran his hand over the stock.

"I've waited my whole life for this," Rafael said.

"Yes, this is your time." Muerte nodded at a satchel in the corner. "There is your second payment. If you are successful, the rest will await you in Mexico."

The man's eyebrows rose. It was the most emotion he had ever displayed to Muerte. "I will succeed."

35

J. D. SPRINTED TO CATCH MARIA but she was too far ahead. When she reached the front of the building, the door opened and she was yanked inside.

J. D. pulled up to catch his breath. Where were the police when you needed them?

Behind him he heard drums banging and a marching band. The crowd was at fever pitch. J. D. took off again and didn't stop until he reached the front door. The glass was tinted and he expected someone to open fire, but as he cupped his hands, he saw the elevator door closing on Maria. She had tape over her mouth and her hands were secured. The guard next to her held two guns.

The front door was locked. But behind him was a garden with decorative rocks. He couldn't budge the biggest one. He chose one half that size and tossed it at the door. Glass shattered

339

but didn't explode. An alarm sounded. He threw the rock against the glass again and made a hole big enough to unlock the door.

Her elevator had stopped on the twenty-third floor. He hit the Up button and the door of a second elevator opened. He punched 23 and let his heart slow as the car ascended. *Deep breaths. Think. Focus.* It was a fast elevator and his stomach, empty since the night before and still woozy from the medication, spun in the enclosed space.

When the elevator car stopped, he stepped aside and let the door open all the way, bracing himself. No one fired. The alarm sounded faintly through the elevator shaft. He took a deep breath and a quick look into the hallway but saw no one. He stepped out of the car and the door closed, leaving him feeling small and alone. The floor had the smell of an ultraclean doctor's office. Intricate patterns wound through the carpeting and the walls were tastefully decorated. There was no reception desk, just a list of offices with arrows.

J. D. had no idea where to go. He walked to his right, straining to hear anything. He tried one door, then another, but they were locked.

At the end of the corridor was a stairwell exit and a large window that overlooked the side street and parking garage. The street was dead except for a homeless man who had evaded the sweep.

Then something caught J. D.'s eye. A security guard was pushing Maria in front of him toward a car in the open parking garage. Lights flashed and the trunk opened and the man shoved her inside.

Behind them came another man, stocky and block-like. He held a gun to the guard's head and fired. The man crumpled and the shooter moved the body slightly, closed the trunk, and stepped into the car.

J. D. hurried to the elevator, fumbling with his phone, dialing Muerte. Anything to slow the man.

The license plate. He could get the number and report it. The police would stop him and find Maria.

He kept his head down, running for the elevator, concentrating, scrolling through the numbers dialed. Then a voice. Faint. Trying desperately to be heard. Was it his imagination? He passed the elevator and the voice became more clear. Pulled by some unseen force, he continued.

". . . and this is clearly the moment the crowd has waited for. The preliminary speeches are over and here comes the man who may become the next president of the United States. Let's listen."

Cheering and music and noise. J. D. stepped into a dentist's waiting room. The sound came from a room behind the front desk. The outer door was locked, so he scooted over the wraparound counter and spotted the reflection of the rally in a window straight ahead. With a thud his feet landed and he cringed at the noise.

"*¿La agarraron?*" a man shouted from the room. Where was he?

"*Ahí viene,*" the man said.

J. D. had no weapon or experience, just a beating heart and more adrenaline than he had ever felt. He noticed a glass paperweight in the shape of a heart and grabbed it. On the floor of the exam room lay a man in a prone position with a rifle sticking through a hole in the window.

On the wall to J. D.'s right was the TV screen with the sound blaring. The candidate shook hands in a sea of placards that waved like an angry ocean. Chandler stepped to the podium.

"I guess we'd better get started before the rain comes!" he shouted.

The crowd went into a frenzy and the man on the floor cursed as the signs rose higher.

"We need some rain here. Some relief. And I've come to tell the good people of Arizona, and in particular the good people of Tucson, that we are not going to put up with the violence and the killing and the drugs and the illegal immigration anymore."

"Perfecto," the man on the floor whispered. His finger tensed.

J. D. brought the glass heart onto the back of the man's head and heard a sickening crunch. The man went limp and the rifle pitched forward. A red stain pooled in his hair and ran onto his starched shirt.

J. D. pulled the gun from underneath him and headed for the elevator. How close had he come to the kill shot?

He placed the rifle at the security desk downstairs and ran into the hot wind that blew every scrap of grit not tied down. Walking steadily toward Win's truck, he dialed Detective Ross's number.

J. D. gave him the address of the building. "There's a guy in a dentist's office on the twenty-third floor with a bad headache. That's your shooter. The rifle's at the security guard's desk."

"Slow down, J. D. What are you talking about?"

"Muerte had a shooter. He's not in any shape to shoot now. But Muerte took Maria."

"What is he traveling in? Where is he headed?"

"It was a grayish color—foreign car. And I don't know where he's headed. But unless he has another shooter, Chandler is safe."

"Where are you? Let me bring you in."

"No, I got something to do."

"J. D., we'll find them. Let us help you. Win said you have Muerte's phone number."

"Yeah, I do. What good does that do me?"

"Give it to me. We can track his phone, find out where he is."

"I know where he is. He's about five blocks from here. And I know he's headed south. That's all I need to know right now."

"I can have someone to you in two minutes, J. D. Tell me where you are."

J. D. walked straight up to a black-and-white cruiser but didn't break stride as he crossed the street. "I'll be in touch."

36

AS MUERTE PASSED the outskirts of the rally, he expected to see people fleeing, screaming in horror at the shooting. Instead, the scene was calm and ordered. A police officer leaned against a cruiser. Muerte nodded and the man looked away.

He turned on the radio and found the local talk station covering the speech. Governor Chandler was heavy into the rhetoric, tearing into the current administration for its lack of attention to the border violence, making promises to change things when he was chosen by "the good people of Arizona." Rafael should have taken the shot right then.

Perhaps something had gone wrong. Perhaps he had gotten cold feet. Surely that hadn't happened. He would not back down. Unless the gun had malfunctioned. But Muerte had checked and double-checked.

As the speech went on, Muerte heard several moments when a well-timed shot would have been the ironic, spectacular coup de grâce he had planned. Why was this man still breathing, still speaking into a microphone and receiving enthusiastic applause?

His cell rang.

"Hey, Gabriel," a man said with a drawl. "Looks like there's a glitch in your plan."

Muerte tried to control himself. "J. D. What a pleasant surprise."

"Well, what I got to say isn't too pleasant. You're listening to Chandler, right?"

Muerte didn't respond.

"He should have been interrupted by your Zeta friend by now. Guy with the rifle and scope."

A sickening feeling entered his stomach.

"Now don't get upset at him. He was ready. I could see his finger tensing up."

"What are you talking about?"

"You know what I'm talking about." J. D. laughed. "This was supposed to be your big moment. Take out a future president. Silence him and cause a big stink. I don't think it's going to work out."

Muerte took a left onto I-10 and headed toward the I-19 exit. As he gunned the engine, something hit his windshield with a splat and he recoiled. Through the darkening skies a raindrop fell and spread in his field of vision. Just one.

"And here's the bad news. After the speech, he's moving down the road and probably into the White House. Not good for you and your business associates."

Muerte wanted to disconnect, turn around, and hunt him down. Maybe cut off his head.

"I'm real sorry this didn't work out," J. D. continued. "I know you hoped to get the manure stirred up with that particular rifle. The authorities will find it and the fellow on the twenty-third floor. He won't be available to help you for quite a while, I expect. But don't worry about repairing that window. I took some of the money from the satchel and left it so the dentist won't pay out of pocket."

"What have you done?"

"What any red-blooded American would do. I smacked the snot out of your hired gun. A little too much snot, I'm afraid."

Muerte could hardly contain his anger. "How did you find him?"

"Doesn't matter. What does matter is the rest of this money. It appears to be the proceeds from some transaction you two had. Unless you were getting wisdom teeth taken out and you decided to pay cash."

How had J. D. found them? Muerte pushed the question aside and focused. "All right, J. D. I applaud your resourcefulness. I never thought you'd survive this long. As payment, keep the money until I have an opportunity to . . . meet with you."

"Well, I don't like that idea. I suggest we get together sooner."

"And why would we do that?"

"To trade."

"Trade?"

"Maria for the satchel."

Muerte chuckled, feeling the upper hand. "Ah, yes. Maria. Your love. You know, J. D., this woman is dangerous. For your long-term health, I think you should stay away."

The man's voice changed. Instead of the country bumpkin,

he was fixed and precise. "I'll decide who I stay away from. Just like you can decide whether or not you'll stay away from the border. I just talked with a detective who called the Border Patrol, giving them a description of your vehicle. Your license number. I don't care how many people you've paid off—you so much as sneeze toward Mexico and the squad cars will make your head spin."

"I do appreciate your concern."

"This is not about me being concerned. I'm offering you a deal. Give me Maria. You get the money. And a chance to slither off and hide until this blows over."

Muerte didn't hesitate. "She is already dead. And I'm planning on cutting her into small pieces and scattering her from here to Sonora."

"She's in your trunk. She's alive. And if you so much as bruise her, I'll hunt you all the way to hell."

Rain began to fall like bullets and Muerte switched on his windshield wipers. "Such bravado, J. D. It is much easier to be brave from a distance, on the telephone."

"Which is why I'm asking you to meet me."

"You have no idea what you're getting into."

"I'm getting sick of hearing that. I know what kind of man you are. You kill police officers who pull over the wrong car. Pastors who come back to their churches. I'm not appealing to your sense of goodness. I doubt you have any. But you're scared and you're cornered. And if I give the police any more information, they'll swoop down like a hawk on a rattler. Now you decide. I can go that way or we can settle this. Clock's ticking and you don't have much time."

Muerte thought a moment. He would kill the girl and J. D. and be done with them. Be done with the entire plan. Then he would make sure Sanchez died, if he hadn't already, and go to the Zetas. It would take time, of course, but better a new beginning than a brick wall.

"All right, J. D. Drive south toward Nogales. I will call you."

"I'll be right behind you."

37

J. D. RAN FULL TILT through the rain, splashing through puddles that seemed to form instantly. The rain had begun slowly with single drops as if testing the concrete. Then something let loose, the drops becoming sheets, falling straight and blinding. Cold drops from the other side of eternity.

He dodged cars and crossed the road through flowing water to Win's truck, threw the satchel inside, and started the engine. He tossed water from his hat to the side, the spray hitting the passenger window. Breathing heavily, vapor fogging the windshield. He wiped a spot clean and pulled onto the street.

Maybe Muerte had killed Maria. Maybe when he shot the security guard, the bullet had hit her. Why would he keep her alive? His hatred was evident. But now J. D. at least knew she wasn't manipulating. She had been running *away* from her chance to assassinate and *toward* her enemy. That heartened him.

Something else brought him hope that sprang up inside as he drove. Was his need to save someone his Achilles' heel or his strength? Perhaps it was the spark of life, a seed planted suddenly taking root.

The gas gauge was nearing a quarter of a tank and the balding tires hydroplaned as he took the exit from I-10 to I-19. Several cars were parked on the side because of poor visibility, but J. D. accelerated, pulling to the leftmost lane and finding a groove in the pavement where he could keep the momentum.

The shotgun was still on the passenger-seat floor and he wondered if it was loaded. It had to be. And then the images of the past few days flooded him—the gunman he had hit on the lonely road, the look in the doctor's eyes, the pastor in Tucson. Win, Iliana, Ernesto. Maria. His son. Faces of people who knew little pieces of his puzzle. Faces that fit into his life like chambered shells.

An 18-wheeler sprayed a line of water from the other side of the median and the world turned blurry. He took his foot off the accelerator, then mashed it down when his windshield cleared, speeding past timid and unsure drivers.

The only face that didn't flash through his mind was his wife's, and somehow that felt good. Was he free? He didn't want to be. Ever. But perhaps he was moving past this lonely mile marker.

The rain didn't let up—it intensified as if the clouds were following, guiding him on a wave toward destiny, toward the climax, pushing him further to an end he couldn't anticipate.

He flipped on the radio and found a news report. A reporter on scene spoke with the roar of the storm around him. A recap of the speech. Business as usual when the world had nearly stopped spinning.

When a semi braked in front of him, J. D. swerved, barely missing a road sign. He slowed for debris and came upon an accident—two cars blocking three lanes and emergency vehicles approaching. J. D. skirted the scene and rolled onto the clear roadway. A sign listed the number of kilometers to Nogales and he recalled the push to convert to the metric system.

The forecast called for flash flooding in certain areas and gave reminders not to enter a roadway awash with water. That was impossible now. Water was everywhere. He'd never seen this much come down at once and hoped he never did again, but he couldn't help thinking there might be an upside to it.

J. D. began to piece the what-ifs together. What if the events of the past few months hadn't happened? What if Alycia had survived and his little family had stayed in Tennessee? They would have seen this rally on TV, or at least a replay of it, and the horror that would have ensued. Instead, a coyote crossed his path on a Thursday morning and on Sunday he was stopping a trained killer. God, if he really was there and cared, could have struck the gunman with a bolt of lightning, but J. D. had been the instrument. He shuddered thinking about it. Was this happenstance or a razor-thin wire tugged by the Almighty?

Darkness hovered in low-hanging clouds and gave a womb-like feel to the landscape. From the moment he had moved here, the sky had been clear, the sun and moon passing without hindrance. But now the light was gone and his path had never seemed clearer. Maria had talked about overcoming fear with love. Maybe that's what this was all about. He was being moved by some force, not to "rescue," but for the simple inclination to participate, to *be*. With all the uncertainty and questions and conflicting desires, he realized his greatest need was to live.

Traffic slowed and he jockeyed through the downpour for a faster lane. Frustrated, he pulled out the phone. "Where are you?"

"Just keep driving," Muerte said. "You act as if you have never seen a monsoon."

"I need to know she's all right."

"She's fine. You have nothing to fear."

"Where are you taking her?"

"I am going to make sure we're alone. That you have not brought the authorities."

"I'm alone. I told you that. I wouldn't risk endangering her."

"Of course you wouldn't. When I'm convinced, we make the exchange. Call me again when you are nearing Nogales."

The line went dead. It sounded like a song—"Last Exit to Nogales."

J. D. drove through the pelting rain, passing San Xavier, though he couldn't see the old mission church. When the red needle hovered at empty, he found an exit and pulled into a Shell station. He prepaid with a hundred-dollar bill from the satchel. Then as the gas pumped, he found a trash bag underneath the full garbage container, emptied the money into it, and placed it inside, underneath the trash. His bill was sixty-five dollars, but he didn't return to the cashier.

He sat, staring at the rain, shaking his head at the thought that Maria might be an assassin. How could he have missed her heart? There was so much more to know about her life, her hopes and dreams. Did she have a love interest in her little town? Had Muerte killed a boy who had a key to her heart?

More questions brought more anxiety. He drove through the rain-swollen parking lot and waited for a line of cars coming off the interstate.

Then came questions about his son. About their lives. Could Jonathan love him after the abandonment? He was ready to move back into the boy's life no matter what hurt it stirred inside. Move toward love instead of fear. That was his resolve. But what if J. D. faced jail time? He was innocent, but it wasn't about innocence; it was about proof and defense. He decided he couldn't let that hold him back either.

The line of cars passed, and J. D. pulled onto the interstate.

38

MUERTE WAS STUCK behind a semitrailer, but instead of fighting his way through traffic, he remained behind it, enjoying shelter from the driving rain and a chance to assess where he had gone wrong. This was a strength. He could concentrate, slow his heart, and see things others couldn't. He could see the truth and act rather than claw and clamor. If a plan didn't work, he would adapt and change. That was a mistake most made: they acted on things the way they wanted them to be rather than the way they were. They kept digging holes that eventually became graves.

He'd had a nagging thought when the girl went missing that her flight signaled something he couldn't anticipate. He had pushed this feeling down. Now, with clearer vision, he would use her flight to topple the Sanchez empire. Miscalculation would become the avenue of victory.

And the truth was, he had underestimated her. She was

much more resourceful than he had imagined. She would have been an asset to his work, but it was clear from her attitude that she had no real interest in him. She had despised him from childhood. Even if she never said it, he could sense it, and this would make her death more satisfying. She needed to die painfully and slowly.

And so did the bumpkin who kept calling. If Muerte killed both before crossing the border, he could hide and lean on the Zetas to clean up his problems. It was clear they were willing.

His breathing in control, the brake lights of the semitrailer directly ahead, he forced patience. He had been spared by his failure. The installation of a hawkish president would be better for his concerns. A fumbling administration appeasing the Right and Left, one that wanted two terms more than a secure border, would be a positive. Gabriel Muerte was in a fine position.

His foot tiring and the muscles in his leg tensing from covering the brake pedal, Muerte pulled off at an exit and found a Shell station. He drove through standing water to the back and watched the deafening rain. He took in the smell of the fresh ozone and listened to the sound on the roof and the clanging of the water on garbage bins. Water changed everything. Water coursed over fields and made furrows in the concrete if given the chance. It was an impressive show and he wished he could enjoy it, but he was tired and hungry and there was much to do. In a normal monsoon there were pockets of rain, patches of landscape bathed in bright sunlight while others were drenched by an isolated cloud. But this storm seemed to move with him, straight through the southern corridor leading home.

"I'll be right back, sweetheart," he said.

More kicking and a muffled scream from the trunk. Exactly what he wanted to hear.

He picked up a hard sausage biscuit still out from breakfast and a bottle of orange juice. Something to give him quick energy.

The kid behind the counter was speaking with a coworker about how a man had prepaid for his gas with a hundred-dollar bill and left.

"Probably phony," the other kid said.

The cashier held it up to the light and Muerte asked to see it. "I know a counterfeit when I see one."

The kid handed it to him reluctantly. There had been new bills in the satchel. He handed it back and nodded. "Congratulations. It's real."

"He only got sixty-five dollars' worth of gas. That means a forty-five-dollar tip for me."

"That's thirty-five dollars, numskull," the other kid said.

The cashier put a ten back and laughed.

"What was he driving?" Muerte said.

"What was who driving?"

"The man who gave you the money."

"Oh, it was a beater, an old brown truck. He was still there a minute ago."

Muerte nodded, paid for his food, and hurried to the car. Back on the interstate, he maneuvered to the fastest lane and searched for the truck. J. D. had obviously passed him as he was caught in traffic. Would it be better to take care of him before Nogales? Then he could take his time with the girl. No, there was something about watching them die together that interested him. A fitting end to their adventure and the trouble they had caused.

Three miles later he spotted the vehicle with a taillight out, zigzagging through traffic. Muerte pulled in a few cars behind him. He liked the feeling of the hunt. So many opportunities. There were many ways to handle a problem. So many ways.

His cell rang. Through the phone hash he heard a voice but couldn't make it out. The service was spotty in this area and the continual rain didn't make it easier.

"Say again," Muerte said, glancing at the number. It was from Mexico.

"Gabriel, where are you?" the man said.

Panic. The Zetas. One of their top men. *Control. Stay in control. Do not give in to fear.* "I am still in the US."

"Things did not go as you had planned. What happened? Or should I say, what *didn't* happen?"

A catch in the throat. A skip of a heartbeat. "There were complications. Obstacles I could not foresee."

"Gabriel . . ." The voice carried derision, disappointment, perhaps menace. "You assured us there would be no complications. We trusted you to complete the task."

Evenly, with measured breath, he said, "Yes, I understand. It is the way I have always treated my employees."

"Perhaps it would be better if you remained there."

"What are you saying?"

The man took a deep breath. "Your failure changes the agreement. The Sanchez operation is no longer our interest."

"He controls most of the—"

"It is no longer of interest. There is too much attention there. From both sides of the border. It is a no-win. Stay where you are."

"You will regret this."

"I regret many things. I regret believing you would deliver. And you will regret returning. I will not warn you again."

Muerte hung up and stared at the truck that had moved into the next lane. He would make this man pay for his insolence. He could see the plan begin to form. Late at night the man would be asleep. Or perhaps he would come home to find his family dead. The last image in J. D.'s mind before he died would be Gabriel Muerte's face, reminding him of their conversation. With enough planning and forethought, he would make it happen.

First, he had to retrieve the money. If the Zetas had turned against him, he would have little recourse. He could not go back to his old life. There was enough in the satchel J. D. carried for seed money.

It became clearer—where he would go, how he would cross. Clearer with each mile he drove toward the border.

39

AS HE APPROACHED THE BORDER, J. D. slowed and watched the rain dissipate and clouds hover like spaceships over the hills. He rolled down his window and the wet air blew like a fan. He held his hand out and watched water run from the windshield and he didn't care about getting wet.

His phone rang.

"Where are you?" Muerte said.

J. D. told him.

Muerte gave him instructions for the next exit and several street names.

J. D. pulled over and wrote down the turns on a scrap of paper. "How do I know this isn't an ambush?" he said.

"Do you want to see your friend again? Come now or you can come later to her funeral."

Ten minutes later he parked in front of a nondescript house on a nondescript street. He could see the border fence nearby and the mountains surrounding the neighborhoods. He had heard of the hills of Mexico. Now he was seeing them spill over the horizon.

There was no car in the driveway. The garage door was closed. Window blinds were drawn. Sunflower plants stretched toward the moisture in a little garden at the front.

J. D. reached for the shotgun and checked the side and rear mirrors. A sense of calm washed over him as he got out of the truck holding the gun and satchel. His whole life had come down to this moment, this setting, this front yard.

A car passed and he watched it slow, then continue as the driver glanced at his gun. He pecked on the front door with the gun barrel and the door opened a few inches. The peaceful feeling slipped through his stomach. He caught a smell—something dead or dying.

"Muerte?" J. D. said.

The garage door scrolled up and it felt like his first concert. Heart racing. Sweat beading. Behind him, an expensive engine. The passenger window came down and the muzzle of an automatic weapon appeared.

"Put down your gun, J. D."

All the man had to do was pull the trigger. But not here in the front yard. That would be too messy even for Muerte.

"I'll drop mine if you drop yours," J. D. said.

Muerte smiled. The guy looked exactly like J. D. had pictured him. Shady, dark around the eyes, and with that confident madman look.

Muerte pointed the gun at the backseat. "Keep your gun

pointed at me and I'll finish your friend in the trunk with a quick burst. Is that what you want?"

It wasn't. J. D. flipped the gun in the air, caught it by the barrel, and placed the stock on the ground. He'd finally gotten the nerve to pick up a gun and now he was surrendering.

"Let it fall," Muerte said.

J. D. did.

"Kick it into the rocks toward the street."

J. D. complied and Muerte exited his car. He picked up the shotgun and placed it on his front seat, then motioned for J. D. to come to the garage. Inside, J. D. saw the origin of the smell that permeated the house. A man's bloated body.

Muerte pulled in and closed the door. "Turn on the light," he said.

J. D. did and stood by the door leading into the house. He searched for any tool he could use as a weapon. He felt helpless, impotent.

Muerte released the trunk and it popped open. "Help her out," he said.

Maria's wrists were taped and she was bleeding from her nose. Tape was wrapped around her head too. J. D. ripped it from her mouth, tearing it so she could breathe more easily.

Muerte tossed him a pocketknife and he cut the tape that secured her legs. She rubbed her wrists and limped when he pulled her to a standing position.

"You okay?" he said.

Maria nodded, but when she looked at Muerte, her face grew tight. She wiped away the blood and glared.

"He is dead?" she said. "The governor?"

"No," J. D. said. "His plan didn't pan out." He folded the knife and Muerte held out his hand. J. D. tossed it to him.

"What happened?" she said.

"Please," Muerte said. "Spare me the gloating."

"His shooter had an accident. A paperweight fell on him as he was taking aim. Strangest thing."

Maria glanced at the body and covered her mouth and nose.

"Let's move inside," Muerte said.

"I got what I need," J. D. said. "Let us go."

"No, you must join me for a moment." He pointed the gun. "I insist."

"Do you have another gun?" Maria whispered.

Muerte fired the automatic into the ceiling. J. D. took Maria by the shoulders and guided her toward the door, looking for something—anything—to put up a fight.

"You ought to know something," J. D. said to Muerte.

"And what is that?"

J. D. and Maria passed him and walked into the kitchen. "I don't have the money."

Muerte leveled the gun and motioned them farther, toward a table. It was the only furniture in the room. His face had gone red. "What did you do with it?"

"On my way down I got to thinking. The only way I walk out of a meeting with you alive, as much trouble as I've caused, is if I don't have the money on me. Or in my truck. So I hid it."

"You fool," Muerte said. "I followed you. I saw every move you made."

"Really?" J. D. said. "I noticed somebody getting close after I gassed up, but I don't think you followed me before that. I may look stupid, but I try not to live it."

Muerte grabbed Maria by the arm and dragged her into the living room. He threw her down and she skidded on the dusty wood flooring and hit her head on the hearth.

Muerte pointed the gun at her temple and shouted at J. D., "Tell me where you put the money or she dies right here."

"You pull that trigger and you'll never get it," J. D. said calmly. "I can promise you that."

The man's arm tensed. He seemed to be deciding between his need and his lust to kill.

A noise. Something blipped. It was Muerte's phone and he studied the screen. J. D. noticed movement behind the man. A door that was ajar swung open. Maria gasped and Muerte smirked as if he would never fall for such a trick.

The figure aimed, fired, and a hole opened in Muerte's right shoulder. He whirled and fired wildly, the spray of bullets leaving a trail from ceiling to floor and crossing the bedroom door and the man's body.

"Father!" Maria shouted.

The man slumped and dropped his gun. Maria ran to him.

Muerte tried to kick the handgun away, but J. D. jumped on his back, knocking his head against the doorjamb. Another wild spray of bullets. When Muerte fell, J. D. put a boot on his shoulder wound and he cried out, releasing the gun. The weapon was hot and smoking. J. D. grabbed both guns and stepped back.

Maria helped her father sit up, blood staining his shirt.

"You were right about him," the man said. "I should have listened to you."

She brushed hair from his forehead and cradled him. "It's okay. Everything is okay now."

"No, everything is not okay, *mi hija*."

Muerte struggled to rise but could only drag himself into the bedroom. Blood poured from his wound.

"Shoot him," Sanchez said.

"He's not going far," J. D. said.

"How did you get here?" Maria said.

Sanchez waved a hand and his eyes rolled back. Each breath was a struggle. "I found out about the tunnel to this house," he gasped. He put a hand on her face. "I came for you."

J. D. kept his eyes on Muerte. He was crawling toward an opening in the floor, pulling himself along slowly, pitifully, the life coming out of him with every move.

"You never told me of this house, Gabriel," Sanchez said.

"There was much I didn't tell you."

"Shoot him," Sanchez said again to J. D. There was a rattle in his voice.

J. D. set down the automatic and stepped into the room, looking into the hole. A metal ladder attached to the concrete wall. He pointed the handgun at Muerte's head.

Muerte stared at him, helpless. "Why are you waiting? Can't pull the trigger, J. D.?"

Something inside clicked, like a light switch. Facing such evil, the man who had been responsible for so much violence and death, was unnerving and yet clarifying. It wasn't that he couldn't shoot. Anyone could pull a trigger. It took something more to wait, to allow life to take its course.

"Go ahead, shoot me," Muerte said.

"You don't deserve to die that easy," J. D. said. He grabbed the man's ankles and pulled him away from the hole. More blood oozed onto the tile. J. D. dialed 911, telling the operator he needed the police and an ambulance.

Maria wept softly. Her father stared into the distance. No rattle from his lungs.

"You need to go," J. D. said. "Before the police get here. Get on the other side. Go home."

"I have no home," she said. "I have no place to go."

"The people in your town. You have them. That's what this was all about. You can help them."

"Can I? And what about me?"

"You told me once that when God is at work, it doesn't matter how big the problem is. He can do mighty things. He can move mountains. You still believe that?"

She nodded and wiped away a tear.

"This is your chance to crawl under them. Go."

She looked up at him. "We stopped him, J. D."

"You stopped him. You kept him from his plan."

"The police are going to ask a lot of questions, aren't they?"

"I'll handle the questions. Just go."

Maria kissed her father's face and placed his body flat on the floor. She stood and held J. D. in a long embrace.

"Will I ever see you again?" she said.

He pushed her back and looked into her eyes. "We'll have to move some more mountains for that."

She smiled sadly and stepped toward the tunnel, then screamed. Something moved in his line of sight and he saw the flash of a blade and then felt pain in his thigh. J. D. brought the handgun down hard against Muerte's forehead with a sickening thud and the man collapsed.

Sirens in the distance. Pain in his leg. A knife sticking out. J. D. went down on a knee.

"Go," he said, holding his leg, trying not to pass out.

"I can't leave you."

"You have to."

Maria looked at the tunnel, then turned and kissed him. The pain mixed with pleasure and death, and he knew he would never be the same.

"I will see you again," she said. It was more like a prayer than anything.

Sirens grew louder and the rain began again, the sound on the roof like a washing.

The front door burst open and all J. D. could do was drop the gun and hold his hands in the air. "In here," he cried. "I need help."

DECEMBER

40

J. D. AWOKE IN THE MORNING HALF-LIGHT, with the sun rising above the mountains behind him. He looked over the heads of the dozing and caught Win's eyes in the rearview mirror. Behind their van was a makeshift trailer filled with clothes and toys. Another van trailed, half-filled with people and the other half with a tent and donated food. He couldn't get over the goodness of people who heard of a need and responded with open hands. Hands, hearts, and pocketbooks were, in the end, intertwined. At least that was what he had come to believe.

The salmon-colored light bathed the hills ahead of them like a rainbow and cascaded, spilling gold and red shadows. The world seemed brighter now, like he was looking at it for the first time. Every small thing had meaning. A bird in flight. Bees flitting from one flower to another. His frosty breath in the chill of a December morning. He had not asked for these feelings, but here they were, replacing something that had died with Alycia. He felt as if the darkness he had held inside had been illumined and the light brought life like he couldn't believe, along with power and strength and possibilities opening like spring flowers.

He did not know what he would find. He did not know if she would be there. He had tried to communicate, first through the authorities in the US, then through the Mexican authorities, then through private channels. He had tried calling, contacting her via e-mail, and had written several letters, but there had been no response. He held out hope that something good was about to happen.

The boy stirred beside him and stretched and yawned. A face full of life and a head full of questions. J. D. could have missed this. That took his breath away. He could have missed these days and the living he was meant to do. Could have missed the freedom of a heart released. Would have missed the moment when he stood at the door of the house in Tennessee and felt the embrace of his father and the sobs that came from somewhere deep in both their chests.

His father and mother had taken care of Jonathan while J. D. was away, while he was searching for himself or for what life would be like after Alycia. They had driven from Tennessee to Arizona in midsummer after the legal issues J. D. faced were over. They stayed two weeks, and every day his father had mentioned the blistering sun and the heat index. He'd taken them to Old Tucson, and though his father couldn't stop complaining about all the cactus, he could tell the man was warming to the idea of perhaps selling their land in Tennessee and making a fresh start.

"Are we there yet, Daddy?" Jonathan said, a little too loud. Almost three, he had a cute way of talking halfway through his nose.

J. D. gathered him in and hugged him. Long gone was the summer heat. It had been replaced by a chill that grew colder as they rose in elevation.

"Not yet. We'll be there soon. Go back to sleep."

A woman in the seat next to them smiled warmly and shifted. J. D. stared out the window. If someone had told him a year ago he and his son would be in a van with a church group headed to Mexico, he would have called them crazy. Even crazier was the fact that he wanted to be here. He had always heard about the mysterious ways of God, from Alycia and others, and if this was how he worked, well, he could believe it was mysterious. Something next to crazy.

Late in the morning the group stopped to eat, and his son sat with Win and Iliana. They were like another set of grandparents.

"Where's Ernesto?" the boy said.

"We're hoping to see him today," Win said. "He'll be glad to meet you. And I want to see you kick his new soccer ball to him."

"That's not a real sport, you know," J. D. said.

Iliana laughed. "Don't get me started. We'll be here all day."

It was after noon when they drove up the mountain road into Herida. He'd seen pictures of the squalor and the people too frightened to walk the streets because of the violence. At this time of year it was a fight to stay warm with winter wind whipping through their adobe homes. But there was something different, something that didn't align between the pictures he'd viewed and the scene before him. It took him a moment to realize it was the people. Instead of a barren street and shuttered windows, there were people. Flesh and blood and hearts and dreams walking anywhere they pleased.

Children ran from hidden spaces into the light, some barefoot or with shoes so tattered they might as well have been. One sight of the vans and supplies and the group was engulfed. Children clamored and waved and ran dangerously close to the vehicles.

Win parked the van near a field that J. D. had seen in a brochure the church created. A grassy area where kids kicked ratty soccer balls through netless goals. He helped Jonathan out of the van and they stretched and began to unload. First it was the trailer and equipment—a sound system and tables and chairs. Men from the town arrived, and soon J. D. stood back and pulled out his guitar. It would be a challenge to keep the strings in tune in the brisk air.

"We're hoping your voice will draw them in," Win said.

"Won't be my voice; it'll be the toys in the trailer."

Win smiled. "I'm glad you were able to come."

There were coats and sweaters and shoes and socks to hand out. No sense waiting until later because kids were cold. No sooner had they slipped on their shoes than the soccer balls flew and the field filled with children and laughter. Jonathan watched, keeping close to his father.

"You want to play?" J. D. said.

The boy shook his head.

"Okay. But you can if you want."

Streams of people poured into the venue, and the smell of freshly grilled hot dogs and burgers brought even those without faith. Townspeople knew this was a church group from Tucson, and surely some stayed away, but J. D. guessed this was most of the town.

When a ball rolled near them, J. D. stopped it with a boot. A girl no older than Jonathan bounced up to them, her dark hair swaying. J. D. kicked the ball gently to her and he scooped it up. Instead of turning, she looked straight at Jonathan as if he were an alien. Big brown eyes pleading like a Precious Moments figurine, a wide grin and stubby teeth.

"*¿Quieres jugar conmigo?*"

The boy looked up, half for approval, half for translation.

"She wants you to play. Go ahead."

The girl rolled the ball to him. He kicked it and it skittered to the right. J. D. tried to show him how to angle his foot, but Jonathan scooped the ball up and ran, squealing as the girl followed him.

J. D. laughed and felt something stir inside, not so much an ache as a promise. A distant memory reflecting in the faces and lives around him. She would have loved this place.

It did not happen as he pictured it. In his mind he had played the scene again and again. He would see her far off, through a cloudy haze. She would be kneeling in front of a child or perhaps helping an old woman try on a coat. She would be in action—moving, walking toward him, or playing—and then she would see him across a street or some wide field and they would move together and embrace.

That was how he thought of it just before sleep overtook him or while reading some Bible verse she had quoted. But how it actually happened was not as romantic. He simply heard a voice that set off a chain reaction, like the rumble of a volcano. He shivered. It could have been from the cold or her voice or both—he didn't know and didn't care.

"Are you going to play that or just tune it?"

He turned and saw her white smile, hair up, jeans and boots and a sweater. A vision. He wanted to embrace her, but he held back and stood the guitar between them.

"I was thinking about playing you a song. A new one."

"What's it about?"

"It's a country song. About losing and losing some more and finding out you don't need much of what other people say you do. It's about getting life in focus."

"I'm glad you're singing and writing songs again."

"I am too."

She looked at the soccer field and the blond-haired boy in the middle of a group. "I wonder which one is your son?"

He laughed. "Not hard to pick him out of the litter. I can't wait for you to meet him, Maria."

When he said her name, she drew closer. "I prayed you would come. I prayed things would work out for you and the authorities."

"It worked out a lot better for me than Muerte. They're still haggling over whether to ship him back to Mexico."

"It's difficult for me to even hear his name."

"Well, we're both standing. I guess there's something to be said for that."

"Yes, Win must have prayed. And Iliana, too."

"Wore out their knees for the both of us, I'm sure."

A boy ran to J. D. and hugged his legs and it took him a moment to recognize Ernesto. The boy's mother and father followed and Maria introduced them. The mother said something in Spanish, ending with "Thank you, very much."

"You don't need to thank me, ma'am. Maria's the one who saved your son."

The father smiled and shook J. D.'s hand. There was an awkward silence until Jonathan arrived. J. D. introduced Ernesto, and the boys stared at each other as the parents beamed.

"Jonathan, this is Maria. She's the friend I told you about who helped me when I lived on the farm."

The boy peered up at her and Maria knelt and looked him in the eyes.

"Hi," Jonathan said.

She smiled and touched his shoulder. No condescension. No big-girl-to-little-boy talk. "I am very glad to meet you, Jonathan. How do you like it in Mexico?"

"Okay."

"Do you like the soccer field?"

"Mm-hmm."

"I was hoping you and your father would join me for dinner. Would you like that?"

He looked at J. D. "Can we?"

"I think we can work it out."

The boy hugged Maria, then said, "I want to play soccer." He went back to the game.

"Where are you staying?" J. D. asked when Ernesto's parents left.

"At my father's house. We have taken in some of the orphan children in the area."

"We?"

"A friend of mine who helps with the church. Her husband is the pastor. You will meet him. He will probably ask you to play at the service tomorrow."

"He better wait until he hears me." A pause. "Did you get my letters?"

She smiled. "Yes. Not right away, because of what has happened with the authorities. They were beautiful."

"The police down here—the authorities know you're not taking over your father's business, right?"

"I convinced them eventually. It's a slow process showing that you are not like your family."

They walked to the other end of the field, Maria leading and J. D. following with his guitar.

"What happened to your wedding ring?" she said.

"Took it off on the anniversary of Alycia's death. I think she would have wanted that."

"And you put it away?"

"Yeah, a box at home. I might need it again someday."

"No, if you ever get married again, you should buy another ring."

He stared at her and she looked toward the hills as she spoke. "It seems like a lifetime ago, what happened to us."

"Do you ever think about it? Dream about it?"

She nodded. "More than I want. We were close to death."

"Sometimes you have to get close to death to know what living's all about."

"Is that in your song?"

"It's between the lines."

He gazed at the vineyard growing its way up the hillside to the villa overlooking the town. The soil was rich and loamy, a good place for a garden. From the looks of the trees they got plenty of rain.

She asked where he was living and what he had been doing in the months since they had seen each other. He told her about the Slocum family and how he had helped them get back on their feet after the farmer's death.

"The kids took it hard. Mrs. Slocum decided to sell. Going to turn the pasture into a big power generator. Solar. She'll be okay financially."

"And your son?"

"He's living with me now."

"And?"

"And he's a handful. But he's a good kid."

"You're living in Tucson?"

"Right. I don't think I can go back to Tennessee. At least not right now." He paused a moment. "How about you? Have you recovered from the loss of your dad?"

"I think of him often. I try to reconcile the evil he did with the man I remember."

"Usually a person isn't all good or bad. They're somewhere in between. I saw something tender from him in that house in Nogales."

"Yes, he seemed as if he cared for me."

"I'm sure he did. In his own way."

"So you'll stay in Tucson? Or would you move here? There is a need for music and the arts."

"And a new movie theater," he said. "I promised we'd go. We should do that."

"I would like that very much."

He dipped his head. "So is this an invitation?"

She blushed. "Do you want it to be?"

He leaned the guitar against a post and took her by the shoulders. "I've lived my whole life with fences. I didn't know it until I lost Alycia. I suppose borders are there for a reason. To keep countries separated. To keep neighbors in line. But I never knew how many fences were around my heart till I met you."

She kept quiet and just watched his face, watched him form the words.

"Every heart has a turning point. And once you get there, once you cross the line, you can't go back. I think I've crossed it, Maria. And I don't know what that means exactly, but I'm willing to keep moving forward if you are."

Her face was like the sunshine itself.

In the shade of his Stetson, on the edge of the field, on ground that felt like a new beginning, their lips met.

Maria moved back to look into his eyes, something welling in hers. *"El amor no tiene fronteras."*

"What was that?"

"If this is to work, you will have to learn another language."

"You know anybody who can teach me?"

"Love has no borders. That's what I said."

J. D. pulled her to his chest and kissed her hair, then her forehead. "It surely doesn't."

ACKNOWLEDGMENTS

FOUR YEARS AGO our family moved to Tucson for health reasons. We've met some wonderful people through the journey. Pastor Steve Lindsey welcomed us to his cowboy church even though we're not cowboys. Pastor Eddie and the men of the "Fishermen's Club" welcomed me as well, and I'm grateful for their friendship.

Kristina Townsend and her family walked the same health road, though a little ahead of us. Dr. Michael Gray helped us identify our problems and put us on a good health path.

Jeremy Breach, the Camachos, Nancy Powell, John Carruth, Melissa Simmons, Pam Bateman, Steve Hayes, Jay Webster, Kathy and Andy O'Brien, and Kim Newhouse have all been instrumental in our lives.

Thanks to Pastor Rob Landry and the people of Two Green Lights Ministries who have risked much to love the people of Sonora, Mexico, and beyond. And special thanks to Tina and Jim of Walking J Farm (walkingjfarm.com), who run an organic farm that does not resemble Slocum's place, for the technical assistance.

Sarah Mason made this a much better book. Thanks for your editing perspicacity. And thanks to Karen Watson and my Tyndale family for letting me tell stories.

My father, Robert J. Fabry, passed away during the writing of this book. His hands were at home in the earth and I owe any authentic love for farming that comes through these pages to him.

ABOUT THE AUTHOR

CHRIS FABRY is a 1982 graduate of the W. Page Pitt School of Journalism at Marshall University and a native of West Virginia. He is heard on Moody Radio's *Chris Fabry Live!*, *Love Worth Finding*, and *Building Relationships with Dr. Gary Chapman*. He and his wife, Andrea, are the parents of nine children. Chris has published more than seventy books for adults and children. His novel *Dogwood* won a Christy Award in 2009. In 2011 *Almost Heaven* won a Christy Award and the ECPA Christian Book Award for fiction.

You can visit his website at www.chrisfabry.com.

DISCUSSION QUESTIONS

Is your book group reading one of Chris's books? Chris would love to join your discussion, either via Skype or by phone. To submit your request, please visit **www.chrisfabry.com/contact** and fill out the **Book Group Request Form**.

1. At the beginning of the story, J. D. muses that "he was a stranger here, and the thought comforted him." Why do you think he feels that way? Given what you learn about J. D., what do you think drove him to Arizona in the first place?

2. In many ways, J. D.'s sojourn in the desert parallels stories of biblical characters driven to the wilderness. Can you think of any examples? Have you ever experienced a period of "wandering in the desert"? If so, what did you learn?

3. Why do you think J. D. decided to help Maria instead of calling Border Patrol as Slocum had instructed? Both Slocum and Pastor Ron later accuse him of having the same motive. What is it? Do you agree?

4. Late in the story, J. D. looks back over the events that brought him to this point and begins "to piece the what-ifs together." What questions and possible outcomes does he consider? If J. D. hadn't met Maria, how do you think the next five years of his life would have unfolded?

5. Why does J. D. have such a negative view of God? Have you ever experienced a tragedy that caused similar feelings, even on a smaller scale? Were you able to move past it and still believe? If so, how?

6. J. D. remembers his father telling him that "small decisions lead to big ones." What did he mean by this? How do you see this idea play out in the story? Have you seen it illustrated in your own life?

7. J. D. often refers to the racist attitude prevalent in the small Arizona town. How does Maria turn the tables on him? (See p. 99.) Have you ever had to confront this kind of stereotype, whether in your own thoughts or in other people's assumptions—even their assumptions about you? How did that feel?

8. On p. 94, J. D. muses that Maria "was a jigsaw puzzle, and the more edge pieces he found, the more he felt like he shouldn't empty the box. Just put it back on the shelf and walk away." Were you skeptical of Maria? Why or why not? Did your view of her change as the story went on?

9. Several times throughout the story, characters argue about whether or not it's right to help an illegal alien. What are the arguments on both sides? What side would you fall

on? Can you think of any stories or passages from the Bible that would apply?

10. On pp. 169-170, J. D. says that he used to think his life was up to chance. And if it wasn't, that would be more frightening to him. What do you think he means? Which do you think is more frightening to believe—that we control our destinies or that God does? Why?

11. Consider Pastor Ron's response to Muerte's question about the existence of evil in chapter 21. What did you think of their conversation? If someone asked you why God allows suffering, how would you respond?

12. When Maria asks J. D. why he helps her instead of going after the million-dollar reward, he replies, "Money can't give me anything I don't already have." How does this compare to the old adage "Money can't buy happiness"? Do you agree with J. D.'s perspective?

13. The desert setting plays a big part in the story. What obstacles does the desert present that the characters must overcome? Are there any ways that the setting also helps them?

14. In chapter 22, Maria tells J. D. that she believes the opposite of fear is love. How does this discussion influence J. D.'s decisions? Do you agree that "you cannot love and fear at the same time"?

15. What struggles do J. D. and Maria have ahead of them as the story concludes? If you were to write a sequel, what do you think would eventually happen?

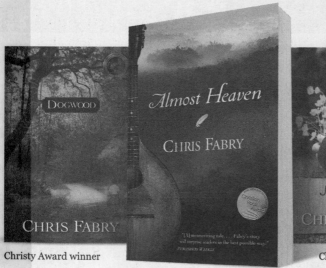